# C✦DA

# CODA

Emma Trevayne

RP|TEENS
PHILADELPHIA • LONDON

ISBN 978-0-7624-4728-2

Library of Congress Control Number: 2012945893

E-book ISBN 978-0-7624-4840-1

9   8   7   6   5   4   3   2   1
Digit on the right indicates the number of this printing

Designed by Rob Williams
Cover art by Rob Williams
Edited by Lisa Cheng
Typography: Minon Pro, OCR, and Univers

Published by Running Press Teens
An Imprint of Running Press Book Publishers
A Member of the Perseus Books Group
2300 Chestnut Street
Philadelphia, PA 19103–4371

Visit us on the web!
www.runningpress.com/kids

To Britlany and Brie,
with all my string, and all my yes.

I'm drawn toward the door. I can't hear it yet, but I can feel it. A pulse, a heartbeat. The floor shakes.

Inside, the cavernous, soundproof room is already packed, black and neon and flashing lights and stifling heat from the crush of bodies. It will dry my hair back into some semblance of the platinum-and-blue spikes I'd arranged so meticulously at home, hiding the wire for the fiber-optic cerulean tubes in my own real hair before snaking it down to plug into the socket at the back of my neck. My own energy will make them glow, just as by day it helps power the Grid. They're an indulgence since I should conserve myself for work, but I love them too much to care.

My body shudders with relief inside wet clothing as I fully register the music that pounds around me: heavy, rhythmic percussion, the cut-glass of keyboards. Speakers line the walls and hang from the ceiling to prevent recurrences of the early disasters, when people pushed to get closer to the music coming from corners of the room, and trampled bodies fell under brutal boots. A more even distribution makes sure we only get the happiness we crave.

And hate.

In the few minutes I have before the effect takes hold, I find my friends, weaving my way through a tangle of euphoria and sweat. Scope has his arms around some guy I don't recognize whose lips and bones are outlined in harsh yellow. Haven's next to them, all legs and spiked heels and her favorite shade of hot pink. Why she slums it down here when she should be at a Sky-Club, being worshiped by rich men, I have no idea. I've asked and gotten only an arched chrome eyebrow and a shrug of a slender shoulder as an answer.

Sticky mouths kiss both my cheeks at once. Haven and Scope shout something I can't hear above the music, but I nod as if I do. Scope goes back to his latest nameless guy, and Haven focuses on the luminous sticks in her hands, transfixed as they slice through steamy air and pulses of light. My own are in my pocket, blue to match my hair, like hers are pink. I reach for them with fingers just starting to hum.

It's working. I just need to let it.

*Sound is everywhere. I can't see, but I don't need to. The music moves my arms and legs around the square foot I've claimed. A crash of drums and I am eight years old again, held by my mother during a thunderstorm that rages in window-rattling fury. Everywhere else I'm forgetting her face, but here, here I can remember her eyes so like mine, and her smile back when she smiled. Scope is grinning at pretty things shimmering just out of reach no matter how high I stretch my hands to grab them. Maybe they're down, not up—I'm not sure if I'm flying or falling anymore, but either way I'm throwing laughter back at the thumping bass in a conversation everyone else must be able to hear because they are laughing, too.*

*With drumbeat shackles and guitar-string ropes, I'm a willing prisoner. It's miraculous here: light and sound and color and shape coalesce around me before exploding into fireworks of bliss. Rainbow sparks tumble down to sizzle on my clothes.*

*I try to catch the pink ones.*

*Songs change. Sweat flows. Energy gathers and releases and gathers again. This one's my favorite. It sweeps me away, floating, until waves of a thousand keyboards break all at once, crashing into my frantic body, tossing me higher, higher, higher.*

My mouth tastes like the carpet that's scraping against my face. Boots nicer than mine, heels tall and sharp, sit at the end of an empty bed. Scope always goes home—almost never alone—but Haven sleeps here a lot because it's closer to the club than her place. Through the painful, expected withdrawal that scratches at my insides and fills my mind with fog, I vaguely remember a good time, which is the problem.

Good times turn you into my father. After a while, they turn you into my mother.

I throw off my blanket and stand to scan my wrist at the console on the wall. If I could brace my eardrums, I would. They say we're not supposed to hear the beep, that the frequency's too high.

The Corp says a lot of things.

My eyes close. The whine ricochets around my head and the chip vibrates subtly against a vein. Text pops up on the display, but I don't need to read it. Male. Eighteen. Six-one. Not heavy enough. Blond and blue. Conduit. Mother deceased; father and two siblings living. Citizen N4003. I pull a headset from a hook. The screen glows too-bright blue and my eyes water.

One song, one hit. I'd have to track for a long time to equal the strong high I can get at the club, but the first rush does come faster here. I scroll through the menus of uppers, downers, and meds until I find something that will take the edge off and not chew up too many credits.

Better. I stop shivering, and the headache fades to a dull throb at my temples. Each deep breath loosens my chest, clears the haze from my thoughts, and prepares me for the day ahead.

Barefoot, dressed only in my underwear, I pad to the hygiene cube to clean up. The mirror's cracks scar my face. Tar soap scrubs away smudged black and blue paint and leaves me stripped to pale under the shower spray.

My fingers loosen and tap out a beat. Drums *here*, one, two, three, and now a keyboard, and now, *now* a guitar, strings screaming and wild.

My clubbing clothes stay in a crumpled pile of stitched-together rags on the floor; I trip over my gas mask and swear. It's not needed anymore—a relic from the war—but it makes a good accessory at night, hanging loose from my neck. A joke, because it can't protect me from the poisonous, sound-saturated air. By day, I wouldn't dare turn up at work in anything but a suit, the collar of my ironed shirt falling just below the jack at my hairline.

"Have you even moved since yesterday?" I ask my father as I cross the living room. He ignores me, or isn't with it enough to hear. A headset hangs from another console on the wall over his head, untouched since the last time I put on a track for him. The TV screen is filled with the face of a polished Corp spokeswoman, babbling something about new developments in hydroponics. Interesting, sure, but knowing how the farms in the skyscrapers at the North Edge *work* isn't going to do anything to put food on our plates.

Neither is the lump on the couch.

"Ant!" my little sister says, racing across the room to throw her arms around my waist. It's a nickname of a nickname, left over from when the twins couldn't pronounce my full handle. Sometimes it feels more appropriate than the one I actually picked, chosen before I fully understood what it meant.

I return the hug. "Hey, Alpha." She's little and blonde, like our mother. Omega's darker coloring comes from our father.

"Haven made me oatmeal the way I like it."

"I don't know why," Haven teases Alpha from her position on the floor, where she's tying Omega's frayed shoelaces. "It's practically soup."

"I like soup," Alpha says with all of her nine-year-old dignity.

"All done." Haven finishes a final knot and stands, stepping back to lean against the counter. Free of makeup and all her pink accessories, she looks different, not as polished as she does at the club. Sound-sensitive implants sit quietly black against her olive skin, banded around her arms and embedded into the backs of her hands. One of them flickers dimly when Omega drops his spoon.

Natural instead of glamorous. I'm not sure which is sexier, and it doesn't matter. She's been awake for a while—long enough to track, judging by her alertness—and her hair hangs in one long, wet rope down the back of her T-shirt, the pink streaks darker than usual against the natural black. This is not the time to think of her in my shower. It never is.

Omega joins the hug and I hold on, trying to be a kid again for a second. "*Thanks*," I mouth over their heads.

Haven smiles easily. "No problem."

"Was the music good, Ant?" Omega asks this every morning, so I'm expecting it, but it's not a simple question to answer. Good, yes. Healthy, not so much. But there are things they don't understand yet—or at least things I'm not ready to explain. In three years, they'll be taken into a large room at school and exposed. All I can do right now is pretend it isn't going to happen.

"It was great," I tell him.

Alpha tilts her head back, her expression daring me to lie. "Did you eat the chocolate I left for you?"

"Yes," I answer, tickling her. "But what have I told you? Keep it for yourself next time."

"Whatever." She rolls her eyes, and Haven tries not to laugh. Like I don't know where Alpha picked that up.

"Don't listen to him, Alpha," Haven says. "What he really meant to say was *Thank you*. Boys are all the same."

"Whose side are you on?" I ask.

Haven shrugs, her bare lips twitching. "Mine."

"Gee, thanks."

"Eat," Haven orders, throwing a green apple at me. It's from one of the North Edge farms. With the first bite I wonder, not for the first time, whether things tasted different when they were grown in soil, beneath real sunlight.

"I want to visit Mommy," Alpha says out of nowhere. Ow. I taste blood on my lip. Shit, that stings. Haven's eyes widen.

"Okay," I say. "I'll take you after school. Go get your stuff."

The twins run off. "You ready for that?" Haven asks.

"Has to happen sometime. They asked; I'm not gonna say no."

"Maybe it's better, that they see just her, before . . ." Her glance flicks toward the living room, and I don't need to ask what she means.

"Yeah." I give him another couple of months, maybe less.

"If you need anything . . ."

"Thanks."

"I've gotta go," she says with that distracted look she gets when her thoughts have turned to lines of code and she can't wait to get back to her computer. She leaves a few minutes later, boots laced on, calling good-byes to the twins and waving to me with hands full of pink stuff. The track I sneak before getting Alpha and Omega out the door further banishes the looming headache and lets me float down the stairs from our apartment to the trans-pod stop nearby. All the kids from our Quadrant are there—pale and small, their clothes washed until faded and paper-thin.

"Behave yourselves." I wait for them to pull themselves from their friends long enough to say they heard me, then leave them to it.

My trans-pod, crowded with commuters, goes in the other direction, up into the middle of the Web. The name fits. Corp headquarters—home of the Grid's power source—crouches, spiderlike, in the center, watchful for the slightest disturbance. Clothing stores, food depots, an old library slide across the view from my window seat. Sunlight has been coming in weak, dim bursts for days, as if the sky is some kind of old-fashioned camera—black, hulking, shapeless—watching over the city for something to happen, its flash running low on batteries. Still too bright for my eyes this morning. I squint and measure the distance of my trip by how much nicer the buildings get with each mile and how much cleaner the streets.

The Vortex sucks us in, a dizzying sprawl of reclaimed metal and power-sucking lights. Every vertical surface except one glows, flashes, and whirrs with neon, more and more concentrated as we near the center. Corp headquarters isn't as tall as the buildings around it but still casts a shadow that covers the entire island.

My tracking buzz has worn off by the time the pod stops outside the Corp. Good, since I have to work, but it means my morning dose of anger at the statue isn't dulled by anything.

Asshole. It sits there in front of the entrance, formed from iron that was probably once an innocent bridge or fence, a likeness of the man who is behind all of this. Only the guards watching my approach keep the spit under my tongue. Their black uniforms reflect off the smoked glass behind them, normal human outlines fractured by shotgun barrels rising above their shoulders.

I don't get so much as a *Citizen* or even a nod from the guards when I pass; they know why I'm here. The cuff of my shirt resists a little when I pull it away from my ID chip and wait for the scanner to beep.

My headache refreshed, I'm allowed inside a lobby of sharp edges and sharper suits. Typical Corp types. Suspended TV screens play the news channel and a receptionist sits at a marble desk. Behind her, sealed doors are set into a curved wall, one cylinder inside another. The entrance to the mainframe that stretches into the sky.

The hum is everywhere; I've never managed to get used to it or tune it out. It raises the hair on my arms. This is less a tower containing computers than it is a tower made from them—a huge network that knows us, controls us, and makes sure we have food and water and the right number of credits in our accounts, however much or little that might be.

And music. It delivers the music.

Doors hiss. I step into an elevator along one of the outer walls and ignore the dismissive sneers of the other occupants when I press the button for the lowest basement level. It's too much to ask that they be grateful for what I do. As if they're so much better. Underground floors are reserved for menial, unwanted jobs. Conduits are literally the lowest of the low.

Alone, I step out into what we dub the Energy Farm, though not with any affection. One massive room, walled in by uncovered concrete and divided into more cubicles than I've ever bothered to count. After five years, I don't need to watch where I'm going to find mine.

"Morning, Anthem," says the white-coated tech in charge of my sector when I walk into the few square feet of space Scope likes to refer to as my *office*. He's not as funny as he thinks.

"Hi, Tango." She's been my tech for a while, and she's okay. We're close enough to know each other's handles, anyway.

"*You look tired*," she mouths. "Are you feeling well this morning?" she asks at normal volume.

It's never safe to assume we're not being overheard. "I'm fine," I lie. The answer matters. If I'm sick, tired, or depressed, I have less to offer the Grid, and I need this job.

"Excellent," Tango says, frowning at me. I stand beside the chair where I'll spend the next eight hours, unmoving, my limbs getting heavier as my own energy is sucked from me and poured into the Grid. Sometimes, I'll look at a flickering TV screen, or glowing billboard, or listen to a track and think, *that's me*. That's one minute off my life. Another. Another.

Tango checks my vital signs before I'm allowed to sit down, my neck jack resting over a gap in the headrest. Her purple hair smells like Hydro-Farm lavender today. I wonder if she matched the color and scent on purpose. Only when I'm close enough to smell it do I notice the reddened, swollen rims of her artificially violet eyes and the tremor of her hands on my wrist.

"*You okay*?" I ask, keeping my voice low.

She shakes her head. I raise my eyebrows and her shoulders slump. "*One of my friends was caught stealing food from a depot*."

Oh. I point at my ears, but don't really need her nod of confirmation. After the pain subsides and withdrawal passes, there'll be another Exaur roaming the Web, relying on the kindness of the Corp to feed them, clothe them in telltale uniforms, give them shelter. "*I'm sorry*." There's really nothing else I can offer.

"What do you want?" she asks, too loud, too cheerful.

"I haven't finished *War & Peace* yet."

"I'm surprised that book doesn't put you to sleep." The point is to keep me awake. Conduits are given whatever mental stimulation we want while we're jacked in, barring a few specific subjects. Another few months and I'll be done with the Russians. "I'll put you on drain-level six. Hold still."

Being jacked in will never *not* be weird. A feeling that I'm part of something much bigger than just me takes over. I am the machines, the power that buzzes everywhere.

Green text begins to scroll across my mind. I close my eyes.

Alpha and Omega hold my hands as we cross the street from the trans-pod stop to one of the nicer old buildings that survived the war; the only new addition to the facade is a plaque beside the doors bearing the words CITIZEN REMEMBRANCE CENTER: QUADRANT TWO.

CRCs are the Corp's brainchildren, one of their many attempts to convince us that they're benevolent. Generous, even, in giving us this special, different kind of library.

We climb the stairs; I briefly let go of Omega to scan my wrist. The doors swish open, and inside we climb to the third floor.

The twins stop, eyes wide, on the threshold of the huge room.

"She's here?" Omega asks.

"It's just like Fable said," Alpha says.

Rows of small, glass-fronted lockers stacked to shoulder height run all the way to the far wall. Every twenty feet or so a round pedestal rises a few inches from polished marble that swallows and spits back the clunk of my boots. A metal tower stands in front of each one, covered in lights that wink at intermittent intervals, a touch screen sitting on top.

I come here a lot, but it's been a while since I thought about what my first time was like.

"Wow!" Omega exclaims, running up to the nearest viewer. "This is cool!"

"It's not even doing anything," Alpha says. "Ant, what's it for?"

"Quiet, okay? I'll show you," I say. Their voices are a little too loud in a place that demands respect for its inhabitants. Right. Left. Along the stack. Five lockers in from the end, three from the top.

Citizen T25641, otherwise known as my mother, is contained in a memory chip on a block of foam behind the glass door. Unlike ID chips, which are implanted at birth, the Corp waits a few years before putting these in. My mother's memories start at about age three—so do mine—but I doubt there's anything interesting to see before that, anyway. I barely remember waking up from the surgery. The day the twins came home from theirs is clearer. I looked at the bandages over their ears and pictured the chips inside, their dual function of recording memories and ensuring maximum receptiveness to the music. Back then, I was still naïve enough to believe those were both good things.

When I come alone, I take a minute to remember her as clearly as I can, a luxury Alpha and Omega don't have. Once again, I pass my wrist in front of a sensor—this one will only work for a family member or a Corp master chip—and the door swings open on its hinges.

"What do you want to see?" My fingers run over sharp corners as I carry the chip to the nearest viewer.

"When we were little," says Alpha. Beside her, Omega nods in agreement.

I smile. "You're still little."

"Am not!"

"Shhhh."

The screen comes to life as soon as I slide the chip into the slot on the side of the tower. There, in white text on a blue background I'm sure is meant to be soothing, is a menu of my mother's life. Or most of it.

The whole benevolence thing would be a lot easier to swallow if the Corp didn't edit the memories after death. They say it's to protect the living from things we don't want to learn about our loved ones. I'm sure it sounds like a reasonable explanation to them.

Organized by date, type, location, and finally by who else the memories contain, my mother is reduced to a list, a catalog. I scroll until I find a day in the park before she really started to go downhill.

"Ready?" They both nod, eager and awed. I select the final option. A halo of lights blooms above the pedestal and then the holograph appears. Compiled and extrapolated from both her thoughts and what the Corp knew about her, the translucent image is an outside view of her holding the twins, round-faced toddlers, while my father and I watch from a few feet away. Like a muted TV, there's no sound. I don't ask if they can remember her laugh.

I look so young, and I'm ashamed, now, of the scowl on my face.

Knowing stuff I didn't then, I can see signs of the illness that eventually gets all of us: dull eyes, yellowed skin, bones prominent beneath not enough flesh. But she's smiling. The twins had been unexpected, later in life than most people risk. They'd given her a temporary energy she hadn't shown in a while.

I pull Omega's hand back. "Don't touch."

"She's so pretty," Alpha whispers.

"She was. You look like her."

Our hologram selves sit down on the grass and my mother pulls food from a bag. I smile, knowing what's coming next, and laugh outright when, beside me, Alpha punches Omega in the arm.

"You stole my cookie!"

"Eat faster next time." He sticks his tongue out at her.

"You get your revenge, Al. Here," I say, grinning as I skip ahead a few days to a scene at the kitchen table and Alpha dumping an entire bowl of noodles over Omega's head. They hang down to his collar, and my mother is torn between chastising Alpha and laughing.

"I look good with long hair," Omega muses, straight-faced, and they both collapse into giggles.

We stay until it's dark outside the high windows and we've watched every kind-of-happy memory I can find that contains the twins. More days in the park, family dinners. She was a much better cook than I am. I tell them everything I can remember and indulge faint daydreams of introducing Haven to her. They would've liked each other.

"Tell you what," I say, the last memory I can show them fading from the viewer, "why don't you guys go hide and I'll find you, like we do in the park? Just stay on this floor."

They run off, smiling, in different directions as I pretend to count to a hundred. My fingers tap through menus for something I've watched too many times.

She's a ghost of herself in this one, gaunt and faded and weak, white as the pillows she's propped against.

*"Promise me, Anthem."*

I say nothing.

*"They need you. They will need you. Promise me they'll always come first, that you'll keep them safe. And promise you won't ever make someone watch this happen to you, the way you're all watching me."*

My younger self squints. I remember the tears, the way they burned.

Bony fingers grip mine with surprising strength. *"Promise!"*

I'm already breaking the first one.

✥

"Lunchtime." Wafts of something hot and unappetizing and nutritionally balanced come into the cubicle with Tango. She moves behind my head to de-jack me so I can eat.

"Good book?" she asks. When I can turn my head, I look at her, see her eyes darting between me and the doorway.

"Interesting." Actually, my mind's been wandering for a while, occupied with my plans for later. It's Wednesday.

"You were humming," she whispers, stepping away to grab the edge of the cart and slide my food over.

Heat, then cold washes over my skin. I hadn't even noticed. "Did anyone hear?"

"Just me, I think. Most of the sector's empty until shift change. But you need to be more careful."

If she only knew. "I will. Track from this morning must've stuck in my head."

"Sure," Tango agrees through thin lips. "I'll be back in twenty minutes."

Fear makes my lunch tasteless—a blessing. I'm not usually so careless or stupid. There's nothing the Corp punishes more cruelly than unauthorized music. *Unauthorized* being everything except the tracks they make available through the consoles we have at home, or the songs played at the clubs. No humming. No singing. I once saw someone pulled into a patrol-pod for whistling. As if we'd all give up tracking completely if unencoded music was around, as if our addictions wouldn't sink their claws desperately deeper to pull us back.

Again, I think of the statue.

My book picks up where I left off, though I've lost the thread now. Wednesdays are the only day of the week I really look forward to, and the closer it gets to the end of work, the harder it is to concentrate. Today, I mostly focus on not making any sound; it's not just me who will get in trouble if I'm heard.

"See you tomorrow, Anthem," Tango says later, after helping me stand. Dizzy, exhausted, and disoriented, I find my way to an elevator and I'm kept on my feet by the crush of other conduits leaving so the next shift can take over. I'm fortunate they let me work during the day, when the twins are at school.

"Usual?" asks the man in the store around the corner from headquarters.

"Yeah, thanks." I wait while he maneuvers his prosthetic arm into a refrigerated case; a bottle of grape juice emerges held in a metal claw. A swipe of my wrist hurts my ears and debits a stupid number of credits from my account.

The trans-pod trip to Quadrant Two is long enough to allow the sugar to take effect and for me to daydream about Haven for a while. Feeling almost human again, I get off at my stop and walk a few quiet blocks.

The bottle rattles into a recycling container as I round the corner. My heart and feet stop in perfect unison; my eyes focus on the red cross, stark and bloody against the pristine white of the med-pod parked outside my building.

It can't be. He was fine when I left him.

Sand fills my throat. Not today, please. It's Wednesday. Any day but today. My boots hammer the sidewalk; my pulse races. I reach the steps the same moment the doors open; a tech backs out and looks over his shoulder to make sure the way is clear for the stretcher before he nods to his partner.

"Who—?" I swallow. "Who is that?" Wheels scrape against concrete; the covered body bounces and stills when they come to a stop beside me.

"Who wants to know, Citizen?"

I look at the med-tech by the body's feet. "I live here." The shapeless lump under the rubber sheet gives me no clues except maybe height. It could be. Blood thuds in my ears.

He shrugs, and the other tech flips back the sheet. Spots dance in front of my eyes; I blink them away to see that I'm allowed to breathe again. I've seen her around, this girl whose lips are naturally blue and whose skin is ghostly pale. She's about my age, I think, but we've never spoken more than a greeting in the hallway. I know she lived alone, and that she was too young to die from whatever killed her— it can't be tracking, not yet—and I'm sorry she's gone, but I care who she isn't more than who she is right now. I push past the stretcher, up the steps, scan my wrist, and take the stairs to my apartment three at a time. It could have been him, and I need to know.

The living room is quiet except for the TV and my father's gentle snores. He's fine, for a warped value of *fine*, anyway, and we all have that. Relief relaxes my muscles one by one as I stare at him.

We do okay without his help, me and the twins. Conduit pay gets them food, clothes, tracks and club cover for me so that the Corp sees I'm following the rules, staying high. If they come for me in the middle of the night, it won't be because I haven't been doing enough of their drugs.

It'll be for something else, and as long as my father's long, painful breaths continue, I can convince myself that Alpha and Omega won't lose their whole family if I'm caught.

I change my clothes and ignore the call of the console. A track would really help right now, and my body is used to a hit at this time of day, but it's Wednesday. Instead, I watch the news while I persuade my father to at least drink some water. There's nothing new, just the usual announcements of songs that will be played at the clubs across the city and an interview with one of the Corp's musicians.

They're treated royally—all for the low, low price of agreeing to help enslave the rest of us.

"I'll be home before the twins," I say to my father. Alpha and

Omega spend afternoons with a friend whose mother needs the credits I give her.

I think he understands—a good day for him.

The green-haired singer is still on the TV, gushing about how great his studio is. If I ever see him in the lobby at work before he goes upstairs, I'll be torn between restraining myself from hitting him and telling him how much I like his music. The guy's talented.

So am I.

Scope meets me on a corner by the South Shore, our footsteps matching up without a pause. The vivid red streaks in his hair catch the light.

"You look wrecked, man."

I laugh. "It's my job, okay? I can deal." He doesn't need to know about my panic back at my apartment. Scope has it pretty easy. He finished school a couple of years ago, then trained as a chrome artist. Haven's eyebrows are his handiwork, so I have him to thank for knowing her at all. His brother, Pixel, runs the club we go to most nights.

"Yeah, okay. How's your father?"

"The same. Your mother?"

He shakes his head. She's held on longer than a lot of people do, but it's coming for her. Her death will be more comfortable than my father's; Scope and Pixel together can afford some of the more specially encoded tracks. The powerful ones that numb pain and bring restful sleep.

Permanent sleep, eventually.

"You weren't at the club last night."

"Yeah. The twins, they asked to go to the CRC. Didn't want to leave them alone after that, you know?"

"Ouch." He winces. "They handle it okay?"

"Better than I did my first time. How was your night?" That smirk. I used to be in love with it. Now it's just another accessory, like the silver ring through his nose or the chains hanging from his belt. "Never mind, spare me the details. Did you see Haven?"

"See, you're not asking if *I* saw her. You want to know if *other* guys saw her."

Heat rises in my face.

"Both of you could just stop being stupid, then you wouldn't have to worry about this."

"We're being smart."

"You're the luckiest bastard I know. I'm just saying. You fall for the one rich, gorgeous hacker chick in the entire Web who feels the same fucked-up way about relationships you do."

"Fate," I say.

"Do you ever wish you'd never met her?"

My heart lurches. "No, but Haven's got a normal life expectancy. Mine's shot to hell." One year off for one year on, that's the accepted ratio, and I've been hooking up to the Grid for five. I think of my mother, my father. "I haven't changed my mind, okay? I'm not putting Haven through that. And I already spend more time away from the twins than I should."

"Not even if she wants to?"

"She doesn't. And I couldn't keep this secret from her if . . . Next topic." I can't talk about her anymore, not down here. *She* and *this* can never be in the same place.

Scope holds up his hands. "Fine. Your life, man."

Such as it is.

Our feet know where they're going; our eyes check often to make sure we're not being followed down to the warehouse on the edge of the island. There are a lot of abandoned buildings down here, empty of the fruits of commerce for which the first incarnation of this city was known. Less damaged ones have been turned into needed housing, but ours is echoing and bare, swathed in razor wire and silence. Squeezing through the hole in the fence takes care embedded by years of practice.

Inside, twisted pieces of junk litter the floor, too worthless to be scavenged. A frayed square of carpet is folded back; the edge of a trapdoor is visible in a patch of floor a little less dirty than the rest.

We descend into an apparently empty room; our boots clang on the ladder's metal rungs. "Just us," I call, and faces emerge from shadows thrown by the single lightbulb, bodies half-hidden by old generators we've rebuilt and strange shapes that don't look like what they are. Mage, whose skin is so dark I can find him only by the whites of his eyes, and Phoenix, who is busy examining a lock of her red and orange hair with affected boredom.

"Hey, guys," says a voice above us that I know almost as well as my own, the way it meshes with my own when we sing.

"You're late," I reply. Johnny's usually the first one here. He grimaces, disappears into the shadows, and reemerges, looping a strap over his head.

"Yeah," he says, frowning. "I think I was followed."

Mage, Phoenix, Scope, and I all stare at Johnny.

"Patrol-pod was paying a little too much attention to me. Had to double back and come through the alley to lose them," Johnny says. His fingers reach almost reverentially for a tuning peg. Johnny's the only one of us who's scraped together the exorbitant number of credits a real instrument costs on the black market. It's like the thing's plated in gold, he's so protective of it.

Not that I blame him. If I had a guitar, I would be, too. I'm lucky that he lets me mess around with it sometimes when the others aren't around.

"You sure they didn't see you come in here?" Mage asks.

"Wouldn't be here if I wasn't. If they knew something, they'd have tried harder to see where I was going. Probably just bored. We're cool." I know him better than the others and I see from his expression he's not convinced by his own words, but Johnny wouldn't put the rest of us in danger.

"Okay," says Scope. "All here. Let's play."

"One sec." Mage picks up a brick and beats out a dent in one of his old oil drums. Each heavy blow makes me blink. "Thing's been screwing with my sound."

"Can't have that," Phoenix says, blowing a speck of dust off a homemade stick.

We use what we have. What we can find, build, break, and deform into the things we need. Hammered sheets of steel, glass bottles, a xylophone I spent months crafting from scrap metal and salvaged wood three summers ago.

It takes a few more minutes to set up, slipping past each other in the damp, dusty, moldy space with its cheap attempts at soundproofing on the walls and ceiling, avoiding lengths of rusted pipe that stick out at dangerous angles. Mage shifts his drums into position, moving them in increments of inches. Scope prepares to extract glittering melodies from glass, Phoenix stands behind the xylophone, and Johnny holds his battered guitar. I get ready to sing.

None of it is perfect. Perfection would be something like the studios the Corp shows off on TV sometimes. Perfection would be amps to crank high, and no fear of using them. As it is, we only have two hours while the guards in the pods head back to base to change shifts.

Definitely not perfect, but this is real.

Mage lifts his drumsticks and counts us in.

I exhale.

*This* is music. Scope starts, an eerie drone into which Phoenix rains clear, metallic mist. Long, languid notes slide from Johnny's guitar, and Mage hits a drum once. Just once. Stale, ordinary air transforms to song in my lungs, a cloud of warmth that spreads out from my chest and sets my limbs buzzing. Johnny's heavy, darkly sensuous song surrounds me and imbues me with a secret energy, like kissing at night.

I'm part of an intangible *hugeness*. We're all connected, united, looking to each other for cues and playing our parts. A dance, but here my mind is *mine*, and I can control every movement.

Down here, only the music needs me. My family and the conduit chair and my mother's hologram are too far away to ask me for anything. Here, I'm not haunted by faces. Energy builds, refilling me for another week. *Thump. Thump.* Mage starts up again behind me, the guitar gets louder, and Phoenix fights for footage in the sonic space, punishing her metal keys. My voice is deep, almost growling for this one. As I move my feet around Scope, he grins up at me and strikes the glass again.

Johnny and I trade lyrics in a race to the sudden end. *More.* Panting and energized, we launch into another. A slow song, almost lazy, its power from the near frustration of restraint, then a faster one, hard and loud and almost violent. *More.* Adrenaline heats the room, sweat paints our faces, and my feet feel like they're not touching the ground, buoyed by the flurry of motion and sound.

⊕

The two hours go by too fast, divided into common measures and Johnny's recent experiments with weird time signatures. Scope's watch goes off—discordant, jarring—and we stop right away. There have been close calls in the past; now we don't play even a second longer than we should. We're not stealing food. The Corp would have to come up with a whole new creative punishment just for us.

"Phoenix, you were a little off on that last bridge," Johnny tells her. His ear is incredible; more so when I remember that he, like the rest of us, plays almost totally by instinct. What little technical knowledge we have comes from an illegally traded, prewar textbook.

Phoenix flips her hair in front of her face to hide a sulk. The flaming strands ripple when she talks. "Who cares? Not like anyone's going to hear. None of us are going legit."

"That's not the point. Wanting music to be what it *should* be is why we're all here."

"Just work on it next week, girl," Mage says. Phoenix shrugs. "Fine."

We cover our instruments with scraps of threadbare cloth and hide them in dark corners before we leave. I hang back with Mage and watch the others go one by one. Scope pauses with one foot on the ladder.

"Club tonight? Heard there'll be some new tunes."

"Yeah," I say. "See you there."

We can never escape.

◆

Mage and I hit the depot on the way home, where stalls of Corp-licensed vendors hawk food and other necessities. If you know the right ones, they'll sell things that definitely aren't vegetables and soap. Mage goes off to talk to a man named Imp about some black-market piece of computer gear I wouldn't have a clue how to use. I buy a loaf of rough bread, a bag of rice, vegetables, nuts, a small cheese I hope will tempt my father. Red meat is almost nonexistent down here—the only land on which large animals can be kept is the giant park in the middle of the island, and even those are weak, over-cloned from the ones brought in before the siege began. An upper-Web luxury. The chicken I pick up is small and anemic, a product of one of the skyscraper farms. We say good-bye back on the street, Mage's arms full of delicate electronics wrapped in cheap cloth.

"Where've you been? You look . . . happy."

I nearly drop one of the bags at Haven's feet, which are resting against the bottom step below the door to my building.

"Shopping."

Haven looks at the two rough cloth bags in my hands. "It took you an hour?"

"Yeah, well, that's how long it takes when you don't have people to do it for you," I say, realizing too late that it was a genuine question. She inhales sharply at the hint of bitterness beneath the teasing.

"Shit, I didn't mean that. I didn't know you were waiting. You should've messaged me." My tablet is in my pocket, but it hasn't buzzed all afternoon.

"What can I say," she says, standing and kissing my cheek. Her perfume makes me lightheaded. "I'm full of surprises."

"Well, mystery girl, how was your day?"

"Busy. Working on a new project."

"Oh?"

"You'll see when it's ready."

I pass my wrist across the scanner and refuse her offer of help with carrying the groceries upstairs. Alpha and Omega get home a few minutes later, both making a beeline for us and then the couch.

"Daddy!" Alpha says, carefully climbing onto his legs. "Guess what we did today?"

Omega sits on the floor by his head, and he and Alpha trade excited descriptions of their days. I can tell the effort he's expending to open his eyes and talk to them will exhaust him later, but I'm glad for their sake that he tries.

The high I'm still riding from band practice gets me through the evening without needing a hit from the console. Haven and I make dinner for them, too close in my cramped kitchen. Really, she mostly watches and slices things.

"Wake up." My father's eyes flicker, and I shake his shoulder with the hand not holding a plate of bread and cheese.

"Anthem," he says through cracked lips. "Thirsty."

I get a bottle of water and hold it to his mouth. He drinks as well as the weakness will allow, atrophied muscles slack in his face. The collar of his shirt darkens, hiding the stains already there, and he coughs.

I wonder if he felt this way when my mother was dying, torn

between wanting her pain to be over and wanting her to live for his own selfish reasons.

"You need to eat something," I tell him. He shakes his head. We go through this pretty much every day. I help him sit up a little, then take a spot on the floor next to the couch and feed him, watching the TV during every protracted chew. From the kitchen, I hear forks clattering against plates and Haven encouraging Omega to eat his tomatoes.

"And now, a message from President Z," says the spokeswoman. The screen goes black, but there's nothing wrong with it. Assassinations during rebel uprisings were a pretty common cause of death for our first several leaders; now all we know of anyone in the job is a disembodied voice and a single, probably invented initial. We know even less about the Board, the group of nine who assist the president, because they don't bother to go on TV. They sit in their offices high up in headquarters and make it illegal to reveal their identities.

"Citizens!" President Z begins, the timbre screechy from digital modification—or I hope so. I might actually have a little sympathy for the woman if she sounds like that in real life. "We have good news to share. A small skirmish was detected in Quadrant Three, but it has been taken care of. I wish to remind you all that your Corporation works for *you*, and we will go to any necessary lengths in order to protect you from those who wish to send our peaceful oasis back to the chaos of earlier times."

I shake my head. A guy probably just had a bad reaction to a track, and others got swept up in the chaos. It happens. Disorganized riots break out and are quelled quickly by guards who blast strong drugs from speakers mounted on their pods.

"In addition, I am pleased to announce that more power has been allotted to the Grid to address a shortage in Quadrant Four, so we can all enjoy the music to its fullest tonight. Enjoy your evenings, Citizens, and long live the Web!"

*Long live.* Right. The Web might, but nothing else has longevity. At eighteen, I'd be middle-aged if I had a normal job. As a conduit, I'm on the downhill slide to old.

I throw a crust of bread at the TV.

"Turn that crap off," says Haven from the doorway. She shoots a disgusted look at the screen and retreats back into the kitchen.

I follow her. "Are you two finished?" I ask the twins, putting my father's half-eaten meal down by the sink. Omega still hasn't eaten his tomatoes, and Alpha's left most of her rice. With promises of a treat—a piece of chocolate I splurged on at the depot—I persuade them to clean their plates.

"Ant?" Omega says, licking his fingers of the last traces of sticky chocolate. "What's a drug?"

Fine hairs around my neck jack stand on end. "Why?"

"Fable said that's why Mommy is in the citizen-place."

I'm going to kill that kid. I'm not paying his mother credits so he can open his bratty little mouth around my brother and sister. Haven is frozen, silvery eyebrows nearly at her hairline, when I look to her for help or inspiration or . . . something.

Lies tickle my tongue. Fable's wrong. He's making it up. Drugs aren't something they have to think about. But however okay I've been with keeping the truth from them until the right time came, I can't bring myself to lie outright. I do try for a minute, fail, and force air into knotted lungs.

I should have known there'd never be a right time, and now they're *both* looking at me.

"It's something that makes you feel good. Or bad. Sometimes it's something that makes pain go away."

"Why would anyone want to feel bad?" Alpha asks.

Haven's expression unsticks, like someone's poured warm water over it. "It's not that simple, kiddo. You remember how I brought you that chocolate cake on your birthday and you ate so much it made you sick?" Alpha nods. "But other times, it's the best thing in the world, and you eat just enough that it makes you happy, right?"

"Yeah." Alpha smiles, the gap showing where she recently lost the last of her baby teeth.

My chest actually hurts from gratitude, but this isn't Haven's responsibility. "So it's a little like that," I say, forcing a smile because the twins need one and Haven deserves one. "Only it's music that does it, and the Corporation makes sure that all the music we hear makes us feel something. Mom had too much, and it made her sick. Someone figured out how to do it a long time ago, but it's not good for little kids, which is why you haven't heard any yet." Close enough.

"That's weird," Omega says. "When will we get to try it?"

My stomach churns. "It's nothing you need to think about right now," says Haven. "Why don't you go get ready for bed?"

They disappear to their room, kissing our father goodnight on the way. I can't make it to my own fast enough. My natural high from this afternoon is gone, ruined by the Corp, the way they poison everything.

*Fuck.*

*Three years.* I stab at the console screen. *Three years before they're exposed.* It doesn't sound like a long time, not to me. The fewer minutes you have, the shorter they feel.

Haven joins me, pacing the length of my room while I attempt to still my whirling thoughts with a track. It doesn't work. Over and over, around and around; there is no way to twist the twins' blossoming understanding into something okay. My mother died before she had to watch the drug fully sink its talons into me; my father might as well have done the same.

In three years, I'll still be lucid enough to have to watch the two people I love most fall into the inescapable abyss. While they were in the dark, I could close my eyes and join them.

Soon the twins are going to figure out the whole truth. Then they'll realize it'll happen to me, too. And how do I tell them that none of us have a choice about going to the clubs or tracking at home? Even if trying to abstain didn't make my body shake and turn my mind to sludge, the Corp monitors that stuff. They know when we're not listening enough.

Three years. The days will run into each other, one shade of gray blending into the next, and suddenly I'll be sending them off to school worrying that today is *the* day.

And on that day, everything will fall apart. They'll come home with dreamy, complacent smiles. Food will taste like colors, and the music they've just heard will light their minds with sunshine.

I'll never forget that first hit. Nothing really compares. We all spend the rest of our lives hoping the next new release will recreate it. Sometimes it comes close, and the high from those can last for hours or even days. The first time a track did that for me, I wound up in an OD station for a week.

That was just before Johnny found me, and that's the worst part of this. I *know* what real music is. Untainted sound, the pure beauty it's supposed to be, and I can't tell them. Not before it's too late, not at all. Nothing could make me break the promise of secrecy I swore to the guy who gave me something to live for at a time when I was too dumb to realize what I already had, not even the twins.

"Anthem," Haven says. I read my name on her lips and pull the headphones off as the final beats of the track fade away.

"Don't." I shake my head. "Just . . . don't say anything."

Arms slide around my waist. She smells like roses from the park.

"You know they were only eight when they picked their handles? I was almost twelve," I say.

"They're growing up fast, I know. You didn't have an older brother to worship. They watch everything you do."

"What if I'm doing all of it wrong?"

"You're not. You make this a real family, Anthem. Not like mine," she whispers.

I lift my head from her shoulder and step away because everything's just too close right now and my willpower is wavering. "Go without me, I'll meet you there."

"You sure?" she asks.

"Yeah."

"Okay." She reaches out to take my hand and squeezes my fingers.

The twins wait for me, curled under blankets in their beds. I sit by Alpha's feet and tell them about sprawling fields between sunlit cities, the way people could travel to the next town or all the way to the other side of the world. I describe the grand adventures I've read, of people crossing oceans in huge boats or climbing mountains a hundred times higher than the Hydro-Farms.

I hope that the ideas of brightness, of blue water and clean air and healthy ground, will be enough to give them sweet dreams, and don't remind them that, these days, we can't even go to the other side of the river. Tunnels were caved in, bridges were dismantled. To keep us safe, of course. To keep us protected in a fortress of glass and steel and concrete. The airports didn't survive the war, and the last planes fell out of the sky when the pulse bombs went off, but we've been shown footage taken on flights in restored helicopters.

There is nothing out there. We're trapped here. *I'm* trapped here, with them, and the future is coming fast, pouring grains of time around my ankles. It won't stop until it buries me.

# 0110010101051011010110

Light from the TV flickers across my father's face as I sit on the floor to lace up my boots. Expressionless, blank . . . there's almost nothing left of the man I once knew.

I press my palms to my eyes, careful not to smear my makeup. It doesn't help, anyway. The darkness just makes it easier to imagine the scars creeping along neural pathways, fault lines ready for an earthquake.

"I don't know what I'm supposed to do," I say into the silence. He blinks once, which could be a coincidence. "They'll ask me why. What do I tell them?"

Nothing. I check on the twins. I fight off the urge to superimpose dull eyes over closed ones and imagine what they'll look like in ten years. They're healthy and strong, just sleeping.

Wind blows in off the river; it's easier to think out here. All of it started innocently, I guess. Supplies of most medications were depleted almost to nonexistence during the war, so people had to think of other ways to help the sick, the injured. Playing music for them worked better than anything else at tempering pain.

If only it'd stopped there.

I kick the doorframe on my way in. Pixel opens his mouth, painted sticky green, then shakes his head. The streaks in his hair match his lips.

"Only half an hour late, I'm impressed. How goes the life of the con artist?"

Rolling my eyes, I scan my wrist. "Don't call me that, and I'm fine. You?"

"Same old. They're on the balcony."

"Cool." I can't hear it yet, but I can feel it. Tracking at home last night kept me going, but my body itches for the better fix I'll get on the dance floor. "Take it easy," I say, my hand on the door to the soundproof room.

"Always do."

Inside, the music hasn't reached its full addictive momentum yet. Gentle tracks play to ease us in, selected by a computer in a glass booth that would once have held a person. I climb mirrored stairs to the table where my friends are waiting, voices raised above the noise. Implants and ultraviolet makeup seize rotating lights. Haven's saved me a seat beside her; I slide into it and catch that something is *choice*.

She reads too many trashy prewar novels when she's not here or at my place, or doing strange things on her computer.

"I wasn't sure you'd come," Haven says, leaning over so I can hear her, long legs inches from mine. I think she wears that skirt to torture me. In my lap, my knuckles turn white.

Scope waves at me from across the table. The guy beside him puts a hand on his thigh, the nails painted noxious yellow. The DJ-comp ups the volume coming from the speakers and I don't grasp what I think might be an introduction, though I don't miss the look.

Guess they've already reached the past-relationship-talk stage. Unusual for my ex, since me at least. I edge my chair closer to Haven, trying to remember to breathe, but whether the new guy gets the hint, I don't know and it isn't my problem.

"Yo," Scope yells over the music. "What's wrong with you?"

I sigh. "The twins found out. Their friend Fable spilled about the music, about tracking. About"—I gesture to the club—"this."

"Shit."

"Yeah."

"That's your little brother and sister, right?" Yellow Guy asks. I nod. "So what?"

He's a moron. Haven touches my knee, and I take a deep breath. "Because it's fucking *dangerous*, that's why. Yeah, I remember thinking this was cool, too. Couldn't wait to listen. Begged my parents to let me start tracking early. Even tried to sneak on a console when they weren't looking, but my chip wouldn't work yet."

"Look around you," he shouts. "Any of these people seem like they're having a bad time?"

"Fun isn't the point. You're only here because you want to be?"

He concedes with silence and settles back against Scope. I lean forward. "One day, they're going to feel like I do. And they're going to know I didn't protect them."

A group at the next table turn to look at us. "Anthem," Haven says. "Not here, okay?"

She's right. And a bad trip's the last thing I need right now.

The songs thrumming from speakers—louder now—are still mild doses, encoded with happiness, a general sense of good feeling. Like the descriptions I've read of the first few alcoholic drinks.

These days, they just need our ears to keep us in line. If necessity is the mother of invention, greed is its father. Experiments begun in overcrowded hospitals were continued; the Corp was formed by men and women already accustomed to power, technology, innovation.

A hum starts; power lines are threaded through my bones.

"C'mon, guys," Haven says, standing. Scope and Yellow Guy pull apart, and the three of us trail behind her to the dance floor, a throng of metal and glow. Implants on arms and faces flash to the beat, pressure-sensitive body paint changes colors and turns skin to moving sunsets or rippling waves.

Hands reach for the music, magnets beneath stretched skin

pulling them into the sound.

We find a place in the middle, Scope and his . . . whatever immediately twining to become one person. Haven shouts something, and I shake my head, pointing to my ear.

"You're crooked," she says, her lips an inch from my skin. She reaches up and carefully rearranges the blue fiber-optic tubes. Soft fingertips find the wire and follow it down to my neck jack. "Perfect," she whispers, stepping away.

I shiver, icicles of tension breaking free, the music hammering in my ears. A low bass note gongs through the club, drawn out like a held breath as monochrome strobes slow time to half-speed. We wait, expectant, knowing. . . .

Keyboards kick in, rainbows explode overhead, and from the speakers, sound is turned to sight and taste and smell by chemical-sounding, computer-driven noise.

For now, the pleasure is worth it. Worth everything. Which is the point, of course, but I can't bring myself to care when the melody is pulsing through me and I feel alive, human, expansive. Memories turn to fantasies and back again. Here, everything is good and right.

I let the drug pull me into its lies. Welcome the relief.

*The earthquake comes suddenly. The land is mad and it scares me. I'm at the kitchen table doing homework while my mother cooks. The utensils on the wall begin to rattle, and I hear her call my father for help as she pulls me into the doorway.*

*She pulls me with fingers closed around my arm while I try to reach for something I really want on the table. I can't leave it, and she won't let me go! My hand is there, nearly there, but I'm stumbling backward and it's gone, falling into the shaking earth.*

"Help!" The hand on my biceps pulls harder; my arm falls away from Haven. Blinking, I open my eyes to grin at a face that morphs from lines of neon into Scope's. "Anthem, come out, I need you!"

His panic makes me grit my teeth, and I search my mind for the *self* hiding behind layers of sound. My eyeballs feel like they're about to explode. I force them to focus. Yellow Guy is on the ground, his back arched and his limbs flailing. There's no time to drag Haven out, so Scope and I go without her, picking him up and dodging wild bodies to carry him through the crowd.

"Overdose," is all Scope says to his brother. Pixel nods and rushes to press buttons on the wall that will call for a med-pod.

The feeling music gives is the light. This is the dark. Receptors in the brain overload with sound and vision and memory until the whole thing is forced to shut down. I don't envy Yellow Guy the pain I know must be crashing through his head no matter how hard he presses his hands to chrome-embedded temples and screams.

There's nowhere to put him except on the floor. Scope kneels next to him, barely flinching when each punch lands, offering comfort that—best case—will only make Scope feel better.

I concentrate on keeping my feet glued to one spot. The music is calling.

Forever passes in the length of a single track, the med-pod arriving as the vibrations change against the soles of my boots. Uniformed techs let themselves in, nod once at Pixel, and turn their attentions to the body on the floor. Only practice could give them the expertise to bind and gag Yellow Guy so quickly, then strap him to a plastic stretcher. One of them runs a portable scanner over his straining left wrist.

"I want to come," says Scope. I stare at him.

"Medical pods only hold one citizen," says the tech nearest Yellow Guy's head, speaking as if Scope's a child. Then again, it was a pretty stupid question.

"Where are you taking him?" There are a bunch of OD stations not far from here. I've seen the inside of three.

The techs lift the stretcher. "He may contact you when he has recovered," answers the same one, in the same tone. For a second I wonder if the other tech, silent and indifferent to us since they got here, is an Exaur, for some reason not in an orange uniform, but that's ridiculous. Scope's not the only one thinking like an idiot.

Pixel puts his arm around Scope, holding him back from the opening door. Yellow Guy's muffled screams extinguish when it closes again.

"He'll be okay, little brother," Pixel says. "Was he tracking earlier? Were you with him?"

"Don't know. I met up with him here."

"Yeah, well, it happens. Probably just the song. Go back inside. You should have enough time to go under again. I'll come since I don't need to wait for Anthem tonight." Pixel jerks his head in my direction and reaches over to press the button that will seal the doors. "About time I got my own fix on."

Scope looks at me. I shrug. "It's that or go home," I tell him even as I start moving toward the door to the inner room. His heart's not really in it, I can see that, so the music won't work as well as usual or he'll have a bad trip, but there's really nothing else we can do for Yellow Guy tonight.

"Leave him to me," says Pixel. "Go find your girl."

"Thanks."

Some jerk with too many credits to spend on chrome and blood-red contacts is trying to dance with Haven. It doesn't look like she's noticed. Sobered—mostly—by now, I can feel every degree of the molten heat that wells in the pit of my stomach. "Leave her alone!" I shout over the music. He just smiles, too far gone to really understand, and my patient streak narrows to slide into the inch of space between them. My push sends him reeling into the crowd. There. He can understand *that*. I take his place, keeping my hands to myself but letting her fill my other senses, whirls of pink and heat rising from her tawny skin.

She smells like her name. Like everything safe and good. We dance until the club closes; my drugged fog, when I help her back to my place, is lighter than normal. I cover her laughing mouth with my hand to keep her from waking the twins; she kisses my palm and my knees go weak. The bedroom floor seems harder than usual. I toss and turn to the sound of her breathing above my head, my hand clenched to hold in the echo of her lips.

$\phi$

"Scope with his *friend*?" Haven grins and examines the budding leaves on the stunted, disfigured trees. I watch her, drinking her in because she was busy with some family thing last night. Her hair catches the sunlight and holds it until she steps forward.

I keep to the path. Ahead, it turns a corner and winds its way through the leisure area of the park. "Yeah, Scope says he's doing okay."

"Rest and antidote will do that. How are the kids?"

"Fine. With Fable." I haven't strangled him yet.

"They can't really understand it right now," she says. "Kids are too accepting of weird stuff at their age. I was."

"Same here."

We walk more, find a comfortable patch of grass. People pass us—others out enjoying the first warm day of the year.

"I got further into the mainframe yesterday. That system is

choice. Bastards can build a network, I'll give them that."

I look around to make sure no one's close enough to hear us. "What'd you find?"

"Nothing. Boring stuff. Corp employee records, birth and death files. Why anyone would bring a child into this . . . Anyway, the point is I've never gotten that far before."

"You are careful when you do this, right?" It's kind of an asshole question; I've never asked Mage that.

"Anthem." She rolls her eyes. "One, I'm not an idiot. Two, I physically *can't* make any major unauthorized changes, the security is . . . intense. I can get past some of it, but not all. And I just like to play around. It's beautiful in there."

I wonder if I'd wear that expression when talking about the band. "You're kind of a geek, you know."

She pokes me in the ribs. Hard. I fall back, laughing. It feels like music. The darkness of worry is chased away by the sun on my face. When I'm quiet again, Haven joins me, our arms almost touching. I bend my knees and dig my fingers into my thigh. The moment stretches—fifteen quiet minutes I want to bottle and keep.

"Anthem?"

"Hmmm?"

"What if we . . . the twins . . . what if there *is* a choice?"

I turn my head. Her eyes are closed, body relaxed, in contrast to mine. All my cells are like taut rubber, about to snap. "How so?"

"I hear things, sometimes. Like, about people who play stuff that isn't encoded."

The park swims and blurs around me as I sit up. "Keep your voice down." An old couple, maybe in their late thirties, walk past us on the path. Expensively dressed, they stare a little too long at Haven, and I wonder if they know her. "Who told you people do that?"

"No one, exactly," she says, looking up at me. "I overheard my father talking about it. They were discussing ways to get inside the groups. Like, catch them in the act. I . . . I think they're worried. There are more people fighting the music than there used to be, like, immunity or something. I don't know."

The sun is too hot. "The Corp would know if the twins weren't tracking after being exposed. And there's nothing we can do to stop that first time."

"Yeah, I guess." She sighs. "I'd like to hear it, though. Just to see what it sounds like. How it's different. I think a lot of people would."

"You have to promise me you won't get involved in that," I say, grabbing her wrist. "It's dangerous, Haven. Your father was talking about catching them for a reason. Please, promise me."

Hypocrisy tastes like burnt toast. She raises herself on one elbow to properly look at me, and I see my own omissions reflected back by her eyebrows.

"Okay," she says finally. "Okay, chill. It was just an idea."

A tempting one. Just for a second, I let myself think about what it would be like to somehow spread the word, the sound of unencoded music. To be able to sing for Haven, alone, or with the band around me. I could teach the twins about real music.

"I know. Come on, princess, let's go find something to do." I'm still holding on to her, my thumb against the tiny area of skin over her ID chip. She frowns when I let go and stand up.

We leave the park, and I hide my shaking hands in my pockets. I need to get to a console soon.

I glance at her face. I can wait.

The streets this far north are lined with stores, faces of steel and neon beckoning, a mobile rainbow brighter than the sun. Haven would probably go in if she were alone and spend credits on outfits of latex and lace that would make me want to blind every man who could see her.

She leads me into a dusty, hushed library. Everything in here is old. Few new books have been printed since before the war; the ones that have been are Corp manuals. There's enough here for anyone's lifetime, especially mine. When I was younger, I wondered why the Corp let us have books. In my mother's last months, she finally told me. I guess by then she had nothing to lose.

Neither does the Corp. Relics of the past aren't indulgences or evidence of generosity, they're reminders. Warnings. Look, they say. Look at how the society that produced these things ended. The lessons, virtues, morals, and freedom they teach are something to fear, not covet.

An hour is lost in brittle pages: Haven finds the funny stuff she likes while I rifle through novels for mentions of music overlooked in the cull.

I creep up behind her. She's somewhere else, head bowed, submerged in an old world.

"I should go home," I whisper.

The book hits the floor with a heavy thump and a cloud of dust. "You ass!" She wheels around. "You did that on purpose."

"Yeah."

All the way downstairs, she tries not to smile. The doors slide open and noise floods in, too loud after the reverential hush. We step outside, one single step before I freeze.

She's an Exaur, the woman who is crossing the street away from us in a creased orange uniform, her head bowed, oblivious. I don't have time to go through a list in my head of all the things she could've done to earn the worst punishment the Corp can dish out and still keep the person alive.

"Stop!" Haven yells, her voice joining the wail of the patrol-pod's siren as it turns the corner too fast. "Stop!"

Almost too late, I grab Haven before she runs out into the road. The woman crumples on impact with the pod; blood sprays up the windshield like drops of acid rain. Once, twice the body bounces, skidding to a stop near the opposite curb.

"She couldn't hear you," I say into an ear that won't stay still because Haven is shaking violently. "She . . . Exaur. She couldn't hear the siren."

"I—" Haven gasps, doubling over. Vomit sprays our shoes, staining the air sour, and I tighten my grip on her arms, holding her until she seems steady again. I grit my teeth and breathe to quell the nausea.

A crowd has assembled behind us. I don't think I'm the only one who wants to look away from the bloody figure, just as I'm not the only one who can't.

Everything's stopped. The only movement is from the guards emerging from the pod. "Didn't you see her?" Haven yells at them. "Or didn't it matter? What's wrong with you?" Her voice is full of tears. One of them shrugs as he surveys the woman and takes out a tablet to type a message.

"Haven," I hiss. "It was an accident. Be quiet."

She pulls herself free of my arms, stepping off the curb toward the guard striding over to us. "Identify yourself, Citizen," he says, mouth twisted into a smile that promises pain. "I repeat, identify yourself." One of his hands moves to rest on the barrel of the gun in a holster at his waist.

Actual shootings are rare. I look at the woman again. The Corp prefers other methods.

With his free hand, the guard takes out his scanner. "Don't touch her," I snarl when he reaches for Haven's arm. He laughs at me.

"You, too," he says, waving the little device. Maybe if I cooperate he'll leave her alone. I step forward and show my wrist. The sensor hovers over my skin for a fraction of a second before it beeps. "Conduit scum," he snorts above the ringing in my ears.

"Go to hell," Haven says. I'm not quick enough to stop him from grabbing her; the beep sounds an instant later. Hot, thick fury oozes in my gut, but it's worth it for the way his eyes suddenly bulge. His recovery is quick, but not quick enough.

"You should choose your company more wisely, Citizen." His voice has turned from ice to oil. It's not an improvement. "Surely your family doesn't approve of this trash?"

I'm impressed by her aim. The gob of spit barely misses his eye. It lands on his cheekbone and slides past flaring nostrils to a faltering smile. The stillness of the crowd is palpable. No one breathes until the guard steps back and wipes his face on the sleeve of his uniform.

"Feisty little thing, aren't you? I like that. Let me know when you're tired of him."

"Yeah," Haven scoffs. "Sure."

"Disperse," he orders. Feet scurry, and when I pull Haven away from the curb and the sight of the body being dumped in the back of the pod, it's impossible to tell anything happened.

As soon as we're around the corner, Haven collapses into my arms. Tears sink into my clothes. "That poor woman. I hate them," she says, hoarse and defeated. "I hate who I am to them."

"I know. You should track. We both should."

"Yeah." She pulls away, wiping her eyes. "Your place? I don't want to go home."

I pull out my tablet and send a message to Fable's mother. A minute later it buzzes with her agreement to keep the twins another few hours.

It's a long walk back to my apartment, but neither of us feels like getting into any kind of pod right now. Clouds move in and a light rain starts to fall when we hit the other side of the Vortex and descend into Quadrant Two. The streets run slick with grime, the same nothing-gray as concrete and the river. It coats the soles of my boots, knee-high indulgences of black plastic and gleaming metal.

Shoes are harder to make than they look. I gave up after ruining too many pieces of good material.

Haven presses herself into my side and I tighten my arm around her, only letting go when I have to swipe my wrist. Towels from the hygiene cube and the extra headset hanging above my father. She uncoils her hair, and I flip through menus on the console in my room, ignoring the stronger meds that would eat up too many credits in favor of a list of mood stabilizers that should help.

"Thanks." Her voice cracks. I take the towel from her cold hands and run it over her hair until it's as close to dry as it's going to get.

"Come on," I tell her. We sit on the bed, headphones over our ears, a blanket pulled over us, boots and all.

Despite the shivers that wrack her body, she's so warm next to me, and I'd be more than a little okay with just staying like this forever. I'm not even sure I need the tracks that work to leach the chill from my bones, calm my stomach, and drag my mind from dark places. Haven relaxes by degrees until her head is on my shoulder, plastic headset digging into my collarbone. I don't move.

I concentrate on remembering to breathe. My eyes close for an instant; I see red and snap them open again. Slowly feeling returns to my toes.

The static hiss of near silence signals the end of the music. I edge out from under her, lay her head down on the single pillow, and adjust the blanket. She's not completely asleep—a word I can't make out forms itself on her lips—so I set up another handful of tracks and leave her to rest.

Alpha and Omega burst through the door an hour later, cheerful and loud, fighting to tell me and our father about the games they played with Fable. It's impossible not to smile, and in any case I don't want them asking what's wrong, but I put my finger to my lips and tell them Haven's asleep. While I cook and all through dinner, I compose lyrics in my head—a sad, slow lament—while they compete to see who can be more quiet.

It's Omega, but I give them both a square of chocolate for dessert.

Haven joins us in the kitchen, creased from sleep, her face streaked and swollen. The twins jump up, homework forgotten on the table until she reminds them. Even then, she's the one who clings to them for another minute.

"Hungry?"

"No." She shakes her head, her hair spilling into red-rimmed eyes. I toast a slice of bread anyway, and make tea from peppermint leaves and the last of the sugar. Crumbs land on the table when she leans over to help Omega with a math problem.

Later, when they're in bed and I've failed at getting my father to eat, we go back to my room. "Your mother," she begins after a long silence. I hold my breath. "Is that why you could handle it? I've never seen a body before." Her voice tightens, and I lace our fingers together.

"I guess? Mostly I was worried about you."

A smile flickers dully on her full lips. "You never talk about her."

"You don't talk about yours either."

"True." She looks out the window.

"Do you miss her?"

Haven shrugs. "I miss the way she was, before . . . When she was herself."

Yeah. I miss the way my mother was *before*, too.

"I hate them, Anthem. Everything they do. The Corp. They wreck people. I wish they'd all just . . . die."

"Maybe you should tell your father what we saw today."

"He won't care."

I can't believe that's true. She's too good, too generous, and she must get it from somewhere. But I know she believes it, and she's the one who matters.

"I wish it didn't have to be like this. I just"—I shake my head—"I don't have any answers."

"Maybe I do," she says, her head jerking sharply away from the window to look at me.

"If you mean what we were talking about in the park." It feels like that was days ago.

"No, not that. I mean getting into the mainframe. Changing things." Her set jaw could smash glass.

I grab her shoulder, rigid under my hand and a layer of purple lace. "Haven, what do you want to do?" I ask slowly.

Quiet. "Nothing," she says finally, a smile appearing on her face, too bright and wide. "Come on, lie down with me." I hesitate and she rolls her eyes. "I'm not going to attack you."

"Yeah." My laugh sounds false even to me. The bed creaks as we move around. She must be able to hear my heartbeat, fast and loud, when she puts her head on my chest, but she doesn't comment. I inhale through fine, rose-scented hair that tickles my nose and shift on the hard mattress. She asks if I'm comfortable and I just tighten my arms. Sleep finds her first. I stare at the ceiling, wishing I could be down in the basement, screaming my lungs out, the wail of Johnny's guitar erasing the siren from my mind. Eventually I give up, disentangle myself, and head for the console.

Just for one track. Maybe two.

⊕

*Blood pulses to the beat of harsh machine-driven noise; the music's texture is like shattered glass, each note precisely jagged, edges hard. They fit together in a melody that moves my feet inches and sends my mind miles away.*

*Freedom. I move, fly, float on memories, and sink into dreams.*

*I am nowhere. And everywhere. One day maybe someone will look, scan through my thoughts and find this night, this club, this floor on which I'm dancing. They'll see the neon lights brushing over my skin, red hotter than blue, green that tingles a little, purple soothing as a warm shower. They'll see Haven through my eyes and know that I loved every pink, glittering, fierce inch of her.*

*If it's the twins who look, they'll know I couldn't make it stop, but that I wanted to and maybe that will count for something in the favorable light death casts on the dead.*

*The sound presses in and crushes me. I can't move in this tiny box and my hands beat against the door. I can see them through the glass, why can't they see me?*

*Someone's coming. Pounding, rhythmic footsteps. A halo of lights bursts outside the door and I see myself, my own pale skin, corpse-white between streaks of glowing color.*

*A siren wails. Blood, again. I'm covered in it, watching it slide over me, bright red. Then green, then yellow, and that makes no sense. I don't understand.*

*Cold. So cold. Get me out of here! I'm shivering, gasping, dying. My fists punch the glass over and over. Help me! I scream again with my last breath. Something pink reaches out, opens the door, and touches me as I tumble out into warmth. I gulp the air, and I'm okay. Haven is there, right next to me, the lights turning her face different shades of happiness. Scope is here and the twins are safe at home, wrapped in the kind of sleep that can only be had by the innocent, the unknowing, the untainted.*

*I stay above for as long as I can, fighting the pull long enough to compose myself.*

*I'm okay.*

*I dive back in.*

◑

I'm pretty sure the couch is going to have a permanent dent from my father's body, lying on his side with his eyes on the TV. He's getting worse. His favorite foods don't tempt him anymore, and flesh is dropping from his bones at a rate that can only mean one thing.

The music itself isn't the only cause of death, but it's the guaranteed one if starvation doesn't get you first, or if you can't summon a last, fatal burst of energy to put an end to all of it.

I wonder what my brain looks like. Not as bad as my father's, but the damage is there already, growing every time I put on a track, building with every song I dance to at the club. One day it will be a scarred, twisted mess and I will be nothing at all. A chip in a locker, stored memories lying by omission.

Maybe I should move him back to the bedroom and sleep on the couch myself. No. The twins deserve as much time as possible with whatever's left inside his shell. The pain is intensifying, though—I have to pry clenched fists open on the rare occasions he agrees to eat—and he whimpers through his dreams.

He's not the only one having nightmares. Mine are jagged, bloody, horror-filled with sirens and screams. I wake, gasping in the sour scent of my own cold sweats, and pad to the console. I'm not sure whether I track to calm myself down or for the reminder that I can still hear.

It's Wednesday again, so I only use the console to check the balance of my account and find an expensive pain-killing track for my father. His reddened ears are hot to the touch.

It's fine. I'll just have to shop more carefully the next time I hit the depot.

◆

Scope isn't waiting for me on our usual corner. I hang around for a few minutes and lean against the window of a cheap clothing store until the old woman who runs it bangs on the glass and shouts at me through gapped teeth. I walk a little farther down the block and take out my tablet.

You coming?_

*Buzz.* Go without me. See you there._

Phoenix and Mage are arguing about something in the corner, probably just for something to do. Mage isn't taking her bait, and I laugh at Phoenix's indignant scowl.

"No Scope?" Johnny asks around the stub of a knife-sharpened he's worn as long as I've known him and writes something down, hand trembling a little as it skates across the page. Maybe he needs to track.

"Running late, I guess."

"Here. Burn it when you know them." Johnny passes me the lyrics he was scribbling. I scan them quickly. Nice. A strain of melody plays through my head, something almost cynically upbeat to underscore the seething words.

"Sorry, guys." Scope jumps down from the ladder. Phoenix clears her throat. "And girl," he adds.

I'm about to point out that Scope's left the trapdoor open, but a single footstep overhead freezes my voice and turns us all to statues with faces carved into masks of fear.

All except Scope's. "I—" he begins. A boot hits the top rung, its laces neon yellow.

I don't wait to see the rest of our . . . guest.

Scope tries to wrench his arm away. I'm bigger and pissed. "What the hell, man? What is he doing here?" In a shadowed corner, as far as we can get from the others, his expression turns defiant.

"He wanted to hear us play."

"And he knows we do . . . how, exactly?" Johnny asks, a few feet behind me. "Decided to show off or something? Damn it, Scope! Are you forgetting I was fucking *followed* here last week?"

"Then it's his risk to take! It was after his OD, okay? He said that, just once, he wished he could hear real music. Pure stuff. Was I supposed to ignore it?"

"Uh, yeah," I say, my eyes narrowing. "We all agreed."

His lip curls. "Just because you're too scared to tell anyone . . ."

"Fuck you." I let go, ball my fists at my sides, and try to remember that there's a whole group of witnesses to this and only Phoenix will find it funny. I'm surprised she's not already laughing. "You think it's only her I'm trying to protect? What about the twins? My father? *Your* mother and Pixel? You think the Corp won't go after them if they find out about us?"

"Johnny, Anthem," Mage breaks in, "nothing we can do about it now."

Scope and I glare at each other.

"What's your problem? Still hung up on me? *You* ended it, remember."

My laughter fills the room. "Yeah, sure, that's it."

"Then what?"

"My problem is you're an idiot. At least when we were together your brain was in your head, not your pants."

Johnny puts his hand on my shoulder. "Scope, man, you should've asked me."

"Sorry," he mutters.

I turn away. "Mage is right. Unless we can get a hold of a memory track, we're stuck with this." I'm only half kidding, but though I know the encoding to wipe memory—in a living subject—exists, I've only heard of it being used in special circumstances. "Look," I say, squinting to find Yellow Guy in the gloom, "it's nothing personal. We just don't know you, and this is Johnny's band. His rules."

"Should I leave?"

We all look at Johnny, who shakes his head. "Doesn't matter now. But tell anyone . . ." He trails off into a silence more menacing than anything he could have said.

Yellow Guy holds up his hands. "Got it."

"You feeling better?" I ask.

"Back to normal. Don't remember much, honestly, except the pain." He grimaces. "But the techs fixed me up."

"How long were you in?"

"Got out on Monday. I've done nothing but sleep since."

"We're wasting time," Phoenix says, irritable now that the entertainment's over. "So if you boys are all done, we should get in some actual, you know, *playing* before the switch."

"We only practice during the guards' shift change," Scope

explains. Yellow Guy nods and moves to lean against a pillar, his hands behind his back. I have to give him credit for not asking a million questions while we set up. He just watches, eyes bright in the dimness.

I have to give Scope some credit, too. Johnny hasn't even picked up his guitar yet and this feels different, even just with an audience of one guy whose taste in music is hopefully better than it is in favorite colors. Sure, we've all played solo for each other before to make sure we're getting something right, but this isn't the same. My voice quavers a little during a quick warm-up and I realize I want Yellow Guy to like us. To think we're good.

Doesn't stop me from wanting to punch Scope, though.

"Ready?" Mage asks.

"Five minutes ago." Phoenix flips one of her sticks over in her hand.

"Yeah."

"Let's do it."

It's easy, so easy to fall into this music. Behind me, instruments come in one by one and I inhale, my pulse setting itself to Mage's beat. Gathering energy crawls over my skin. I close my eyes and open my throat, ready for the words we always start with.

It never gets old.

We sound better than we have in a long time, since before the stumbles experienced when we added Phoenix to the mix. Johnny sings about the girl he loves, a theme that'll never die no matter what the Corp thinks up to mess with music next. Even the stuff played in the clubs—what's not all about glorifying the Corp, anyway—is boy-meets-girl.

The urge to write about that is something I understand. My own songs stay in my head because it's Johnny's band. He's the one who found us and, after deciding we could be trusted, let us in on the secret of this room.

Mage hammers on his drums with fists like an angry god and Scope hits one of the bottles so hard it skitters away to smash against the wall, the sound a new layer to the rising crescendo. The next time he does that, it won't be an accident. Phoenix throws her sticks in the air, catching them before her next note. Johnny's guitar wails and screams, his fingers a blur.

Over it all, I weave new flourishes into Johnny's lyrics and he laughs midbeat.

A flash of red catches my eye, but it's just Scope's hair.

One song fades into the next, and the next. We play through Johnny's view of the world—his wish for freedom, his hatred of the Corp that employs him. By turns our instruments are thunderous and frenzied, whispery and simmering.

Maybe anger only needs the right melody, the right rhythm to be beautiful.

Practice is too short since we lost precious minutes at the beginning, but when the alarm sounds we're breathing hard and bathed in sweat. Johnny is serene and Mage is smiling. Phoenix looks truly happy, which deserves to be on the news. I high-five Johnny and turn away from Scope's upheld hand.

"And here I thought you were just trying to impress me," Yellow Guy says to Scope, pushing away from the pillar. Their fingers tangle; we all look away. "You guys can really play," he adds, the kiss over. "You should go legit. It could be you people dance to at the clubs."

"Never gonna happen," says Johnny. "I'd rather play down here for the rest of my life, with *my* stuff, than let the Corp get their hands on my tunes and turn them into tracks. What they do is *evil*."

Yellow Guy raises his eyebrows. "So, what? You're not hooked?

How do you make that work?"

"I wish. I'm as addicted as the next guy, man, but I don't want to be. I tracked *hard* my first few years, OD'd, like you. A bunch of times. Then, the last time, I'm recovering and just keep thinking *what would it be like to really play?* Took a while to put this together, but here we are. Now I just track to get by, same as everyone else here."

"Unreal. So is it just the five of you?"

"There's other bands around. Don't know where, don't care. Not like we can all get together for some big-ass party. Better to stay hidden," he says, aiming the last part at Scope.

Gear is packed up and stowed away while Yellow Guy asks Mage and Phoenix their stories—less filled with venom than Johnny's, but they don't have any more love for the Corp than he does.

"You coming?"

I look at Scope and shake my head. Eventually, he disappears up the ladder behind yellow-laced boots, leaving Johnny and me alone.

"How's everything?" I ask.

"Good, I guess. Life in the Web." He leans against the pillar Yellow Guy adopted earlier and folds his arms. "Except . . ."

I wait.

"I don't know. It's . . ."

"What?"

His eyes flick to the trapdoor. "I didn't want to freak everyone out again, but I keep seeing that pod."

"They're all over the place," I say, trying to ignore the flutter in my stomach. The band is the only thing that keeps me sane. "You think we should find a new spot?"

"Or I should stop." The thought looks like it causes him physical pain.

"C'mon, all the patrol-pods look the same, man. You're thinking about it because you're looking for it."

"Yeah." He exhales and uncrosses his arms. "You're right. Anyway, good sound today."

We move on and talk about new stuff he wants to try, more weird shit like Scope breaking the glass.

I'm all for it, but I just can't figure out why he wants to. Why he bothers. The tiniest taste of actually performing makes me ask myself why Johnny works so hard to perfect a sound no one but us— and Yellow Guy, I guess—will ever hear.

# 011100100**1071**00101010111

Lights wink at me; Mage's fingers click instructions that flash across a monitor.

"I'll never get that," I say, and he grins.

"It's not so different from what we do. Being in there, it's almost transcendent. Code is pure, man. Clean. And a little dangerous."

"Think I've got enough of that in my life already."

"Yeah. Okay"—he hits one last key—"done. One sec." Doors open and close, not quite muffling the scrape of a vent screen being pushed aside. He's back inside within a minute, holding out a battered book that I bury under a pile of old sweaters in my bag until I can hide it under my bed. "Give it back to Johnny when you're done?" It's not safe to keep it in one place all the time, and Johnny's already worried about being watched.

"Thanks."

"Sure."

Typical Mage, not to ask why I want it, and I'm glad because I'm not sure. There's nothing in these pages I don't have memorized. A book on real music can't tell me how to protect Alpha and Omega's young ears from the Corp.

"Water?"

"I've gotta get home before the twins do," I say. "Have fun with that."

"I'm telling you, it's a whole different level."

Outside, there's a crackle in the air like the moment before a thunderstorm, even though the sky is as close to blue as it ever gets.

I step into the street in front of his building, slowly, because down here moving fast is a good reason for a guard to wonder why.

One arm wrapped around my bag, protecting it from the people who brush past. Out of the corner of my eye I see a patrol-pod and hug the book tighter.

Fuck, I'm turning into Johnny. My tablet buzzes in my pocket, a message from Haven.

Club later?_

Where else would I be? Good day?_

Productive._ Whatever that means. She still won't tell me what her project is, which I guess is only fair. I smile at the screen, blocking out everything around me except her name as I cross a crowded square. I picture Haven in that short skirt I love and put my tablet away to restrain myself from suggesting it.

It happens too fast. I look up too late, into the wide, wild eyes of a girl on a violent trip a few feet away. A piece of metal flies from her hand, misses someone's head by an inch, and ricochets off a street-lamp. Someone cries out. I reel backward, clutching my bag, but there's nowhere to go. A guy tries to grab her arm and she throws him into the crowd, her face lit like a fuse. A dozen precious eggs smash on the ground.

I don't know who throws the first punch, or the second. Who pushes first. I have to get out of here. Glass shatters somewhere on the other side of the square and an alarm starts to scream.

I can't be caught with the book. It's too precious to drop. People close in all around me, a violent, formless mass. A single elastic second stretches when no one is touching me, and I can feel the heat, the beauty in the turmoil. The *life*. Someone kicks me and the moment snaps, pain echoing around my knee as I stumble back, am shoved forward. My fingers tighten on the fake leather strap.

"Citizens! Disperse!"

It's too late for that, and I know what's coming next. The crowd roars as if it's one thing instead of hundreds, a song made up of notes. The air twists and the crowd unites against the pod, streaming around me to charge it, and from the back I hear it tip, the strangled crackle of the loudspeaker smashing to the ground. I step back, away, turning as another patrol-pod careens into view, a third, a fourth, closing in all around us. *Free drugs for everyone.* The music starts to flow from the speakers mounted on top of the pods. Hard and electric, strong and heavily laced with some of their most powerful drugs. A guitar plays and I think of Johnny. He's better.

He should be playing this.

We . . . should . . .

I can't . . . think. I can't think. Are they dancing? Music, anger, energy. Everything goes black.

◆

The green text of *Crime & Punishment* blurs, the plug in my neck jack feels deeper, more invasive. I hate this job. It gives me too much time to think about the things I'll never say or do because of all the things I've already said and done.

At three, I'm de-jacked and I drag myself up, into the elevator, out onto the street. Haven is waiting for me by the statue, holding out a bottle of grape juice. I sigh and push my feet toward her.

"I've told you not to meet me here."

Her eyes narrow the tiniest fraction, then she smiles. "And I choose to ignore it. That's how we work. Besides, I was here anyway."

Oh.

"I want to go see Scope," she adds.

"He's at work," I say, twisting the cap off the bottle and pouring half of it down my throat. Sweetness explodes on my tongue.

"Duh. I'm thinking of having something done."

"Is this about what happened? The Exaur?" Scope's told me about this before, the way people will come in for chrome as some kind of catharsis.

"Maybe a little." She shrugs. "Plus, we never see him anymore. He's always with whatshisface."

"Okay," I say through a yawn that cracks my jaw and makes my eyes water.

"That still hurt?" she asks, reaching up, her fingers skating over the healing bruise at my temple.

"Not really." Thank fuck for Mage. He saw the riot from his window and pulled me out under cover of the confusion.

We climb a trans-pod down to Two, my head against the window until Haven tugs me down to rest on her shoulder.

Scope's chrome studio isn't far from his apartment, on the opposite side of Quadrant Two from my own. The river's acrid scent fills our nostrils on the walk between the pod stop and the storefront, a bitter wind cuts at our skin. Haven shivers, but I lean into it, breathing deeply.

"Hey, beautiful. And Anthem." Scope grins from a stool next to a chair similar to the one I have at work. A huge guy is on it, tipped almost horizontal, the soles of his boots pointing at us as Scope leans over his head. "Gimme a few."

Hard, black regulation Corp chairs line the area at the front. I collapse on one, and a sketch of Scope's work crinkles under my head where I rest it against the wall. Haven settles next to me, close enough to feel her warmth. She crosses her legs, and I focus on a design across the room until it blurs into random shapes instead of a cohesive picture.

I've never seen the allure of chrome, not for myself. There are enough foreign objects implanted in my body. But I do like the way it looks at the clubs, flashing under the lights.

Angry, broken blood vessels edge the new silver swirls on the man's round cheeks when he stands, pulling off the headphones that were definitely playing something to numb the pain. He checks his reflection in a mirror, grins, then flinches, his jowls wobbling. Scope tells him not to smile for a few hours and directs him to a scanner to pay.

Haven wants bracelets, delicate loops around both wrists. I half listen to her discussion with Scope, who promises to sketch something cool for her. This job is really made for him, or the other way around.

A draft of cold air washes over me. I pry my eyes open, expecting to see another customer, but it's impossible to mistake that yellow. I wave at him and he smiles back, but it doesn't reach his eyes. Honestly, I wonder what Scope sees in him. He's cute, in an overdramatic kind of way, but colder than Scope's usual type. Scope goes for guys like himself—happy and trusting, eager for a good time.

Except for me, but he's known me long enough to look past the things that make me the way I am.

"Hey," says Yellow Guy, sliding his arms around Scope's waist from behind and kissing his neck. The blush is such a contrast to Scope's normal paleness that I laugh and decide I like Yellow Guy a little more. Haven manages to roll her eyes, shake her head, and smile at the same time.

"I'll close up," Scope says. "Let's go do something fun."

We wind up at my place, all crammed into my room. Yellow Guy immediately claims the bed, sprawling back and pulling Scope down to join him.

"Mess up my sheets and you'll regret it," I warn.

"Someone should." Scope laughs.

"Fuck you. Just for that, Haven and I get to track first." I tug on her hand until she gets within reach of the headphones and sits on the floor. I choose a pounding rock song that's been one of my favorites since it appeared on the menu a few months ago.

Oh, hell, yes. It erases my exhaustion and sends me into spasms of laughter at absolutely nothing. Haven is giggling at her own shoelaces. Scope and Yellow Guy obviously think we've lost our minds and they want their turn.

We trade the headsets back and forth, swiping our wrists to pay for a stream of tracks that send us headlong into giddy happiness. It's nice to feel. This isn't *normal* for me, but it's nice to have it for a while. Haven climbs into my lap while she has an intense but disjointed conversation with Yellow Guy about water. She smells too good, and she's too warm. Over her shoulder I'm laughing at Scope's amazement about how the paint on the wall feels. I put the headphones back on and let the next track play.

◆

"I said no, Phoenix."

I cross my arms, sigh, check my watch. At least we got a whole practice in this week before a fight started, and this one's all on Phoenix.

She glares at Johnny, her annoyance oddly crazed in the light's erratic swing. "Why not? You found us, how much harder would it be to find other people who won't tell?"

"You think it's that easy? It took a long time to find all of you. I watched Anthem and Mage for months. Anthem's known Scope his whole life, and still it was a year before we brought him in. You don't

68

even want to know how long I spent on you before I was sure."

"So? We play for people we know we can trust."

Johnny's chest rises and falls, too controlled, too restrained. "Yeah, and that trust will last until the minute one of them realizes they can pass the information to the Corp in exchange for whatever they want."

"You wanted a band! Music should be heard, or else what's the point?"

He wheels on her, his nostrils flaring. "Music should be heard," he mocks. "That's what the Corp thinks, too. The point is just to be here. We're taking back something; we don't need to go telling everyone about it."

"*He* thinks we're good enough."

Yellow Guy's eyes widen, like he's surprised he's suddenly part of the argument. Idiot. "He—" says Johnny, then stops. I've probably been rude enough to Yellow Guy for both of us.

Whatever, I'm still kind of mad at Scope.

"It's not about being good enough, Phoenix."

"What do you guys think?" Phoenix asks. It's not really her place, and I glance at Johnny, who shrugs.

Mage twirls his drumsticks through nimble fingers. "I'm just here to play, girl. Don't need anything but that."

"Anthem?"

Across the room, I catch Scope's eye. He's tapping his bottles too quietly to make any sound. "I think it's Johnny's band," I say after a minute. "He's in charge."

"Because that's what you think, or because it's Johnny?"

I glare at her because I don't know how I feel anymore.

"I agree with Phoenix," Scope says. Yellow Guy smiles, and Phoenix grins, triumphant.

"You want to play for other people, go legit or find another band," Johnny tells them. "They're out there, hiding for a reason just like we do."

"What about a few others? Not many, enough to fit in here," Scope suggests.

"A few *more*, you mean?" he asks, gaze flicking to Yellow Guy. "No. You want to do this, you do it without me."

Phoenix presses her lips together and turns away. The argument seems over, at least for today, though I doubt she's totally given up.

Johnny picks up the rag and drapes it over his guitar, a funereal shroud. "You still coming over?"

"Ready when you are."

We climb up through the trapdoor, out, head away from the warehouse under the deceptively open sky. It stretches a lot farther than we ever will.

"It's not that I don't get it," he says quietly, looking around as we approach a corner. His eyes are gray, like he takes in more of reality than the rest of us do. "Playing for people, I get that. But it's risky, and we all have a lot to lose."

"Yeah," I say. "Don't you wonder what it'd be like, though?"

"Sometimes. Then I remember it wouldn't be worth it if it's the last time I ever get to play at all."

Or hear music at all.

White pods pass each other smoothly on the streets—long ones for transporting commuters, little, almost square ones for guards and maintenance crews. No one gives us more than passing appraisal, just two guys walking on a sunny day. I turn my face upward to absorb the warmth.

Maybe he's right. Half the time I only know what day of the

week it is because of the proximity to Wednesday. Jeopardizing that is stupid.

"Stop moping," he chides, bumping my shoulder with his. "We have a secret from them. That's the biggest fuck you there is. Think of how much work it's gonna be for them to edit our memories."

I laugh, a sound right for the weather. "Okay. But you know Phoenix won't give up on the idea."

"Phoenix isn't happy unless she's bitching about something. It's part of her charm. C'mon, in. Got stuff to show you."

Johnny's place is a single room on the top floor of an ancient brown building. Scanners outside other doors wink at us like knowing red eyes on our way up the stairs—watching, waiting. At the end of a silent hallway he opens his door and I follow him inside, weaving through the cramped furniture and mess. He shifts a stack of library books from the couch to the bed to make room for me, and then goes to the tiny kitchen in the corner opposite the hygiene cube. Boots and black sweaters jumble haphazardly on the floor. Every surface is piled with the strange things he collects: wires, pebbles, flowers from the park now dried out and crisp. Nothing's changed in the few months since I was last here.

I think it looks more like a home than my apartment.

Steam slicks the window above a pot of water just starting to boil. Johnny lifts it from the stove and carefully fills two chipped mugs, sending a thick waft of chamomile and honey my way. He has to pick his way carefully across the room so he doesn't trip and slosh tea everywhere.

"Here."

"Thanks." It's too hot, but still soothing to my throat, flayed from the afternoon of singing.

We don't do this as often as we used to. Back when the band was just me and him in the basement we almost always wound up here after, unable to let go of our rebellious enthusiasm but needing to escape the dangerous presence of guards on the street above. We'd hang out, write lyrics, and talk. Then Mage came in, and Scope. Scope and I started our thing and ended it. Johnny met his girlfriend, the twins became more than an unwanted responsibility, Haven turned up at the chrome studio.

"Ever think it was easier when it was just the two of us?"

I grin at him. "Stop reading my mind," I say, and he laughs.

"Don't get me wrong, I love our sound now, just feels sometimes like there's too many people in the room. What Scope did, bringing his guy, that doesn't help. You and me, we hardly even needed to talk, we just felt it from each other. It's still like that, I guess, just not as intense, you know? It's great when it works, but then someone fucks up, you know?"

"It's harder to get it back with so many people," I say. "Yeah, I miss it, too. That why you don't want to play for anyone else?"

"Maybe part of it," he says, shrugging. "Anyway, you doing okay?" He leans back on the couch and runs a hand through his hair. The back of his neck is briefly visible, marred by the round, sunken jack. I'm glad I can't look at my own.

"My father's not going to last much longer."

He nods. It's normal. Johnny's parents were heavy users. He's been on his own since he was fifteen.

"You said you had something to show me?"

"Oh, yeah."

The wooden box he pulls out from under his bed is a prewar antique, worn to glossy warmth by a thousand touches.

I can't hide my smile. "New ones?"

"Yup," he says, the brass latch flipping easily under his fingers, the lid opening to reveal a sheaf of paper he hasn't burned yet because these songs aren't finished. He takes a sheet off the top and passes it to me, one side announcing the collected works of Shakespeare, the other covered with lyrics, thoughts, and words crossed out faintly or with heavy black lines.

I read them, a melody slowly coalescing in my head. Fresh from practice, still buzzing from the raw naturalness of it, it's easy to line Johnny's guitar up with the words, insert Mage's beats and Scope's sounds and Phoenix's clear, bell-like notes.

"Still not happy with 'em," Johnny says.

"They're about death, and you're looking for happy?" I shake my head. "Yeah, no, I see what you mean. Pencil?"

He digs one out of the box and I hold it in my teeth, reading the song again.

"This isn't working." I tap a line in the second verse with the splintered end of the pencil. "It's throwing the rest off." Synonyms march through my head until the right one refuses to take another step. I scribble it down above the offending word. "Here. Then the downbeat comes here instead."

He reads, nodding when he hits the part I just changed. "Got it. Guess all those books with big words you read do come in handy."

"Hey, not all of us can leave the conduit life behind."

"You could if you wanted to."

"It sucks, but it's predictable. I'll take it."

"I'm gonna track. You first?"

I nearly laugh. Even in our addictions there are conventions of politeness, of friendship. "I'm good. Go ahead."

The couch creaks as he shifts, kneeling to reach the console on the wall over our heads. Fingertips hit the touch screen with dull, arhythmic thuds. I pluck another piece of paper from Johnny's wooden box and read it, tapping the pencil on my knee.

"New stuff on here."

"Cool," I say, only half listening.

"Hey, do me a favor and check out that one on the blue sheet? I think—" He stops suddenly.

The pencil scrapes over the paper. "Think what? Johnny?"

The couch creaks again and I look up. Headphones are clamped over Johnny's ears, his eyes rolled back into his head, his body swaying, but not to the music. It's the oscillating swing of someone about to fall, lifeless, to the floor.

# 0110011000000101011111001

Johnny Shell is dead.

I stare out at the milk-white sky, gray buildings, and streets tarred black. The blue sign of a water bar flickers on and off. Guess the Grid needs more power.

Dead. He was young, even by normal standards. Only a few years older than me. I hit the button for a med-pod so hard it cracked, but nothing could've made them get to us in time.

My hands shake. I fold them in my lap. Johnny did for me what I wish I could do for everyone—found me, trusted me, and showed me that something different was out there. A way to satisfy a need I'd only barely identified at the time. Under Johnny's influence, what had been a strange, yearning kind of frustration found its cure.

He helped me figure out who I am.

"What's wrong with you two? Do you need to track or something?" Haven asks from the step above mine outside my building. Scope's at the bottom, legs bent awkwardly up to his chin, expression serious. I shoot him a warning glance.

"Nothing," he says. Relief loosens something inside me at the same time as guilt tightens somewhere else for lying to her. Again. "Just"—he winks—"long night."

"Ew. Forget I asked. What's your excuse?" A sharp fingernail lands between my shoulder blades. I lean back, prolonging contact that's good just because it's with her.

"Tired," I say. Sleep was impossible last night.

Haven touches my back again, gently this time. "Okay. You up for the club later?"

"Yeah."

"Choice," she says, standing to brush lower-Web grime from her short black skirt. I keep my head turned just enough to stare at her legs. "I'm going home to change."

She walks away, pulling her tablet from her bag to send a message. I know she's calling her personal pod, telling her driver to pick her up somewhere away from my place. I've never bought that she doesn't want her family to know where she is; I'm sure they do anyway. But I appreciate the gesture.

For once, Scope doesn't make any of his usual comments when he watches me watch her.

"Johnny," is all I say.

"I don't get it. I mean, OD'ing, sure, we've all seen that, right? But when was the last time someone died from it? The techs are pretty good at patching people up."

"Maybe he was sick already. I mean, more than usual for his age." I hate the idea that Johnny wouldn't have told me something like that.

Scope looks as doubtful as I feel. I lean back on my elbows to look up. A single pigeon flies across the sky, ugly in form, beautiful in rarity.

He eventually leaves to get ready and take care of his mother. I don't move after he's gone; I just sit and watch the street. It's like losing an older brother, one who had the balls to give me the guidance I needed.

Fable answers the door to the apartment below mine, and the twins run to hug me. I just glare at the kid. I don't have the energy for anything else. Upstairs, I sit Alpha and Omega down at the table to do their homework while I hoist my father off the couch and hold him under a shower. Every day he's less able to keep himself upright, and the icy spray doesn't do as much as it used to for bringing back periods of lucidity.

After dinner, the news channel tells me about pod upgrades and mainframe enhancements, which isn't worth much but is better than silence.

Message received: the Corporation is strong, powerful, and doing all it can for us.

Through my open bedroom door, the console screen glows. My nails dig into my thighs, I grit my teeth, my jaw aching from every time I've tried and failed to resist since Johnny died.

If I don't track, they'll come for me.

It killed him.

The twins laugh in their room at some private joke. A few feet away, my father snores. Cold sweat breaks over me as I close my bedroom door behind me and take the headphones from their hook, running my thumb over the edges. The track I choose drifts up, tinny and distant, not strong enough to affect me, thin plastic cutting into my hand. It's so close. The wall is cool and smooth against my forehead. I breathe and lock my knees so they'll stop shaking. I can just stand here, the track playing. They'll never know I didn't listen.

I know. My screaming brain knows. *Want. Need.* I crumple to the floor along with my willpower.

*Loud and perfect, a room of sound. I can just hide here forever, wrapped in these strings, blanketed by warm, heavy drums. The room's edges blur, tinge with color, melt into something soft and liquid. Johnny's here, smiling with his weird mix of cheerful seriousness.*

*It's raining. I can feel the drops on my cheeks.*

*The room reforms, the floor morphing into a conduit chair. Fuzzy green words I can't read slide across the ceiling and my fingers tap out a rhythm until I realize and stop myself. When I stand, Johnny follows me out into the street, catches my arm, and my heart speeds up. I don't know him! What does he want?*

I can help you, *he says.*

*No, no, I don't need help. I'm fine, everything is fine and I have to get home. I have to leave now. Alpha and Omega are waiting for me; they need me.*

I've seen you, *he says.* When you think no one's watching.

*Thunder hammers a relentless beat. The rain falls harder from the sky, then from a dirty basement ceiling, soaking my face. He shows me a guitar, and I smile and laugh as the strings get louder. It's battered, ugly, a relic so holy I'm afraid to touch it, but I do, reaching out, wood and metal smooth under my fingertips. The paper he gives me is thin, creased, but I can read these words. I can sing these words, here in this safe room where no one can hear us.*

*We start and my voice sounds like someone else's in my ears; the guitar is loud, confined in the small space. I laugh again, keep laughing and singing until I run out of lyrics and the music begins to slip away. It can't be over yet. The walls shimmer; the strings tug me one last time before letting go, and Johnny smiles but it's wrong, all wrong that I can see through him to the solid, hard lines of my bedroom. I blink, once, and he's gone.*

✦

They killed him. I don't care if it was an accident. Right now, I don't even care that we're all going to die because of the music. Johnny had so much life and talent, so much bravery.

He was my friend. My fucking *friend.*

Haven and Scope will be wondering where I am; they're probably already in deep at the club. I want to puke.

And I want to be there, which just makes me want to puke even more.

My dark clothes are a blessing, as is the shadowy doorway that hides me from the view of a passing patrol-pod. I could talk my way out of it if they decided to ask why I'm not at a club or home tracking, but I can't promise not to do something stupid if a guard gives me a hard time. I'm not Haven. I can't get away with that.

I'm just conduit scum.

Aimlessly, I wander along quiet streets. I'm almost at the South Shore, in sight of the warehouse, when I realize I was coming here all along. It's as close to a real good-bye as I'll ever be able to give Johnny. I slip through the fence, biting my tongue at the sharp slice of barbed wire into my palm.

Something scuttles in the pitch darkness of the basement and I jump. I don't even want to know what that was. My hand fumbles over greasy slickness for the light switch.

Everything's still, quiet, exactly as we left it before going to his place. Knees weak, I sink to the floor beside it, my back to the filthy wall.

Faces flip through my mind. Johnny, sure, but not just him. Haven, her open expression not quite hiding the hardness in her eyes. Alpha and Omega, who depend on me for protection and safety and *home*. Mage's easy smile. Phoenix, always a wild tangle of emotions that lash out in whipping tendrils when she's unsettled. Scope, who I trust more than anyone, and Yellow Guy, who Scope loves even if he hasn't admitted it to me yet. My parents, who did the best they could and who I can't disappoint, no matter how uneven and backward that is.

I'm not sure how long I sit there; my watch is still on the edge of the sink at home. Long enough that when I shift, stiff-limbed, to a more comfortable position, I have to peel myself from the sticky floor.

The guitar is a mix of textures under the fingertips I stretch out—smooth wood, sharp strings, and cold metal. No sound comes from it, but my own voice is loud.

"I'm sorry, Johnny."

Disapproval settles in the air, his ghost lingering. I doubt it'll ever completely go away, and I don't want it to. I leave and slip wraith-like through the streets, my brain in overdrive.

This isn't right. None of it feels right.

"Yo, man, you're late, even for you. And you're bleeding. What happened?"

I look at Pixel, then my hand. Shit, I forgot.

"Oh," I say. "Um . . ."

He shakes his head, disappears through the door into the club room, and returns a minute later with a roll of gauze. "Programmed the DJ-comp to play something for pain next," he says. "You okay?"

"Yeah, it's nothing." I let him wrap the bandage around my palm. "Thanks."

"Sure. Look, I usually try not to think too much about what Scope does in his spare time, but is he okay? It's just, he got tabbed yesterday and went, like, paler than usual. You don't look much better, actually."

"Yeah, he's fine." The message was from me, hours . . . after. I couldn't get my hands to work.

"Didn't have a fight with that dude of his?"

"Not that I know of."

"Okay, thanks, Anthem. Don't tell him I give a damn, will you?" He grins.

"Our little secret."

Haven and Scope are way too far gone to comment on how late I am. I get a sloppy kiss from Haven that lands dangerously close to my lips; my groan is swallowed by the pulsing sound. Soon my mind is, too, but I don't forget the decision I made. It keeps me lying awake beside Haven and distracts me from my book at work. A week passes, and I barely even notice. The others meet up without me to talk about what happened to Johnny. I ignore my buzzing tablet and close my eyes, the memory of him falling to the floor on an endless loop in my head.

Until Wednesday. If I had the energy to run from headquarters down to the warehouse, I would.

Mage probably won't care, and Scope will say the guitar should be mine. Phoenix . . . well, I'm just not letting her have it.

Johnny would want it to be played, not sit under a section of rusty old pipe forever, gathering dust and grime.

I carry it to one of the crates we use as tables and pull the cloth away. It doesn't look like it should be able to produce the melodies Johnny forced from the four remaining strings. I probably won't come anywhere close, but I have to try.

The strap is made from braided lengths of rough rope that cut into my neck the moment I slip it over my head. Pain doesn't come anywhere close to denting the sensation of having the guitar in my hands.

A single harsh note, then another, and another vibrate up into the cloying, stale basement air. One of them is off, I know just by hearing it, so I gently turn the tuning peg, careful not to snap a string I can't replace.

My eyes close. I remember Johnny's hand dancing along the fretboard, the way he plucked and strummed. Something that sounds almost like music carries through the room and time distorts—not the way I get when I'm tracking or at the club, but just from the feeling of making the music myself. There's only this beat, that note, and this sliding, wailing scale. It's ten times better than anything I've ever known.

I think of Haven.

Okay, ten times better than anything I'm allowed to have.

"Thought you'd take that. Not bad, man, not bad." Mage ignores the last few rungs of the ladder, jumping down and brushing his dreadlocks from his eyes. "A little rough, but I like it."

"Thanks. I"—my voice cracks—"I'm sorry." I'm not even sure what I'm apologizing for.

"Yeah." Mage stares at the filthy floor. "What *happened*, man? What Scope told us doesn't make any sense."

The strings dig more deeply into my fingers. "He just . . . I don't know. We were at his place, composing and hanging out. He decided to track, and . . ." I press my lips together, shut my burning eyes.

"The techs say anything?"

"That bad reactions aren't unusual." The lump in my throat threatens to choke me. "Then they covered him up and carried him out."

"That bad, though? I never heard of someone dropping like that, not from a single track."

"I know. Scope said the same thing." *This isn't right.*

"I said what?" Scope's boots ring on the ladder, Yellow Guy's just behind them.

"Hey," I say. "Johnny. How sudden it was."

"Oh, yeah. Pixel says he's heard of it, though. Recently, like about a month ago. Some friend from the club."

"And it was just like this?" My head starts to spin.

"From what he said, yeah." Scope frowns at me and puts his hand on my shoulder. "You holding up okay?"

I nod, and we stand in silence for a minute.

"He'd want us to move on," Mage says finally. "Guess Anthem's the boss now?"

Phoenix arrives, sparing me from having to answer. She closes the trapdoor behind her, the usual fierce prettiness softened on her face. Mage hugs her, and she clings to him for a second before pushing him away.

"Figures," she says, shaking out her fiery hair and looking at me. "Let's get started."

The guitar is in my hands. I could play. I could try to forget, to not think for two hours.

My hair catches on the strap as I tug it over my head. "No," I say. "Not today."

Four faces stare at me. "Anthem, what—?" Scope starts. My feet land on the ladder, my hands reaching to hoist myself up. I stop halfway, my eyes level with the rusted hinges of the trapdoor.

"Play without me. Or don't. Whatever." I don't want to ask Mage to look, to tell him what I'm thinking until I know. "I've got to talk to someone."

I'm right. It doesn't make me feel any better.

I stare at Haven. Her lips are pursed, waiting for me to say something. She crosses her legs on my bed and I turn around, pacing to the door and back again.

"A list," I say. I can picture it. White codes on a black screen.

"Of targets." Her knuckles are white, contrasting against the lurid pink of her fingernails. "I had to dig deep for it, but I got there. Anthem, they're all . . ."

Dead. Yeah.

"Are you going to tell me why I was even looking in the first place? Whose code was that?"

"A friend. His name was Johnny." I back against the wall and my knees fold. Haven's warm hand lands on my shoulder.

"He used to be a conduit," I say hoarsely. It's the only safe thing to tell her.

"I'm sorry," she whispers.

I look up and wipe my eyes. "Did it say *anything* else? Like why?" Not like I can't guess.

"Nothing," she says, shaking her head. One strand falls into her eyes and she thoughtlessly flicks it back. "Just *Targeted for Termination* and about twenty codes from people all over the Web. Not why, or how, or anything."

They know. Sick certainty curdles in my stomach. They know about us. Or at least about Johnny, which means it's only a matter of time before they start looking around at his known associates. Phoenix and Mage. I've been seen with him. Tango knows we were friends. From me, they'll find Scope and Yellow Guy. Pixel might be seen as guilty by blood.

"What did he do, Anthem? What's all this about?"

I stare at the console and watch the Corp logo bounce around for a while. "I don't know."

$$\oplus$$

I've spent so long trying not to be noticed that I haven't truly looked around me. Haven's words replay in my head, and I open my eyes everywhere I go. Guards here and patrol-pods there during shift change. A single small boat skirting the edges of the island, a uniform at the helm. On my way into work, I stare at the statue until a suspicious guard tells me to move along.

I seriously doubt that the people who came here after the war had this in mind. Starving, filthy, lost, without any governments left to guide them, they had to go somewhere. They picked here, this place that was once known as New York City. A prime target during past conflicts, it learned better than others how to protect itself and so, when it was all over, this was where there were still stores of food, undamaged shelters, and the only computers not destroyed by the final pulse bombs.

They just wanted safety. Peace. What they got was fighting as heated as the war, if not as devastating because there weren't many weapons left. Amidst the repairing and restructuring of the city were bloody battles over who would take charge of it, eventually won by the man now immortalized in metal.

The elevator is packed, hot, and I flash back to the riot.

"What's up?" Tango asks, helping me into my chair.

I nearly tell her, say her friend was lucky to get off with being made an Exaur, but that's not true, and I can't explain. "Nothing," I say. "Tired."

I'm always tired. She doesn't question it.

$$\oplus$$

On the other side of the river, broken concrete juts from the dead landscape, a mouthful of crooked teeth jaggedly reflected by gun-metal water. I stare for just a second, thinking, before I duck through the fence. I know what I'm about to ask of my friends, why I'm taking the risk of asking them to meet me here on a Friday, when even more patrol-pods swarm the streets in preparation for the weekend.

The cramped basement feels smaller, claustrophobic as I pace, stomping, gritting my teeth. I kick one of the old pipes and listen to the dull ring fade away. Decisions have been stacking up in my head since Haven told me, fueled by anger and just . . . complete fucking disbelief.

No, that's not true. I wanted to be wrong, to know even the Corp wouldn't do something like this, but I have no problem believing it.

I want to see red, but instead I see yellow laces.

"What the fuck?" he gasps as I cross the room and push him against the wall. Vaguely, I hear Scope land in the room.

"Did you tell anyone?"

His eyes widen. "What?"

"This. Us. Did you tell anyone?"

Scope grabs my shoulder. "Anthem, what the hell is going on? Of course he didn't."

I look between Scope and Yellow Guy and think of the plans I've started to make. "I'll explain when the others get here."

Mage and Phoenix turn up a few minutes later, curious about why I tabbed. I'm grateful for their arrival if only because it breaks the strained silence.

"They murdered Johnny. Probably Pixel's friend, too," I say. "And I think someone from my building." I remember my fear, then my relief because she was just a girl on a stretcher and not my father. All the color drains from Mage's face.

"No way."

"I . . . my . . . I got someone to hack in to the system. Johnny's code was on a list. All of them are dead. Scope, if you can get the other code from Pixel, she can check," I say. Scope nods.

"The track," Mage whispers. "The track he put on."

"Yeah." I still can't figure out how they did that, but I guess it doesn't matter right now.

"Wait a second. They're *killing* people now? With tracks?" Phoenix asks.

"They always have been. Looks like they've found a way to do it faster." I picture Johnny dropping to the floor. Over and over and over. "He thought he was being watched."

"You think they know about us."

I shrug off Yellow Guy's use of *us*. Whatever. "It makes the most sense, right?"

We're all quiet for a few minutes. I should tell them that letting it sink in doesn't make it any easier to accept. When they look at me again, I find my spot beside Johnny's guitar and start to talk.

"We need to fight back. A friend said something to me. She said she thought a lot of people would want to hear unencoded music, and I think she's right. If the Corp *did* know about Johnny, there's a good chance they know about us as well. The same thing could happen to us any fucking time. Either we're all next, or they're counting on us being scared enough to stop. I say we do the opposite. We might never get another chance. If the Corp are worried enough to kill, they're weak—"

"But this is the Corp," Yellow Guy interrupts. "They won't be weak for long."

"Exactly," I say.

"What are we talking about?"

I meet Phoenix's eyes. "Concerts. Somewhere—here, I guess. Get people we trust, they'll come just to hear what real music sounds like, or we don't tell them why they're coming, I don't know. We'll figure that out. But use unencoded music as a way of gathering, spreading the word somehow. Getting enough people together that the Corp can't ignore it." I think of the riot and the energy that buzzed in the crowd before the drug subdued us. The anger bubbling under all our surfaces. It just needs an excuse to come out. "Enough people that we can overpower them. Take control of headquarters."

"You're serious?" Scope asks. They all stare at me.

"Too much has happened. Johnny. The twins. That Exaur I saw."

Mage and Phoenix look confused; I explain to them what happened that day. The censored, bloodless version isn't an accurate description, but I know they can imagine the truth behind my careful words.

"Fucking Corp," Phoenix spits.

"Which is why we have to do something. And no, I don't know we can make any kind of difference, but what are we supposed to do? Keep going the way things are? Let it be someone else's problem? Leave it for the twins? And what if we *are* next? Our codes could go on some list, and we might not even know. Haven can't watch the whole time even if she knows what she's looking for. If that happens, I'm not going down without a fight."

"You're talking about a revolution," Mage says.

My skin tingles. "I . . . Yeah. I don't know. Something. You know music used to be a voice against injustice? And now it *is* the injustice. I'd rather . . ." I swallow, my throat dry and sticky. "I want the twins to know I tried. And do it for Johnny." Someone needs to stand up for Johnny.

"Well, you don't need to convince me," says Yellow Guy.

Irritation flares brief, bright, hot. I shake it off. He's on my side, so I shouldn't care that he's not really part of this.

"You know I'm in," says Phoenix. "I just want an audience, but a fight makes it better."

"I've been watching the guards and the patrols," I tell them. "It's going to take a lot of us, but I think it can be done."

"Then we, what, storm the Corp with an army and kill them all?" Yellow Guy grins with something almost like relish, and I shake my head.

"Violence is their trick. No. There are other ways of making them stop this. All we need is the manpower to take headquarters."

He raises his eyebrows. "That's not a little naïve?"

"I'm not killing anyone for the hell of it. Not even for revenge," I say. I'm sure of that much. "We'll have to defend ourselves, yeah, but . . ."

"So how far do we take this *fight*?" Phoenix asks. Everyone looks at me, waiting. I close my eyes and see my friend dying, right there, inches away but with no chance for me to stop it. I hear him hit the floor.

I think of the twins.

"As far as we have to," I say. "But no further."

Mage is quiet for a long time; he stares down at his crossed legs and threads his dreads between his fingers.

"Mage," says Scope, "they killed him."

"You really think we can do this?" he asks me.

"I think we have to try, and it's going to take more than just us."

"With music? You don't think that's like using bombs to end a war?"

I almost smile, and I don't point out that in the end, that worked once. "More like fighting fire with fire."

Slowly, he nods. "All right, man. It's not why I got into this, but for Johnny . . ."

I get it. We all do. "Okay." I stand up, nerves buzzing in a way they haven't since before Johnny died. Since our last practice together. "I have no idea how to really get started, but we need to open the circle a little. Scope, we've got to tell Pixel. We're going to need his help."

Scope laughs. "He's going to love me for this. Always says I'm trouble."

"Yeah, well, he's right," I say, grinning. "You want me there?" Yellow Guy reaches over to take Scope's hand, and Scope shakes his head.

"Nah. But if he flips out, I'm telling him it was all your idea."

I'm not that worried. Pixel's never been above breaking the law a little, like the way he sneaks me into the club for free on nights I can't afford to pay cover.

I guess after that it's all just a matter of scale.

"We need the right crowd," Mage says. "People who aren't gonna rat us out. Sympathizers."

"Yeah."

He nods slowly. "Your hacker friend, she ever tell you much about what we do?"

Phoenix, Scope, and Yellow Guy stop talking amongst themselves to listen. "A little. I don't really get it," I say. "She says the security's pretty strong."

"It's a playground. Yeah, there are safeguards, I don't even understand half of them, man, but just being in there is giving the Corp the finger. Doing something we're not supposed to, something they don't know about." He laughs. "Kinda weird; everyone who hacks hates the Corp and we spend all our free time inside its brain."

"Okay? And?"

Mage smiles. "Dude, the only thing hackers like better than getting deep into a system is bragging about it. We leave messages for each other all the time, buried in the code, and the Corp has no damn idea."

✚

We do nothing in the basement but talk, and still when I leave I feel like we played all day. Mage's idea about the messages makes me nervous, though I know Haven's been too busy with her project recently to dig around the system much. The others promise to start telling people they trust. In Phoenix's case I don't even know who that would be, but I assume she has people she loves—and if she wanted us to be aware of them, she'd have said something by now.

We're all bonded by this one thing. Nothing else matters when we're in the basement, pouring our souls into notes.

The crackle along my veins dulls a little when I get home and see the twins. They'll be in danger if I get caught. Haven, too, if I decide to tell her—maybe even if I don't. I haven't made up my mind on that one yet, because what I want and what is smart are two very different things here. My father, Tango, Fable and his mother, others. I'm putting everyone who knows me at risk.

I just hope that if it does get me turned into an Exaur or sends me on a one-way trip to the CRC, the reason is enough to make them forgive me.

I shudder. Of the two, I'd prefer death. If the Corp thinks that strapping a person down, covering their ears with headphones, and playing the track that will deafen them forever is a brutal punishment for the average person—and it is—it would be even worse for me. Never to hear music again . . . I'll kill myself if that happens.

At least I'm right about Pixel. I'm not surprised to find him waiting for me outside my apartment when I get home from work on Monday. He'd probably wanted to talk to me Saturday night at the club, but Omega has a cold and I didn't want to leave him.

At least it isn't anything more serious. The restrictions on music for kids are lifted when one needs medical treatment. I see them, sometimes. . . . Tiny kids, holding their mothers' hands as they navigate the world through drugged, glazed eyes.

I shake it off, focusing on Pixel, the green streaks in his hair catching the light. He's my height, so our eyes are level. I see the acceptance I think is bordering on approval. Inside, I check that my father's sleeping and put on a track for him anyway, more to make sure he can't hear us talking in the kitchen than anything else.

Maybe a track guaranteed to bring instant death isn't always a bad thing. . . . I shake myself and look at Pixel, who seems weirdly out of place here and yet totally comfortable. He's never been here, but the apartment he shares with Scope and their mother on the other side of Two is nearly a clone of this one in appearance.

"You okay?" he asks.

I shrug. "You?"

"I didn't see it happen to my friend."

My mouth opens, the words *I'll live* on my tongue. I swallow them.

"Been thinking since Scope told me everything. Using tracks to kill . . ." He whistles and I cringe. No one's here. No guard heard that. It's okay. "Have some ideas about where to do this thing," he says, wrapping long-fingered hands around the hot mug of tea I made him.

"That's the biggest problem." All night, between checking on Omega's low fever and forcing water down his throat, I'd thought about that.

Pixel's lips—odd without the green he wears at the club—twist. "Or not."

I raise my eyebrows.

"You need somewhere soundproof, right? Scope told me about your basement, and that's all cool when it's just you guys and you're careful, but you can't get a crowd in there."

"You might be overestimating our talents, but anyway," I say.

Grinning, he cocks his head. "I doubt you suck. You think I don't see you when you're into the music, even when you're in really deep? You *get it*, man. Like almost no one else does. Scope, too, and this Johnny guy doesn't sound like he was just messing around."

A twinge pulls at my gut when he says Johnny's name casually like that, but how else is he supposed to talk about someone he never met? I remind myself that the same thing probably happened to his friend. "You were saying . . . about where?"

"Right." He nods. "The club."

"You're insane," I manage in the middle of choking on my tea. "The Corp owns it!"

"Anthem," he says, looking at me like I'm an idiot. "The Corp owns every square inch of the Web. And it's the last fucking place they'd think to look."

Okay, he has a point, but still.

"So the club," he continues. "Sunday nights, when the Corp so generously gives me a night off. I can get whatever you need from Imp; he owes me a favor. The best part? The thing about this city is that there's a whole maze underneath it where the trains used to run."

"Right," I say, not sure what tunnels have to do with anything. The materials from the trains were recycled a long time ago, probably to make consoles or something.

"So there's a way in," he says, looking at me until I get it. We don't have to use the front door. We can bypass the scanners, and any pods on the lookout won't see people going into a club that's supposed to be closed. A club that has everything we need—or at least, a lot more than we have now. Sound gear, lights, enough space.

It's perfect. Crazy, but it's not as if the rest of this isn't.

Pixel finishes his tea and stands, the *clump* of his boots as they make the trip from tabletop to floor provoking a loud snore from my father. I get a sympathetic look and return it.

And still, the first thing I do when he's gone is head for my room and walk straight to the console. I'd love to just set the track to play and not listen, and so many times I try. I'll make it a second, or two, maybe five if I'm having a good day and my head is filled with my own music. Always, though, I'm broken just by knowing that the track is there, a drug in front of a hopeless addict, with the credits for it already gone from my account.

Still, it takes three tries to make myself cover my ears and press the screen to find what I want.

My heart stops—a preemptive strike.

Warmth floods my fingers and toes, tingling and golden and sweet, and I exhale. Not my turn, not this time. If I concentrate really hard before the track has time to take its full effect, I imagine I can sense the melody entering my brain and hear the subliminal messages communicating with the part that's designed for this. Or that the music is designed for. An endless loop that circles me until my mind starts spinning, too, around and around until I lift off and begin to float.

I wish I could keep going, on and on until I fly away from here completely. But I don't think there are enough tracks in the world for that.

⊕

For the rest of the week, I throw myself into plans for the band. Saturday I watch Alpha and Omega play in the park, but my mind is elsewhere. I don't even know what I'm hoping for. All I want is to get by, live out my life, and look after the twins for as long as I can, but that word of Mage's—*revolution*—is a spark in my brain that finds too many fuses. Circuits glow with thoughts of ways to end the Corp for good.

They're definitely going to delete those before my chip goes in a locker at the CRC. I guess they'll wipe out a lot of the past few years, including these footsteps as I follow Pixel through the tunnels below the Web, over ground scarred and uneven where the tracks have been ripped out. Water leaks down the walls; rats and cockroaches run from the beam of his flashlight.

"Keep up, you two," Pixel calls over his shoulder to Scope and Yellow Guy, who have stopped to take advantage of the darkness.

"How are people going to find their way through all this? Shit," I say, catching myself before I fall flat on my face. I'm already disoriented, with not a damn clue which way I'd go to find the entrance we took near the South Shore. It was another basement, kind of like our practice room, with a door that eventually opened, on squeaky hinges, to the tunnels.

"We'll put up arrows or something; I've got some fluorescent paint up at the club. No one ever comes down here."

"And you know this how?" Scope asks, his tongue apparently available for speech again.

Pixel laughs, the light jerking erratically. The sound echoes down the path ahead. "You're not the only lawbreaker in the family, little brother. And that's all you're getting."

Scope can whine more than the twins when there's something he wants, and I'm convinced the only reason Pixel doesn't tell Scope what he does down here is to annoy him. Suits me fine.

I crash into Pixel's back, stumble, and right myself. This stretch of wall doesn't look any different from the miles we've already passed, except for the stack of old crates piled against it. He tosses me the flashlight, its beam arcing over the wall and ceiling before I catch it, and tells me to point it above his head. The crates don't look sturdy enough to hold him, but he climbs them anyway, reaching up to unscrew four evenly placed bolts that are more well-oiled than they should be.

A scrape, a thump, and then a shaft of light pours down, turning Pixel's face too bright against his black clothes. He pulls himself up and through the square with ease that proves he's done this before.

Guess he wasn't kidding. The three of us look at each other for a moment, until Pixel's green-streaked hair appears again and he tells us to hurry up.

I climb into a strange room, squeezing my way out from behind a set of metal shelves, obviously moved to allow for this. They're filled with loops of cable, bars of soap, and bottles of water. Yellow Guy and Scope join me, Scope clearly knowing where he is. His usual smile widens into a grin he aims at Pixel.

"This way," Pixel says, leading us to the door. The hallway we step into *is* familiar, at least once we pass the doors to the hygiene cubes at the end, just before it opens up into the room where I spend so many hours of my life. Daytime-bright, even without windows, I recognize it only by extrapolation. My imagination offers whirling, colored replacements for the static, boring lights overhead, bodies to fill the empty floor as they dance to music blasting from the now quiet walls.

I stand in the middle, staring as if I've never seen it before—and I haven't, not like this, but it's the vision my mind gives me that's more enticing than what my eyes are looking at. A stage will go against that wall, right where Pixel is pointing, and the people who'll fill the club will be listening to *my* music coming from the speakers.

The others are talking about what gear we'll need, how to find it, and where to set everything up. I'm not paying much attention. In my head I'm singing to Haven, who is looking down from the seats on the balcony, eyes focused on me. In my fantasy, she knows the song is about her.

"Earth to Anthem," Scope says, tapping the side of myhead.

"Yeah?"

"I was just wondering when you wanted to get started," Pixel says.

"Oh." I haven't really thought about it. "I guess we need another few weeks to practice?" If we still had Johnny . . . But we wouldn't be doing this if we still had Johnny. He's the reason now as much as he was the obstacle before. That same itch, the one he first cured by showing me there was another way, another path to music, has been crawling over my skin since he died. I have to do something to make this all make sense. I have to do something to protect the twins, even if I fail.

I just have to do . . . something, even if they kill me before I'm done.

"Sweet. Okay, I'll take care of stuff here, but you guys should think about using this place to practice. You need to get used to the acoustics. Plus, I wanna know you don't suck."

Scope hits him and Pixel laughs. I wonder if life would be easier if I had a sibling closer to my own age. A brother, instead of being an almost-parent to two little kids I'd die for.

My mind is too young for this, my body too old.

Work is especially draining the next day, the time spent thinking about my energy traveling in pulses of light along wires to the labs upstairs. I didn't cover Johnny's ears with headphones, but it doesn't make a difference. I help power the Grid, the Grid powers the music, and the music is killing us all.

I think of Haven, angry enough to want the Corp dead, though she's too good to ever act on it. I've murdered, even if I've been apathetic, sometimes barely conscious during the process.

If there's going to be a future without the Corp and its evil, where music is just music, then death is going to have to come first. My own, maybe, if we build enough of a cause that I need to martyr myself for it. Anyone who stands up to fight will be risking themselves. There'll be deaths caused by action, not by the energy sucked from me while I sit in a chair in a basement with a thousand others. I guess that's just a matter of scale, too.

Haven's usually pink lips are stretched white and thin around the rim of her water bottle. We're sitting in a bar mid-Web, dodging dirty looks from the waitress because we're not ordering anything else. Like the water doesn't cost enough.

"I need my own place." She's been upset since we met up, something her father did. She won't say exactly what, but enough that she was torn between shouting and crying when she got here.

"So, do it." *You can afford it* hangs between us. Honestly, I don't know why she's lived at home for this long, except for the fact that she's almost never there.

She chews a pointed fingernail, its once smooth edge ragged. "He wants me to stay."

I love her, but she frustrates the hell out of me sometimes. "You have two choices—that's more than most of us get—and neither one is okay?"

Water sloshes against plastic; the table shakes. "I thought you'd listen!"

"I am," I say, glaring at the waitress who is now too interested in us for a different reason. We're not here for entertainment. "What do you want me to say?"

"I can't stop thinking about what we found out. Every time I go home, I . . . why are they doing that? *How* can they do it?"

"Look." I peel her fingers from the water bottle and link mine with them. "You're at my place most of the time anyway."

That might not be true if she found herself some swanky upper-Web place away from her family. My gut twists. I can't leave the twins overnight. I never leave until after they're in bed, and the few hours of sleep I get every night end when they wake up. I don't want my bed to stop smelling like Haven. I don't want to stop finding long black and pink hairs in my hygiene cube.

She smiles softly. "You're not sick of me yet?"

I shake my head. "Never." I'm pretty sure she knows that. Those words are loud between us, too. "I have to get home to the twins."

"Want me to come over?"

"Can't. I, uh, promised Scope I'd help him with something. Guy stuff."

"Oh." Her face falls, and I want to punch myself. "Okay, well, tab me later?"

"Sure."

I go to the club, via an apartment empty of anyone but my father. Fable's mother was only too happy to accept more credits to look after them, which at least lets me act like I'm doing a good thing.

*This is for them*, I remind myself.

Partly, anyway.

The stage is makeshift, hastily assembled, and ready to be taken apart and hidden before the club next opens for its legitimate purpose. The rough, homemade quality fits in with everything sitting on it. Pixel hasn't run this place five years without learning a little about sound. I don't know where he got the amps, or the parts if he built them himself, but the sight of them makes something itch inside me. Whether it's excitement or fear, I can't tell—or if the difference even matters.

One more week.

We're not expecting a huge crowd, just people we know from Quadrant Two and the ones who've seen Mage's coded message.

I'm still expecting guards to storm in any minute, and the knot in my stomach throbs to the beat of imagined footsteps made heavy by boots and weapons and righteousness.

"Ready?" Pixel asks, carrying in a microphone stand made of pipes held together with silver tape.

"How would I know?"

He sets the stand on the stage and perches beside me on the edge. "You're doing a good thing."

"I'm doing an illegal thing that could get my whole family killed. So are you."

"Yeah," he agrees, "but maybe that's *why* it's good. A sign or whatever. Something easy wouldn't be worth it. You still think it is?"

I think I don't know what else to do, that this feels like the only thing I *can* do. I guess that's the same. Not smart, but right.

Pixel nudges my shoulder with his. "Never pictured you as the type to have stage fright," he says, and the tightness in my chest unfurls a little. Yeah. That's all this is.

We're quiet for a few minutes, staring around at the empty club. "Does Scope seem different to you?" he asks eventually.

"How so?"

He shrugs. "Dunno. Calmer, or something, even with everything going on. Maybe that boyfriend of his is a good influence. Never thought I'd say that again, after you."

I shift uncomfortably. "He's in love. Give him a break."

"That bother you?"

"Not the way you mean."

Mage walks in wearing a black leather trench coat that billows out with his long strides, Phoenix following in a skirt that's really more of a belt. Yellow Guy seems to have become some kind of mascot—I have to fight a laugh at the idea as he lets go of Scope and the four of us climb onto the stage.

The club looks different from up here. The few extra feet of height lets me imagine looking out across a crowd, not being swallowed up in it like I am when I'm on that floor. They're all staring up, glittering and beautiful, their mouths singing my words back to me. The idea that we're still fucking crazy for using the club disappears when I bring my hand down across the strings for the first time today, my guitar across my body. Phoenix pounds her xylophone so it can be heard above the crash of Mage's drums; improbable melodies burst from Scope's growing collection of noninstruments.

Generators hum, a low, buzzing bass line. I don't mind using my energy for this—twice.

We sound nothing like the music that usually fills this room, the stuff that's polished in a studio before it's sent to a lab for enhancement. I'm sure those musicians aren't pouring with sweat as they sing into their microphones, playing harder when the calluses on their fingers threaten to rip.

I'm sure they can't feel *this*. If they could feel anything, they wouldn't have sold their souls to the Corp.

My arms ache, and my throat is raw when I stop midsong to tell Mage his timing is off. Broken glass crunches under my boots. I step back to the mic again, suddenly hyper-aware of Pixel and Yellow Guy watching from the back of the room.

Stage fright. Yeah. I breathe, calm my heartbeat, and sense the others' impatience behind me.

This is our last practice until we do a final soundcheck next week before the concert. I think we sound good. I don't know how good we'd have to sound for me to be ready.

"Anthem." Scope gets my attention.

"Yeah. Sorry."

We launch back in and repeat the verse we were on when Mage

messed up. Every song we know blares out of the speakers, building a wall of noise that begs to be climbed. I want to stand on it and stare down at the Corp below.

Heat bubbles in my chest. I look at the others.

We can do this.

My apartment is too quiet without the twins, filled with only the constant babble of the TV and my father's rattling breaths. I leave my room, a track ringing in my ears, relief humming through my veins, a pink feather held between two fingers. My father blinks and turns his head toward me when I switch the TV off, his eyes going to the feather. I'm never sure how aware he is of Haven, but I think the nod he gives is some kind of indication. Even that small movement seems to exhaust him.

"I need to do something," I say, crossing the room to sit on the floor by his head.

He grunts; the soft wheezing of air could mean he understands me or it could mean nothing at all.

"It might get me into a lot of trouble." Understatement of the year. But his clouded, milky eyes sharpen and his muscles tense. "It's for the twins," I continue. "And me, and all of this. Are you listening?"

"Do . . ." Coughs puff out his hollowed cheeks, and he fumbles for the water bottle I've left out for him. I grab it and hold it to his lips. "Do . . . what you have to," he gasps, shudders wracking his body. "Anthem . . . I'm sorry."

"I know." My mother had said the same many times in her last weeks. "It's okay," I lie. I can't bring myself to yell at this shell of the strong man I once admired, though fuck knows I've wanted to in the past.

He's silent for a few minutes; I think he's fallen asleep again. "What?" he mumbles finally.

I shake my head. "You don't need to know. But if anything happens to me, you *have* to make sure Alpha and Omega are okay, you hear me? I know you can't do it, but Haven will, and Fable's mother. Listen to them. Let them help." I wait until he nods and his eyes flutter closed before I stand and go back to my room. I'd feel better if I was sure he'd remember this in the morning—hell, in five minutes—but there's no way to make sure of that. Death would have to have me by the throat before I stopped worrying about the twins. I gather my last scraps of faith and hope it's the same for him.

$$\oplus$$

Pixel lets us use his office while we're waiting. I've been pacing around the club for hours—since I decided that pacing around at home wasn't getting me anywhere.

Yellow Guy is sitting on the desk and swinging his legs; his eyes are on me when I enter. A small fridge hums in the quiet. I have no idea where Scope, Phoenix, and Mage are, but it's still early. There's plenty of time.

"Hey," I say. He's turned out okay. The anger I felt when Scope brought him to practice that first time is gone, though my embarrassment isn't. We probably wouldn't be here without Yellow Guy, or we wouldn't be ready. He's no musician, but he's been useful in other ways. His hands are still stained with paint—in his favorite color, what else did I expect?—from when he and Pixel ventured down into the tunnels to mark arrows on the walls, and he even found me a new string to replace one of the broken ones on my guitar.

"Your girlfriend coming?" he asks.

I turn away from the fridge, the bottle denting under my thumb. "She's not my girlfriend."

"That day at your place you looked . . . Anyway, Scope said it was why I don't have to worry about the two of you still being friends."

I laugh to myself. Haven isn't the reason I'm not a threat. The truth is much less sexy, but Scope's confidence has always been one of his most attractive qualities.

"I am, and you don't, but she's not my girlfriend."

"O-kay . . ."

I can tell he wants to ask more, but I don't encourage it. Knowing Haven won't be here tonight—and that with one message from the tablet in my pocket she could be—is painful enough without baring my soul about it.

At least until I get onstage.

"So what did happen with you and Scope?"

"A mistake."

Yellow Guy's eyebrows lift. I slump against the wall. "I made a promise to my mother before she died. My little brother and sister come first. For a while, after, I was angry enough to not care about keeping it." I shrug. "Now I do. Anyway, Scope and I never would've lasted. Haven's different."

"They won't be young forever," he says.

That's the truth. "I'll be dead by the time they're not. That's the other reason. What's the point? Love me and watch me die in a few years. No, thanks."

"You give up time with them for this," he says, waving his hand in the general direction of the club. I don't know if he means my nights here or what we're doing now, but I guess it doesn't matter either way.

"I don't have a choice."

He nods, and I walk over to one of the couches that line the wall. Sleep kills a few hours; leather sticks to my back where my shirt's ridden up.

In my head, Johnny puts on headphones, but he doesn't die. He screams instead, screams and screams as the track deafens him. When it's over, he smiles and walks out into the street, right into the path of a speeding pod.

Mage and Phoenix come in, talking loudly enough to wake me. Scope looks as if he's been here a while. He and Yellow Guy seem to think that being the only ones awake is the same thing as being alone.

Seriously, I'm happy for them, but I wish I had their energy.

"Are your tongues made of glue? Can you unstick yourselves for a minute?" Phoenix asks. I shoot her a grin.

Soundcheck shouldn't feel any different from the practices we've had. The empty club is the same, Pixel is fiddling with knobs and switches as usual, but the expectance in the air is new, unfamiliar.

Rope digs into the welt already on my neck. I stare at the calluses on my fingertips while the others get ready behind me.

The first whining note from my guitar echoes around the empty room, and the stage shakes to the rhythm of Mage's opening drumbeats, distorting my voice to a raspy tremor. Scope dives in exactly when he's supposed to, filling out the building with angry sound, but my hands jerk in surprise. I correct myself, hoping no one noticed the slip. My stomach turns over. Phoenix's part is a relief when it comes. Its happy, playful melody unexpected enough in the sonic rage to let me fade into the background until the end.

We make it through the second song, my attention half on the music and half on Pixel, his fingers turning swells to tidal waves, rumbles to earthquakes. Partway through the third, he replaces the bright fluorescents overhead with the neon beams I'm so used to here. I blink.

The next time I see this room, it won't be empty. My breath catches. Footprints on the glossy floor glow in a shaft of yellow light. Green. Purple. Wrong lyrics spill out, a verse I sang already, throwing the others into confusion until I remember the right ones.

Goose bumps break out on my arms. It will be warm later, heated by the bodies of whoever shows up.

"Damn it!" I stop singing and whirl around to glare at Scope, his wrong note ringing in my ears. "You think you could get it right, maybe?" His eyebrows shoot up and his mouth opens. The drumming stops. "And Phoenix, do you even want people to hear you? Stop hitting that thing like a girl." Now I'm hot, too hot. I feel Yellow Guy and Pixel closing in behind me.

"Anthem—" Mage begins.

"Don't you get it? The only thing we have going for us is that we sound *real*, but no one's going to care if *real* sounds like *shit*. They're all gonna run back to the tracks the Corp's polished with all their studio tricks." Panting, I kick a speaker hard enough to make it rock on the uneven planks.

Mage rounds his kit. "You done, man?" he asks, nearing me, his dark eyes boring into mine.

"We *have* to be good enough," I say, gripping the neck of my guitar as if it'll keep me from drowning.

"We have to be *different* enough. Different from those Corp idiots strutting around on the TV who don't feel it like you do. Like we all do. You asked us for this, man. We're here. Whatever happens after this is only gonna come if people see what music can be, and they're only gonna see that if they see *us*, not you being a bastard. Remember that you love it or don't fucking play."

I look down at the blue laces of my boots until my breath levels. "Sorry," I mutter.

"That's the one you get," Phoenix says. "Pull that shit again and I'll kick you in the balls."

"I'll help," Scope offers.

"You're done," Pixel says. "C'mon, Anthem." I follow Pixel's wave into his office and stare blankly at the headset he holds out after scanning his wrist. He knows we play sober, but I remind him anyway. His hand stays in the air, and the weight is pulled from my words by my traitorous feet.

This is different. Not just a bunch of us screwing around in a basement anymore. Live-wire nerves are arcing up my spine and along trembling fingers. I've been trying not to track, but now more than ever we all have an act to maintain. The Corp would notice if even one of us stopped listening, let alone a whole group with known ties.

And I need it. Fuck, do I need it, even if every note will sound like the aural embodiment of hypocrisy. I'll just take the edge off, calm my hands enough to play and unwind my twisted stomach.

I don't breathe until the first verse is over, and halfway through the track my heartbeat slows, my eyes close, and my body folds down to sit on the floor. Pixel's left me alone, so there's no one to see the shame mixed with my relief. I don't know how the music can make me feel so strong, so invincible, when I'm so fucking weak that I need it in the first place. Every track, *any* track could kill me, and I still can't stop.

I pull the headphones off. Footsteps are passing the door; my pulse quickens to match their pace. Our audience, such as it'll be. Some friends of Pixel's are going to try to keep out anyone who'll run to the Corp about us, but that's just to make us feel better. If the Corp wants to find out about this, they will. All they'll need is a hint that there's something to look for.

I find Phoenix and convince her to lend me her eyeliner. It was pretty much a given that I'd forget something at home. In the bathroom, I sing while I outline my eyes with black and hum while I do my lips to match. Sound responsive, it will change to silver when the music gets loud enough. It makes me look fiercer than the blue I usually wear.

Yellow Guy's dirty look is forgotten as soon as I close the door on it. I just want a few minutes alone with the band. Just the band. Yeah, he's been helpful, and yeah, I'm sure Scope loves him, but there's this last link that's only between the four of us. I'd do the same if it was Haven. I think. I push that thought out of my head. I need it filled with lyrics and chords, not the voice screaming that she should be here.

It feels like I should say something inspiring or motivating or at least cool, but I've got nothing. We know why we're here. We know we have to play well. Those people are out there because some part of each of them is willing to believe there's an alternative to what the Corp shoves down our throats. If we suck, that promise is gone.

"So, uh, yeah."

Phoenix turns away, her shoulders shaking. I choose to believe it's nerves.

"We got this," Mage says easily.

"Definitely had more practice than those Corp puppets," Scope adds. That's true. Musicians who audition for the Corp are shoved into a recording studio pretty quick, from what I hear. The ones that make it, anyway. Rejects spend the rest of their lives being watched so the Corp knows they're not taking matters into their own hands. Like we are, except that none of us have ever tried to go legit.

"And we're better," says Phoenix.

"I hope they think so," I say. Outside, the noise is getting louder. It is the sound of impatience. Shuffling feet and voices growing in volume and pitch. "So, we ready?"

Phoenix faces me again, wearing a hint of a smile. A strand of red hair is stuck to her lipstick. "Five minutes ago."

We're just a band. We could be anywhere. We're no different here than we were in the basement. I take the few steps needed to lean down and kiss her cheek. She pretends to puke.

We're still us.

Mage leaves first, high-fiving me on the way, then Phoenix. Through the open door, I hear the crowd's unified inhale when the two of them climb the stairs to the stage. Scope takes a step, stops, and looks at me.

The last time he hugged me was the day we broke up. It would be nice to have that same conviction that I'm doing the right thing again. "Let's go," he whispers into my ear, releasing me and backing through the door.

I wait a second before I follow, brushing past Yellow Guy on my way to the stairs. He says something that might be a wish for luck; I'm not sure because I can't hear him, just buzzing, the hum of the audience taking on a life of its own inside my head.

There's more of them than I expected. I can see only heads and shoulders from where I am, one foot on the rickety bottom step that will take me up and put me on display. Curious faces atop a formless mass of shifting bodies.

I smell sweat, the tangible heat that comes from a crush of people in an enclosed space. Perfume. Scope's cologne on my shirt.

I can do this. The others are up there, waiting for me, bathed in lights that are the only thing making this place familiar. Soon the kaleidoscope will be whirling to my rhythms, painting a crowd moving to my songs.

Mage stands behind his newly enhanced drum kit, Phoenix is at my old xylophone, Scope is surrounded by an array of things only the creative would call instruments. Glass catches beams of blue, green, and purple and sends strange rainbows across unconvinced expressions.

My guitar leans against a speaker. It has a voice of its own, and it's calling.

*Play me.*

# 0010011011121101101110

I am as weak for my guitar as I am for the tracks that come from the console or the cacophony that takes over this place six nights a week. I shove all thoughts into a dark corner and let instinct move my feet the rest of the way. One step. Another. One more and the stage is creaking beneath me.

Whispers rustle. Yes, that's me. Yes, I'm the singer. Yes, I'm the one behind all of this.

Only when I've looped the strap over my shoulder do I look at the audience again. Maybe a hundred people, waiting for me. Chrome gleams, framed by crazy dye jobs and the same fiber-optic tubes that weave through my own hair. I recognize some from Quadrant Two. They're surprised that it's me up here; I'm surprised they've come to see this. There's the guy who helps out his father with the vegetable stand at the depot, the waitress at the water bar closest to my place, and several people I know only from hazy hours of clubbing.

Again, I don't know what to say, but they're not here to listen to me speak. Not yet, anyway. I glance back at Mage, who grins and jerks his head in the direction of the crowd. Scope and Phoenix are both poised to strike their instruments with fierce hands, just waiting for me. The song we're starting with is all me in the beginning, just simple, repetitive chords until Mage gets to jump in with the beat that will keep us all in line.

One, two, and the guitar starts *here*.

It's loud, so much louder than I've ever been in practice. Maybe Pixel has given extra juice to the speakers, maybe it's just my ears catching every vibration of noise through the heavy air. The fingers of one hand fly across the strings, the others find the right frets by instinct. I know this. I *feel* this. Two measures pass and then the floor starts to shake from the hammer-falls of Mage's drumsticks.

I step to the mic and put my mouth an inch from metal that sends static to raise the fine hairs above my lips. To my right, Scope hits a piece of glass. My cue. The first word chimes with Phoenix striking a note, and suddenly we're all playing, singing, a cohesive group of disparate parts.

Nameless, but not faceless. Not voiceless anymore. I look out at the crowd and see open mouths that maybe, one day, will sing these lyrics with me, join in with my anger at the Corp, scream with their last breaths at the complacency that suffocates us all. For now, though, it's just me. They don't know these words, and I'm the Web's most unlikely teacher. But even if they're not what everyone wants to hear, they're what I need to sing. Revolution. That this isn't okay—it never really was, and I can't contain my voice in a basement any-more. We have to take this chance.

Electricity bubbles along my veins, set to the frenzied pulse of the music. I can barely even feel my hands anymore, just sound and strings and relentlessness. Explosive energy pools under my tongue, and the only way to let it out is to sing louder, free my voice until it hits the back wall, send it flying over faces I can't see anymore.

Verse, chorus, verse. We mess up a few times, my fingers slip-ping and Mage banging his drums half a beat too early, but it doesn't matter. What comes out during the coda is so fast it's barely English, just a jumble of syllables I sing with all the power I have. The drums are more frantic now, Phoenix's arms are a blur, glass is shattering and steel is screaming.

The end is abrupt, a crash of notes falling into the abyss of shocked silence. I wipe sweat from my eyes and see my hand stained black. This is the first time these people have heard music that isn't encoded, the first time they've ever experienced a song that didn't leave them flying on their trip of choice. Their faces . . . it's like when I watched Alpha and Omega learn to walk, their tentative amazement at this *thing* which had never been available to them before.

"What the fuck was that?"

I look for the guy, but Pixel's beaten me to it. "*That* was music, asshole," he says, carving his way through the crowd to someone in the middle. Arms crossed, angular face creased with doubt, the guy's eyes pass back and forth between Pixel and me.

"I don't feel nothing."

"Well, then, you're a—"

I step back to the mic. "Pixel," I say, shaking my head when he glances at me. I stare the guy down. "Yeah, you don't feel it. That's because this is *real* music, and you've got to want it. You've got to *let* it get inside your head. Do that, and the high is better than some processed drug. This is what the Corp keeps from you so that they can make us listen to the stuff that'll kill us. So they can keep us under control, use our bodies for energy, take our credits, and run our lives. If that high is worth it to you, go back to your console."

He doesn't say anything. I've started it, now. It's too late to turn back, but I guess it's been too late since the day Johnny first showed me the basement. Everything was always leading here.

"There used to be five of us," I continue, gesturing to the band before I face the audience again. Rapt expressions nearly make me shut up. I'm not the person for this. "Our friend put on a track one day and dropped dead. They killed him, and he's not the only one. It could happen to any of us, any time we put on a track. Have you ever pissed off the Corp? You might not know even if you have. Maybe our friend was lucky. Maybe it's a good thing that he won't go through what happens when the music's finally eaten through enough of his brain. But do the Corp care? No, it just makes room for the next person to come along: someone else for their guards to threaten, someone else to give up their life for the Corp's glory."

Murmurs ripple. "And you're gonna change all that?" asks the guy, raising his voice to be heard. Yeah, I don't really believe it either.

"I'm saying that this is what they take from us." I slap the body of my guitar. "The right to express ourselves. They take it and use it to kill us, instead. I'm saying we take it back, but we need your help. We need people."

"For what?"

I can't see where the question comes from, but it's one I've asked myself a thousand times. "Change," I say. "To show President Z, the Board, and everyone else involved with encoding the music and keeping real stuff from us that we don't want this anymore. That they have to give music back to us and know they can never get away with doing it again. To replace them, if that's what it takes."

"Yeah!" A girl's fist punches the air. I manage a smile for her, breath coming in pants through my stretched lips. Others join in; shouts of *Fuck the Corp!* fill the room.

I'm glad this place is soundproof.

"Ready?" I ask the guys and Phoenix. I am alive, electric. I want to *show* the crowd what I mean.

A sheen of sweat glistens on Mage's bare, muscular arms. "Hell yeah," he says, tossing a drumstick up and catching it again.

We jump into one of Johnny's old ones, a hush falling to make room for my voice when I start to sing. It's fast and dirty and filled with rage that shreds me from the inside and makes me pour everything I have into playing. My hair falls in my eyes, salt stings my lips.

My feet, so used to being connected by sound-threads to my ears, start to move.

When it's over, in a burst of metallic drums and clanging glass, we don't give them a chance to stop us again. Songs blend together on the strings, as incessant as if it were a normal night at the club and the Corp's tracks were sending us all into a spiral of memories and dreams. I have to make them see that this is its own high: playing, being here, *seeing* the music instead of just being another bite for the insatiable appetite of the drug. I know I don't have them, not yet, but through blurred eyes I see bodies find Mage's beat. Sweet-sour adrenaline floods over my tongue and my hands strum faster; I barely notice tearing off a thumbnail.

◈

It's a start. Maybe that's all it'll ever be. Pixel is flashing the blue light overhead; our signal to stop so people can get through the tunnels and off the streets before curfew.

"That's it for tonight," Scope yells while I pour water down my scorched throat. "Same time next week, and bring the friends you trust. Down with the Corp!" His final words get a cheer bigger than any of our tunes have. Blindly, I stumble from the stage and feel my way to Pixel's office and the couch.

"That," pants Phoenix as she flops down on my deadened legs, "was fucking amazing."

"No lie, girl," agrees Mage. Scope and Yellow Guy fall through the door, tangled in each other, their eyes bright.

I'm weirdly light and heavy at the same time, excitement giving life to muscles otherwise ready to collapse. "You think they'll come back?" I ask no one in particular. It comes out as a whisper, but Pixel hears me as he backs into the room.

"Are you kidding?" he asks, handing out an armful of water bottles. I let mine fall to my chest. "At least a dozen people out there were wondering how to start their own band. Another guy already has and wants to play here. I thought maybe, if they're any good, they could be a kind of warm-up act for you guys. Get the crowd going before you head onstage."

"Well, that's what we wanted, right?" Phoenix asks. "To get others to come out of hiding?"

I just nod. In the basement, and even at practice here, I've held back. Tonight was the first time I've ever really let my voice go, tried to embed it in a hundred heads.

"So, now what?"

"Word's gonna spread," Mage says to Phoenix. "Some people will just come because they're curious, but some'll want to fight."

"Mage, can you start trying to find out anything in the system that might help? Like, where the weak points are in the patrols other than shift change."

"See what I can do." He nods.

"We should get out of here. Mage, you make sure Phoenix gets home okay?" Pixel asks, handing Mage a flashlight and ignoring Phoenix's protests that she doesn't need a babysitter. Outside, there's silence; I guess Pixel's friends have cleared the club already. "C'mon, Anthem, I'll take you." He grabs my arm and hoists me to my feet. I think I probably do need a babysitter.

We walk through the tunnels in silence broken only by faint noise ahead, the shouts and echoing footsteps of the last of the crowd. On the street, we split up into pairs and go in different directions, Pixel poised to catch me if I collapse.

I'm fine, really, just . . . I've never felt so alive, so I've never felt so tired when it's over.

"This is you," Pixel says, putting a hand on my shoulder to stop me when I almost walk past my building.

"I can make it from here," I reply hoarsely. He grins.

"You guys really rocked it. You *owned* that stage. You know, when Scope first told me about all of this, I wanted to slap him senseless for being so stupid. But he explained everything, and I came around pretty quick. Still, I wasn't sure that you guys had the chops to pull off what you're aiming for." He shrugs. "But I think you do. Don't lose your nerve, man."

"None of it would have happened without you."

"Eh. I'm just the hired help. I'll take my fee in tab-numbers. There were some *smokin'* chicks there tonight."

My laughter feels like razorblades. "All yours."

He nods slowly, the smile dying on his lips. "Why haven't you told Haven? You know she could help us."

"I should go check on my father," I say, climbing the first few steps before I look back. He holds his hands up.

"Sorry. Night, Anthem."

"Night. And Pixel?"

"Yeah?"

"Thanks. Seriously."

"Yeah."

◈

"You sound sick."

"I'm not," I say, but my voice proves Tango's point, and it's no wonder she raises her eyebrows at me. "Really, I'm not."

"Sit."

I do, submitting to the blood pressure and temperature checks and fighting to keep my eyes open when she shines a flashlight into them. "Hmmm," she says, examining my fingernails and noting the missing one, the calluses on my fingertips. "Anthem, what the hell have you been doing?"

"Rough weekend." I shake my head and meet her eyes to plead wordlessly with her. *Don't do this.*

"Okay." She nods, keeping the contact for a second too long. "Be right back."

It feels wrong to track here at work when I can't warn her about what's going on, not here, but I've tested the limits of our tenuous friendship enough and can't argue when she returns with a small portable console. After last night, it feels wrong to track, period. Nothing's ever going to match that high.

She puts the headphones over my ears and presses buttons. I just wait, my knuckles turning white on the arms of the chair. This isn't for fun, and I don't get to choose.

Soothing, computer-generated sounds fill my head. This is different than the music I make. The collection of samples and tones sounds like a dream, or like I imagine space would sound—each note the bright flare of a star as I fly past.

The pain in my throat fades; energy fills my limbs. It's only temporary, a feeling I get to borrow for a little while before I pour it back into the Grid, but knowing that doesn't take the pleasure away completely. My body is grounded in this chair, everything else inside me is soaring, my own music in my head.

"Better?" Tango asks when the track is over and she's pulled the headset away.

"Yeah." I put my hand on her arm. "How's your friend?"

"Doing okay." She smiles sadly. "Thanks for asking. Drain-level four for you."

The day is normal after that, filled with the complex book I'm reading and a break for awful food. My thoughts are still in the club—which isn't unusual—and on the experience of last night, which is. I don't know how the audience felt, or what they must be thinking right now, but I know what being on that stage was like for me. The power and electricity, the sensation of being omniscient and an insignificant part of something massive and uncontrollable, all at once.

I want to scream about it on the streets and tell everyone I know.

Tell Haven. Pixel's question comes back to me, the same one I've been asking myself for a long time given a different voice. One that's harder to ignore because it's not mine.

I should tell her. I can only imagine how she's going to react if we get bigger, start that . . . revolution. I still can't escape Mage's word. Haven should know before then.

Even to myself, I'm reluctant to admit why I'm holding back. I love her. I need her. I would do anything for her.

I trust her, right?

Opportunities present themselves all week: at my kitchen table, the park, on walks home from the club. But even the inhibition-erasing high isn't enough to loosen my tongue.

Maybe it's better to wait. I want her to see us play well, comfortable on that stage; I want to convince her I can really do this. Yes, waiting is good.

She knows I'm hiding something. I catch her glancing toward my father, eyeing the twins. If only my secret were something that easy.

More people come to the club on Sunday. I'm itching to get out there and guess how many are creating the hurried, heavy rush on the other side of Pixel's office door, but there's business to take care of first.

"This is Crave, guys." Pixel gestures to the guy he's just brought in. Taller than me, his long, curly hair is entirely a natural shade of brown. The smile he aims at me is kind of cute. I shake myself.

"Hey," I say, pushing myself from the couch to shake Crave's hand. "Anthem. That's Phoenix, Mage, and Scope." The others nod from their spots, scattered around the room. "You're in a band?"

Crave shrugs. "Well, sure. We're not as good as you guys—no real instruments or anything, don't have the credits. But we've been going for a while. Practice in an abandoned building up in Three."

"How many of you?"

"Four, like you."

Like we are *now*. Fuck, I miss Johnny. He'd know the right questions to ask. "Okay. Next week, come early. All of you. We'll see how you sound. Are you cool with all of this?"

It's vague, but he gets it. "Dude, the Corp needs to be stopped. I've got a family to look after, a wife and little kid of my own." Well, that settles that—not that it was more than a fleeting thought. "But some things are bigger, you know?"

"Yeah. What do you do?"

"I'm a guard."

Phoenix whirls away from the fridge. "What the hell? Pixel?"

He opens his mouth, but I interrupt before he can say anything. "Phoenix, most of us work for the Corp. I'm a conduit. Mage is a coder. Pixel runs this place. But," I pause, staring at Crave, "you'd better not be thinking of doing anything stupid."

"Hell no. I just gotta pay the bills, same as everyone else."

"And we're just going to take his word for it?" Phoenix demands. I find Scope and see him nod, no more than a tiny jerk of his head. Mage is more confident.

"Yeah, we are. Just like we all trust each other, and Johnny trusted all of us."

She deflates against the fridge door. "Whatever."

I reach out and grip Crave's palm again. "Okay, man. You play next week."

"Awesome. What's the plan?"

"For now, gathering as much info as we can on the Corp. We've already learned some from people who came last week. Schedules, ranks of higher-up employees, that kind of thing. Mage, you found anything new?"

He purses his lips. "Getting there, but I could use some help, honestly. The system's huge, Anthem."

"You know who we need," Scope says.

I glare at him. "Don't start. Crave, can you give a hand with guard stuff? Shift changes, weapons in the armory, anything you think we'll need to know."

"Can do."

The discussion shifts back to music. Mage asks about their gear, predictably most interested in what they use for percussion. Like us—like most or all of the hidden bands around the Web, I guess— their instruments are salvaged, self-constructed. Crave tells us they use old power tools like drills and chainsaws to add to their sound. Scope's eyes spark.

It's almost time. Today feels different than last week because I have a taste of what to expect. I want it now, even more than I did seven days ago. I want to make that crowd move and teach them lyrics to keep in their heads. A secret from the Corp.

Yellow Guy reappears to wish Scope and the rest of us luck. He gives Crave a quick, appraising look before I kick everyone out. It's too early for traditions, and the concept of that word is weird to me anyway, but this time with the band before we go out there feels important.

This time, I don't need to ask if they're ready. I can tell they are. I'm sure they see the same on my painted face, in my taut muscles, in my boots rocking onto my toes. Phoenix fidgets with her skirt, Scope taps his thigh to the rhythm of our first song, and Mage's hands clench around his drumsticks so tightly his nails turn white.

The noise that erupts when Mage appears in front of the crowd is so much louder this week. It swells even more when Phoenix and Scope take their places. I close my eyes, just for a second and let the sound wash over me, giving me back some of the energy I surrender every day.

My steps aren't uncertain. My heart races, but this time I relish it.

I climb the stairs.

President Z's voice comes from the TV, strident and mechanical. I freeze, the spoon halfway to my father's mouth.

But it's nothing. Just more crap I don't care about. What we're doing hasn't made it to the ears of the Corp. I'm sure when it does, President Z will speak and promise the good citizens of the Web that they will stomp out our amusing little rebellion—or that they already have, though in that case I doubt I'll be watching the news.

Someone knocks on the door and I look up, blinking. Alpha and Omega pause in the middle of the story they're telling our father. "Is Haven coming over?" Omega asks.

"Maybe she wanted to surprise you." I smile, crossing the room and opening the door just as another knock starts to rattle the thin wood. "Hey—"

All the blood drains from my face, sucked out by the flat black of the uniforms. "You two, go to your room."

"Ant—?"

"Now." I wait until I've heard them go before I face the two guards standing in the hallway. "Can I help you?" I don't hear my own voice over the rushing in my ears.

"You are Citizen N4003?"

I nod. "Yes," I whisper. Shit. This is it. I clench my teeth so they don't chatter.

"We have received intelligence that your tracking level is borderline. Is there a problem with your console?"

"What? No." No. Thank fuck. I chance a small, relieved breath. Okay. I've been through this before. "I've been busy?"

The taller of the two eyes me carefully, then glances at his partner. "He look nervous to you?"

"He does," the other guard agrees, stepping toward me. My legs start to shake, and I lock my knees. His face is inches away; his vile breath is hot on my face. "What've you got to be worried about, Citizen?"

"I—Nothing. Just need to track more, right?" I ask, pasting on a falsely bright smile.

"If you know what's good for you," the tall guard says. "Consider this a friendly warning. You don't want a visit when we're feeling *un*friendly. Trust me."

I do.

"C'mon," he continues to the other one. "We've got twenty-seven more on the list to do tonight. Be careful, Citizen."

"Yes, *sir.*" I almost choke on the word. It takes three tries to close the door with my sweaty hand. I collapse against it, the wood rattling again.

It's okay. We're still okay. The twins run out of the room and stop by my knees.

"Who was that, Ant?"

"Just some guards checking on something," I say. "They're gone now. Why don't you get ready for bed, and I'll come tell you a story in a minute." I slide to the floor and stay there until my pulse returns to normal.

The fight can't come soon enough. We're not strong enough yet, but we're closing in. On my pod rides to work, trips to the depot, and regular nights at the club before I'm too high to notice, I catch the eyes of strangers who nod once and move on. Every week it gets better. They understand it now, the single, many-headed creature on the dance floor. They absorb the hatred for the Corp that spews from my mouth and out of my hands. Every thrashing chord I play is a *fuck you* to the bastards who say I shouldn't have this. That what I'm doing is wrong.

I tell myself it's only been three weeks, and it's a hundred years since the Corp took power after the war. But I know that people are putting on headphones in their bedrooms and falling, maybe with no one to find them. We've heard of at least five more since we started, all people who somehow broke the law. One of them was at the first concert, and I don't believe in coincidence anymore. The Corp's method is changing. I might be running out of time. Consoles across the Web have become murder weapons. I want to fight *now*.

*Patience.*

◈

Crave's band is pretty good. They played before us on Sunday, rougher and harsher than our sound, their energy more brutal. My envy that they got to go on in front of a crowd already prepared for what they'd hear disappeared when the chants for us got louder, needier. Still, every day it feels like the different parts of myself—brother, father figure, musician, rebel, conduit scum, drug addict, the *me* I am with Haven—are growing further apart.

I'm holding myself together with hands callused by strings.

The front of the Citizen Remembrance Center in Two is flashing green and bathed in late-afternoon light. I don't know why Haven tabbed me, asking me to meet her here of all places, but I come without questioning it. None of her family will be in here. They'll all be in cabinets up in One, where the rich sit and look down on the rest of us.

She's standing in the lobby, head tilted so she can look at the artwork on the walls. That's one creative expression the Corp still allows, probably only because they haven't figured out how to make paintings addictive yet. Anyway, there aren't many people around who do it; paint is expensive.

"What's up?" I ask. She turns to face me, startled. Those legs are encased in high boots below a short skirt and a sweater—her sole concession to the crisp wind blowing outside. The bag over her shoulder is violently pink rubber, covered in comically large spikes.

"Come upstairs with me?" Haven asks. I swallow dryly.

"Uh . . ."

"To your mother," she clarifies impatiently, long nails digging into the strap of her bag. "My project is ready."

"Sure, okay." On the way up to the third floor, I try to get her to tell me what's going on, but her lips stay pressed together. Haven pauses at each break in the stacks, where the pedestals are, to look left and right.

"Good," she says. "We're alone."

Confused, I lead her to my mother's locker. The solid, sharp-edged chip is in my palm for only a second before Haven holds out her hand. Automatically, I lift my arm to pass it to her, then stop. "Going to tell me what we're doing here?"

She shakes her head, unzips her bag, pulls out a computer and a tangle of wires. "I hacked in," she whispers, even though there's no one else here. "You can see everything, Anthem. All of it." Without waiting for me to answer, she walks to the nearest viewer, does something complicated with the cables, and opens her computer on top of the usual touch screen.

My feet stick to the floor. Blood hammers in my ears. I imagine I can feel it swishing around my own chip. Everything I do, every experience I have is recording to it. Even this. Right now.

"I just thought maybe you'd want to . . ." Haven bites her lip.

"I do."

"The information's not gone, just encrypted on the chip itself. I always thought they erased it permanently, but then I wondered. . . . Why would they do that? The Corp's all about having stuff to hold over us, so it makes no sense that they'd get rid of *anything*. It works," she says, coming to pry the chip from my stiff fingers. "I tested it on my grandfather."

"I can't believe you did this." I'm in awe of her. "Will they know we looked?" I glance at the nearest corners of the ceiling. "Is this safe?"

She gives me an *oh, please* look. "They're good. I'm better. And CRCs aren't under surveillance. No point, since they've gotten rid of everything we're not supposed to see. Or think they have." Rapid clicks reverberate down the long room as she types on her keyboard, and the halo of lights bursts to life above us. But instead of my mother appearing, I'm looking at a glowing, three-dimensional map drawn in blues and greens, dust motes breaking up the perfect lines.

"This is the network?"

"Told you it was beautiful."

I'm completely still, but feel as if I'm moving. The hologram in front of us is changing at a dizzying speed as Haven navigates her way through menus and subfolders. Finally, one appears right in the middle, an icon at eye-level, marked *Citizen T25641*.

"Here," Haven says simply, unnecessarily. "Press this when you're ready. After that the navigation's normal. I'll just be—"

I grab her hand to stop her. "Stay."

"You sure?"

I nod. I'm suddenly sure of a lot of things I wasn't last week, or yesterday, or five minutes ago. Whatever's on that chip, Haven's given me an incredible gift—time with my mother without Corp interference. I won't have to look at this image of her and know I'm not seeing the whole story.

There are so many more choices than I normally have. Options for every day of my mother's life since they implanted her chip. Most of the early years I've seen already. I guess there isn't really much a kid can do that the Corp would need to hide.

I pick something at random; an evening when she was about fifteen. The lights flicker almost imperceptibly, the hologram changing from the Grid to a young girl—not blonde the way I remember her in life, but with long, wild spikes of violet hair I've only seen on a viewer. They threaten to poke the eyes of the boy holding her hand as they walk along a street in the middle of the Web, faces and bare arms turned to chameleon-skin by flashing neon.

"I've never seen this," I tell Haven.

"Is that your father?"

"No."

For several long minutes, I watch the two of them. I don't really care who the guy is, but I understand why the Corp removed it. Hard to convince us that the editing is for our benefit if they leave memories in that might be painful for those left behind.

"You look so much like her," Haven says. "The same eyes." She hasn't let go of my hand and I want to grip her fingers more tightly. I would, if I wasn't afraid it'd draw her attention to the fact that I'm still holding on to her.

It's impossible to memorize everything. Often, I land on memories I already know from my earlier trips here. But there are new ones, too—in one, my mother steals an apple from the depot, in another, she lies gray-faced and screaming on a bed in an OD station. I don't linger on that one for long.

There are surprises: an argument with a guard I can't hear but that makes my breath catch, even though she's young and I know she survived past that day. A casual sneer I never saw on her face in real life, aimed at Corp headquarters as she walks past. Physically, I've always known we were alike. Maybe that's not the only way.

*Flick, flick, flick,* I go through the menus, the memories, my mother. The invasiveness should feel wrong, but we all know this will happen to us.

I almost skim past it. My finger is already touching the key that will take me to the next image when my brain catches up with my eyes and my hand recoils. Beside me, I hear Haven's sharp intake of breath and sense her surprise as the hairs around my neck jack stand on end.

She's young, younger than I am now. Maybe sixteen, and too bright and colorful to be standing in the dingy room, its walls blackened with whorls of soot from a fire. A few precious candles sit in corners, their wicks dancing in a draft.

The viewers have no sound, and I've never wished more that they did. Instead, I have to make up the melody coming from the violin in my mother's hand, her cheek resting against old wood. Even without hearing, I know she's good. Her fingers move with graceful confidence, the hand holding the bow steady and strong.

"Holy shit," Haven whispers. I can't say it any better, so I don't say anything. I just watch, transfixed.

That's where I get it from. *She* gave my talent to me.

Emotions play tug-of-war in the hollow space in my chest. Pride. Disappointment. Awe. Envy. Anger.

Why didn't she ever tell me? Why hadn't she prepared me somehow?

When the clip is played out, I restart it. Again and again and again I watch, my feet moving as near to the hologram as they can without disturbing it. Up close, I see the broken hairs on the bow and the scar across the violin's scroll. I'm sure those things didn't matter to her, the way I don't care about how battered my guitar is.

Why didn't she tell me?

I step back to the controls. My fingers scramble over the keyboard as I look for more, skipping past ordinary memories, which would be interesting on any other day.

There it is again. She's older in this one, the sickness already taking hold, but she grips the violin with as much strength as she did when she was younger.

I never had any idea. My mother worked in a library; she wasn't a musician.

Except . . . she was. And she kept it from me.

No more secrets. Especially not from the girl who's given me this.

"We should go," I say. "The twins will be home soon." The door to the third floor swings open—someone else coming to visit a ghost.

Haven is already unplugging the wires, slamming her computer shut, and slipping all of it into her bag. The lights wink and die out when she pulls the chip from the tower and hands it to me. Whoever just came in is getting closer, walking down the aisle next to this one. I put my finger to my lips and Haven nods.

The chip feels heavier in my hand as I carry it to the cabinet. I close the door, checking twice that the lock sealed properly. The woman we pass on our way to the exit is about my father's age, tears streaming down her face as she waves her wrist in front of a small pane of thick glass.

Home is the only safe place for this conversation. We hop a

trans-pod in silence, my head so full my temples are bulging and achy.

I haven't tracked since this morning.

The twins beat us to the apartment by a few minutes. We spent too long at the CRC. Their joy at seeing Haven follow me through the kitchen dulls my frustration at not being able to talk to her yet. As soon as I can, I bribe them with chocolate into playing quietly and drag Haven into my room. She takes the headphones I give her with a raised metallic eyebrow but says nothing and tracks with me.

Calmer, if only because the track didn't kill me, I sit on my bed and watch her legs as she sits down. "Thank you." My voice cracks, and I inspect my fingernails. "What you did . . ."

"Wanted to see if I could, that's all," she says. I don't buy it, but whatever, that's not the important thing. "What happened to the violin?" she asks in a whisper, nudging me until I stretch out on my back. "Do you know?"

I thought about it all the way home. "When she was . . . near the end, we didn't have the credits for the tracks we needed to help her." My voice cracks. "Then, one day, we did."

I wonder if my mother knew, whether my father sold it because she'd asked him to or if he did it on his own, unable to bear seeing her that way.

Will I have to do the same for him? *Can* I?

"She never told you."

"No. She kept that secret pretty well." I try to keep the bitterness from my voice and fail miserably. What else didn't she tell me?

"Anthem," Haven says, propping herself on one elbow and finding my hand with hers. "I'm sure she was just trying to protect you."

Her face is so close, mouth inches from mine. I almost do it, but I chicken out and focus my eyes on the ceiling. "Yeah. Can we just be quiet for a minute?"

She takes me seriously, not even answering, just settling down against my side. The air swells and contracts along with my nerve. In the next room I hear the twins playing. Through the thin glass of my window noises filter up from the street. My father is snoring, someone's shouting somewhere.

"I need to tell you something."

Haven wriggles closer. "What?" she asks, her nostrils flaring against my shoulder. "You smell good."

That isn't helping. I've rehearsed this moment over and over in my head. Now that it's here, I wish she were further away so I could concentrate or even closer so I'd have an excuse to say nothing at all. "Seriously," I say, "this is important."

Fingers still their gentle wanderings over my ribs. "Is this about your friend?"

"Sort of. I"—deep breath—"Well, Scope and I—"

Haven sits up, the side of my body suddenly cool. "You're back together." Her voice is flat.

"What?" Oh. Oh, yeah, I see how she got there. Absolutely nothing is funny about anything this afternoon, but I have to bite my lip to keep from laughing at her confusion. It's just so . . . something. "No. Hell no. It's just that my mother . . . she wasn't the only one."

Green eyes widen and search my face.

"We've been playing. Music." In a rush, I explain everything: the band, Johnny, and what we're doing now at the club. I talk until I run out of words, of breath, of hope that she'll take this well.

And after what she did for me, I am the Web's biggest asshole.

Stillness falls in my room, thickest over the few square feet taken up by my bed. "For how long?" I should have guessed she'd ask this question first. It's the one I didn't want her to.

"Years. Haven, they're killing people now. No warning, no chance to say good-bye."

"You lied to me."

I didn't, not really, but my guilt is the same either way, so I don't defend myself. I was a hypocrite that day in the park.

"Don't you trust me? Think I'd be able to handle it? Why didn't you tell me before? Why did you tell me not to get involved if you've been doing it forever? Fuck, I'll bet you and Scope thought that was really funny."

That pain . . . I did that. I hate myself. "Scope's always thought I should tell you, and of course I trust you."

"Then why?"

"I was trying to protect you." This is less of a good reason than it sounded an hour ago, yesterday, last week. I know now how it feels to hear that excuse.

"Because I'm some weak girl who needs it?" she asks, her voice thick with angry tears.

"Because if I get caught, I pay the price, and you . . . That price is too high." She doesn't answer, and I try again. "You're the strongest person I know, Haven. You don't let anyone else decide what you should do with your life."

"That isn't *exactly* what you're doing?" The bitterness is so sharp it turns *my* mouth sour.

"I almost told you. So many times." I reach for her hand. When she pulls her fingers away, my heart goes with them. I know she feels me sit up; I'm sure she senses my eyes on the face that's pointedly turned away.

"So why are you telling me now?"

"Because I hated you not knowing. Because of today. Because I want you to hear us."

She laughs, a harsh sound with no humor in it. "I don't know whether to be pissed at you for being selfish or happy that you're actually admitting what you want for once in your life."

"I want lots of things, okay? But not all of us are born into a life of luxury. Not all of us get everything we ask for." It's a low blow. I know it before the words have left my mouth and still can't stop them.

Haven's eyes, resolutely closed until now, snap open. They're wet, shimmering. "Fuck you, Anthem," she hisses. A sharp pain shoots up my leg where the heel of her boot catches my knee.

"Wait. Haven, wait!" I scramble off the bed, stumbling a little, and get to the door in time for it to slam in my face. I hope the twins didn't hear that. When I get to the living room, the front door is still vibrating on rickety hinges.

"Did Haven go home?"

I turn and see Omega's innocent smile. I can't leave them. "Yeah." I nod, forcing away the need to chase after her. "Yeah, she's gone."

# 1000011010140101100100

My bed smells like her. I sleep on the floor, imagining heeled boots near my head. Her scent wafts down to cover me, a blanket not big or warm enough. Everywhere I go, I see her in the places she isn't: the club, my apartment, outside Corp headquarters waiting for me even though I've asked her not to. Tabs go unanswered, and I don't know how to find her any other way. The upper-Web isn't huge, but its luxurious towers are tall enough to hide her.

When they ask, I tell the twins she's busy, that she'll be back to visit them soon. Like it wasn't lying that got me into this mess in the first place.

Tracking doesn't help. I do it anyway because I can't risk another visit from the guards, and each time, I hang up the headphones with a mixture of relief and disappointment. At work, thinking of her sucks more energy than the wire plugged into my neck jack. Numb, drained, I go through the motions of caring for my family: cooking, telling bedtime stories, and force-feeding my father.

Word of another tracking death filters down from Quadrant Four. Anger blooms in my chest and wilts just as quickly.

The band gets the rest of my fractured attention, though I think they wish they didn't. Yesterday, during practice before the show, I actually managed to reduce Phoenix to tears with my criticism of her playing. A first, but not one I took more than an instant of pride in.

Alone, I head back to the CRC. Without Haven's toys all I can see are the memories I've always had access to, but today those matter less than my own. I stand in front of the viewer, flipping idly through my mother's life, remembering Haven here beside me. The hologram glitches and reforms back into a drab room, a bed, a final good-bye.

*I promise.*

It was the last time I ever saw her alive, though she hung on for a few hours after that. I've never watched beyond this, never wanted to, and I don't know why my hand reaches now for the controls to flick forward. Maybe nothing can be as painful as what I saw the last time I was here.

Only the figure beside the bed changes. I was in the kitchen with the twins, as far from the bedroom as I could get and away from my parents behind the closed door. Their mouths move, saying things I can't decipher and really don't want to, but I see him take her hand and then, as if that's not enough, move from the chair to lie beside her.

She smiles, and so does he. They fall into silence. It only takes another few minutes before her eyes close, as if she's just falling asleep, and a few seconds after that for my father to realize what's happened.

It's not the first death I've witnessed recently. There've been too many of those—violent, sudden, and lonely. I watch as my father leans in to kiss her forehead, and I pull the chip from the viewer, put it back in the locker, and leave.

◆

"Dude," Scope says from the stairs outside my building. "Spill it. What's wrong with you?"

I finish the last of my juice and sit down next to him. "Nothing. I'm fine."

"Yeah, sure," he scoffs. "That's why Haven's not around anymore. You think I haven't noticed? I'm not always, you know, busy."

"That explains why it's taken you a week and a half to ask me.

I'm not the only one who's different around here."

He shrugs. "Figured you'd pull your head out and fix whatever you did on your own. You haven't, obviously, so I figured I'd give you a hand."

My skin prickles. "What makes you think it was something I did?"

"Uh, because we both know Haven? That girl takes more of your shit than anyone should ever have to. She spends all the time she can with you and treats Alpha and Omega like they're her own brother and sister. If you two want to dance around each other forever, that's up to you, I don't care, but you can at least remember how fucking lucky you are to have her."

"Ease into it, thanks."

"Not my style."

"We had a fight. And don't talk about me behind my back."

"Don't change the subject. What happened?"

Sighing, I lean back and relish the pain of the cement step digging into my back because it makes me feel less tired. "I told her. She kind of freaked out on me." Scope doesn't know about what Haven did with my mother's chip, what I found out that day, and I don't tell him now. It just makes everything worse.

"That's it?"

"Are you kidding? That's not enough?"

"No." He shakes his head, his dark eyes examining my face. "It's more than that. Yeah, she's gotta be angry that you kept this from her. I could've told you that was going to happen. Pretty sure I did, actually. But this is Haven, and you know she'll forgive you once she's cooled off. You're"—he grabs my arm—"I don't fucking believe you."

"What?" I ask, pretending I don't know what he's talking about and wishing he didn't know me so well. I deserve his disgust.

"You're happy to have total strangers come and watch us. You let Crave and all the others in on this even though we don't know them and Crave's a damn *guard*, but you don't trust her? And now you're worried she's going to go tell her father or someone because she's mad at you? Damn it, Anthem, this isn't just about you anymore, okay? Everyone's looking at you for the next move, and you've been walking around in some kind of fucking fog. We need her. Pixel and I trust her even if you don't, and Phoenix and Mage would if they knew her. She knows more about the Corp than any of us. Don't you think we should give her the chance to help?"

Now that it's been given voice and isn't just a wisp of dark thought in my head, I can fully appreciate what an asshole I've been, how stupid that fear is. Scope's mouth opens, closes, opens again.

"I probably can't say anything you aren't already thinking," he says finally. "Has Haven ever given you a reason to think she'd do something like that?"

"No." He's right about all of it.

"You know you're an idiot, right?" Including that.

"Yeah." I swallow. "I want her," I say. "It's just too late." I don't care what promises I made to my mother. She was wrong.

His hold on my arm morphs from angry grip to reassuring touch for a second before he pushes himself from the stairs. "Okay. I've gotta get home. Stop yelling at Mage and Phoenix. I promised them I'd say that."

One side of my mouth curls up. "I will."

Scope looks at me for a long time. "Well, that's why I got the brains and you got the looks. Wait, no, I got those, too," he says, grinning as he walks away. I sit there for a while, watching people pass by. Fear has spread like disease, carried by the truths and rumors of what the Corp is doing. The faces I see are gray, pinched, showing the signs of not tracking enough.

No wonder the guards are busy.

◈

I'm careful to be nicer to the others when we meet at the club on Sunday. Phoenix is holding a grudge, but I think it's just because she's bored while Mage and the drummer in Crave's band are adding something new to Mage's kit.

Practices aren't really private anymore. Crave and his friends mill around the club along with two more bands that have come out of hiding in the past few weeks. Looks that I think are meant to be surreptitious get sent my way all afternoon. It's time, or there isn't much point in continuing to be here. The insidious campaign to gather more people in this room has taken us as far as it's going to go.

We have to be smart. A few hundred of us marching up to headquarters would be a spectacle for the few minutes before we all got shot or dragged off to have headphones clamped over our ears until that most special of tracks deafened us forever. Even if, by some miracle, they didn't do either of those, a protest wouldn't accomplish the kind of change I've read about. The Corp has no reason to alter their ways; there'd be no pressure from anyone they can't quash.

It might still be worth it. The twins would hear about it from someone. I just wouldn't be the one to tell them.

I want to be, though. If we can't change the Corp's mind, we have to change the Corp itself. Get rid of all the people who are responsible for this. Lock President Z and the Board up somewhere they can't hurt us anymore.

Dreams, because we're not ready yet. Anyone important at the Corp is so well-protected there's no way to get to them. We don't even know what they look like. Something is missing.

I am *really* not the person who should be leading this. The crowd should scream someone else's name.

Pixel follows me into his office, saying nothing as he scans his wrist at the console and leaves me alone again. I enjoy the silence for a few minutes, trying and failing to resist the track waiting for me. Every week it gets easier to be the focus of a growing number of eyes, but I still need this false courage. Maybe this will be the one that erases Haven from my mind for more than thirty seconds, or maybe my problems will disappear, along with my speeding pulse. A slow, acoustic guitar starts a simple, three-chord progression in a rhythm like water lapping against the edges of the Web.

*Pink. That's all I can see until it darkens to blood red, dissolving into spatters on glass. I smell her skin, her warm, shaky body in my arms, loving and hating that she needs me as much as I need her. Lying on my bed, her hair splayed across my chest, each fine strand like the hairs on a violin bow that drags across quivering strings. The sound gets harsher, each note struggling for air. Drag, drag, drag, like the breath from my chest, and what does become music is wet, sloppy, and sticky with blood.*

*The siren starts and oh fuck, the pain, I can't. Knives stab at my ears. I can't. There's only pain, and this is it. I'll never hear anything again. My music is gone and the only thing my voice is good for anymore is screaming, screaming—*

The headphones are ripped from my ears. "Anthem? You okay? Come on, over here." I'm lifted, half dragged to a couch. My face slides wet against leather and I can't catch my breath. Plastic is pressed into my hand. I spill water over my cheeks when I lift my head to drink. Fingers hold mine, tendons strong against my skin.

"Better?"

I blink and look up at Crave. "I think so. Yeah. Thanks."

"You were halfway to an OD there. Sure you're all right?" he asks, his thick eyebrows creased in concern.

"Is everyone done with soundcheck?" I ask, sitting up. Only a little dizzy. Good.

"Pretty much. I just came to say I can't play next week. It's my kid's birthday."

"Lucky you did. Come in, I mean. Thanks for telling me. And for, you know."

He gets up from his crouch. "No problem. See you out there?"

"Yeah. Listen—" My gaze flicks to the console, heat drying the last remains of tears from my face.

"Don't tell them you were tracking? I won't. Just stay away from it for now, okay?"

"Promise." I shoot him a grateful smile.

I don't have time to track more anyway. Scope, Phoenix, Mage, and Yellow Guy all come in almost as soon as Crave's gone. The other bands have to cram into an old storage area that hasn't been used since it flooded a few years ago. We get the perks of knowing the manager.

Phoenix not only lends me her eyeliner but offers to do my makeup for me when she sees my hand shake. Guess she's forgiven me, though I'll reserve judgment on that until I look in a mirror. Mage is his usual self, stretched out on a couch, completely relaxed. I really envy him sometimes. Scope and Yellow Guy are in a corner, not kissing for once, but I can't hear what they're whispering about and don't think I want to know. They were both giving me weird looks all afternoon. Scope's probably told him about our talk the other day.

I still can't figure out if it's better or worse, having other bands go on before us. It gives my nerves more time to build, but at least the crowd is ready when we get there.

And the crowds are getting bigger. Last week Pixel had to open up the balcony to people who leaned over the railing, chrome-adorned arms stretched toward the stage. In front of us, above us, they screamed for more between calls to destroy the Corp.

So many people want this—way more than I ever would've imagined. It's not just with Haven that I was blind. So many years holding real music to my chest, a tightly kept secret, meant that I never really considered the world outside our dingy basement.

I want to see the looks on the Corp's faces when they find out about us, even if it's the last thing I do see before the world turns black.

Phoenix mercifully hasn't vandalized my face. The lines around my eyes are as steady as if I'd done them right after a calming track. One that didn't send me into a bad-reaction tailspin, at least. In a mirror Pixel's propped against the wall, I weave blue tubes through my hair and plug them into my neck jack. They come to life, tangled with white-blond spikes to match the reflective strips on my black shirt and the blue laces threaded through the holes in my boots.

"Looking good, pretty boy," Yellow Guy calls. I roll my eyes. If Scope had said that, Yellow Guy would be all over him in a second, marking his territory.

Beyond the door, the club is filling up and the group of girls who'll be going on first are getting ready down the hall. They're talented, with strong voices more powerful than Phoenix's. Mostly they sing, with the occasional beat from a drum or clatter of a homemade tambourine joining in—mellow and soothing, airy, the kind of thing I listen to on the console when I want to float. The Corp has done one good thing by addicting us to all music—not that many of us are really picky about style. Music is music.

I take the other couch, try to rest, but it only feels like an instant later that Pixel's opening the door to tell us we're almost on. I grab my guitar from the corner and give Yellow Guy some silent credit when he leaves without being asked for the band's moment alone.

Nerves get forced down with a swallow of air and I follow the others out. The club is packed, hot—full of every volume from whisper to scream. Lights dance and waving arms try to catch the intangible beams.

I don't think it would matter how packed it is. The thousand people blur to nothingness when I get onstage, all made invisible in contrast to one person whose face I know down to each intimate detail. My brain registers the first flash of pink and the twin glimmers of two chrome arches in the middle of the audience.

I glance quickly at Scope. He's grinning. I wonder what he said to her and when he said it.

"*Hi*," she mouths when my stare is back on her face, more beautiful than I've ever seen it. One corner of her mouth lifts cautiously upward. I hear her as clearly as if she'd breathed it in my ear, despite the rumbling, impatient noise around her.

I say something back; I'm not even sure what. My toes are over the edge of the stage, ready to jump down into the mass of decorated bodies. I clench my fists and step back, still staring. If nothing else, I doubt even the pull of my guitar could tear me from her side again.

But there is one thing I can do.

Before I plug it into the amp, I play a few notes that only the band and the people right at the front can hear. It's not what we usually start with, but a glance at Phoenix and Scope tells me they get the hint. I know Mage will, too.

She's listening. I just hope she understands.

I step back to the microphone, as uncomfortable with this part as I always am. Singing is so much easier than talking. "Thanks for coming," I say, a brief whine of feedback cutting through the words. They must think I'm speaking to all of them. My fingers go to the strings, the notes I played a minute ago repeating themselves. Mage, Phoenix, and Scope all join in, the song swelling through the speakers on the walls.

For the people who've been here before, the change is a surprise, and for anyone new I'm sure this is confusing. They came to rebel against the Corp, not listen to some slow love song.

I really don't care. There's only one who matters, and by the time I open my mouth to sing the first verse, she's all I can see. I think I can smell her perfume, too, heady above all the scents in the room.

It's one of the first songs I ever wrote about her. I sat underneath the cherry blossoms in the park with a broken pencil and a white, blank page from the back of an old library book, scribbling imperfect words with imperfect tools for a perfect girl. It's the first day I saw her in Scope's chrome studio, knowing she was the reason my mother forced me to make that promise. That this was the girl who'd tempt me into the distraction of happiness. Lyrics twist and turn around the peaceful, velvet melody I pull from the guitar, but I don't register that I've sung them until I see their effect reflected back at me. Not the nervous smile of a few minutes ago, but a full one that is somehow not incongruous with the wet tracks on her cheeks catching light in teardrop prisms. Nebulous warmth in my chest eases the ache there.

The coda flows over the audience—soft, rhythmic, hypnotic. Fitting. I push the last word past a lump in my throat and let the music die away under my fingers.

I hadn't thought past this when I started, but Phoenix takes care of it for me. I don't even have time for surprise that it's her, and not Scope or Mage who shoves me away from the mic.

"Go," she hisses before addressing the crowd. "Sorry, guys. Technical problems. Back in five."

I'm gone before she's finished; I ignore the stairs and slide from the stage into a space made empty by the approach of my boots. Hands reach out to touch me and grab my clothes. I pull away from one girl, not even stopping to glare when my shirt rips and a blast of humid air hits my rib cage.

Soft, bare, shoulder-skin is suddenly under my hands. The perfume that teased me through the few minutes of the song floods my nostrils, and it's the first real breath I've taken in weeks. "Hey," I say, leaning my forehead against hers. She lets me, the final confirmation I need that she got what I was trying to say.

"Hey, yourself. This is incredible." Her lips are trembling and I want to kiss them still. A hush falls over the circle of people around us and ripples out like water fleeing a tossed pebble. "I should slap you."

"Scope already did." Laughter bubbles in my chest. "I'm so sor—"

She silences me with a finger. "Later. Don't think you're getting out of it, just . . . later. And I'm sorry, too."

"I've changed my mind."

Her eyes widen, so does her smile. "So have I."

I cup her cheeks and bend to close the gap between us. A drumroll starts. I let go with one hand and give Mage the finger without looking at him. Haven and I are both laughing as our lips meet for the first time, and maybe that's the way it should be.

I can't kiss her deeply enough or hold her tightly enough, but I try. Fingers twist into the hair above my neck jack and catch on the wires and tubes. It doesn't hurt, though it probably should. My tongue flicks at her teeth and she gently bites my bottom lip. *Fuck.* I'm pretty sure the whole crowd hears my groan, but they're getting impatient. I can't stay here forever, as much as I want to.

Haven uses her leverage on my hair to pull me away. "That song was pretty choice," she says, eyes lit with challenge. "Get back up there and show me what else you can do."

Sweat coats our bodies beneath the sheets—old, from earlier at the club, and new. My ragged fingernails travel the bare length of her spine. I should be exhausted. I always am after a concert, but I can't sleep and I refuse to get up to track no matter how much my brain is screaming for a hit. Moonlight streams through the window, illuminating the floor and the bright pink pieces of clothing scattered the length of my room. I keep smiling, reliving how each landed in its spot.

I'm going to hurt in the morning. I played harder, faster than I ever have, let my voice escape louder than ever.

It's *possible* I was showing off a little.

"Tell me what you need," Haven says. Goose bumps follow the trail of her breath across my skin.

"Thought you were asleep," I say, tightening my arms around her. "You. I need you."

Her mouth finds mine in the darkness and it's like hitting a perfect note, or that's like this. Energy gathers in my limbs; my tongue tingles where it slides over hers.

"That's a relief," she says, her lips still against mine. "But not what I meant."

No. We've talked about us already, until my raw voice was even hoarser and I couldn't keep my hands from her skin. She knows everything now, and we're still here. I grin again, trying not to think about what it'll be like the next time I see Scope. He's going to be unbearable.

"The Corp," she continues. "What are we waiting for?"

I laugh softly. "I can't remember right now."

A finger lands between my ribs, not hard enough to burst my bubble. "We have enough people, I think. Waiting any longer is gonna be too risky. And everyone's been sharing information—most of it's useless, but we've got what we need, except . . ."

She waits and I breathe. If I'm right about who her father must be, I'm asking too much of her.

I do it anyway. "Access to the Board and President Z. They're not going to reveal themselves in the middle of a protest. We have to get to them."

A beat. Two. Three.

"Okay," she whispers. "I'll take care of it." Her tone turns more playful. "Anything else?"

I roll us over, hover above her, and gently find her collarbone with my teeth. "Lots of things."

The sun is already a faint purple tinge across the sky when we fall asleep.

It's a good thing the twins are used to seeing Haven emerge from my room, tousled and free of makeup. As it is, Alpha gives me a brighter-than-usual smile that makes me wonder if she can tell something's different. It's only for a second, though, before she and Omega rush to hug Haven, exclaiming that they missed her, and all traces of my guilt over a broken promise vanish. My aching fingers brush against hers over the toaster, our legs press together under the table.

A new kind of normal. My face actually hurts, and even after the downer track I sneak between checking on my father and getting dressed for work, I spend my entire trans-pod trip forcing my smile into a box I'll open again this afternoon. I don't have to try as hard to not spit on the statue, my fists don't clench as tightly when the elevator fills with sneering Corp suits. Even the mainframe's hum doesn't bother me as much as usual.

"Good morning, Anthem," Tango says, following me into my cubicle. Ready to give my usual response, I glance at her. This is not her normal, automatically chirpy self.

"Hi?"

Her lips twitch and her eyes sparkle as she gestures for me to sit so she can check my vitals. "Are you feeling well this morning?" Her shoulders shake.

"I'm fine," I say at normal volume. "*What's up with you?*" I add in a whisper.

"Excellent. Deep breath," she says, pressing the cool metal stethoscope to my chest. Finished, she turns my head and leans in to inspect my neck jack. Not an everyday part of this routine, but she does it sometimes. "*I'll just bet you're 'fine.' That was some kiss last night.*" My heart skips several beats—at least she's done checking that. I jerk away to stare at her.

"*You . . .*" I don't know what to say. She was there, obviously. It's not much of a surprise that I didn't notice her, but Tango is a good little Corp tech—goes to the Sky-Clubs every night to mingle with others of her status and higher. Deftly, she maneuvers my shock-frozen limbs until I'm in jacking-in position, then puts a finger to her lips. A sign. My secret is safe.

"What are you in the mood for?"

Oh, hell. She's worse than Scope'll be. I ignore the tears in her eyes.

"*Crime & Punishment,*" I say, glaring. I'm starting to think that top-of-the-world feeling I woke up with is because the whole damn Web's flipped on its axis since yesterday. I'm happy and Haven is mine and Tango is watching bands play illegal music.

She finally calms herself. "You and those books. Hold still," she says, unfurling the loop of cable that will hook me up to the Grid. *"You're really good, Anthem,"* she whispers as I'm plugged in and that strange sensation takes over me. *"You really think we can make a difference?"*

"Yes," I say, but I can't move my head and I think she's already gone, leaving me to Russian literature and my spinning mind. If word has climbed this far up the Web, to Tango's ears, other people know, too. We can't keep the secret any longer. Electricity hums and flows from my body as I stare at the ceiling. The Corp is looming, powerful, and I'm just giving it more every day. There's going to come a time when I'm too weak to fight, when juice and chocolate won't be enough to restore me.

It takes all evening to recover from the level-seven drain Tango put me on today, apologizing as she jacked me in. I get it. The twins run around, jumping over my sprawled legs on the living room floor. I drag myself up to put them to bed and get ready, covering the dark circles under my eyes with makeup.

Being at the club on an ordinary night feels weird now, like I'm in some fantastical house from an old book where the same door opens on to different rooms depending on the situation. Pixel's greeting is as friendly as ever—the undercurrent of conspiracy wouldn't be obvious to anyone overhearing us. I hope, anyway.

"Took you long enough," he says, running a hand through strands of green.

I shift my gas mask so it hangs over my shoulder. "Not you, too." My tablet exploded with messages from Scope when I checked it at lunch, and again after work. I started to delete them unread after the first twenty.

"Hey, just happy for you. She's in there, and she looks—" He shakes his head. "Lucky she only has eyes for you, I'm just sayin'."

I laugh and open the door. The music grasps me and yanks me into the middle of the club. The harsh drums of an energizing track have everyone's feet stomping, lifting, the people a visual embodiment of sound. Bright mouths outline lyrics, but nobody sings. I feel sorry for them.

I'm late, like always, but it's on purpose now. I won't be recognized by anyone who comes here on Sundays; they're all too high. I can't afford to replace another shirt.

Pixel's right. She looks . . . Black latex encases legs I know intimately after last night, a matching corset is strung with pink laces that reveal an inch of olive skin on either side of her spine. I just got here and already I want to leave, with her, but she's seen me and I'm dancing, pressed against her, my face buried in her hair.

*It starts to work. The music fills my bones with light that spills out, ricochets around the room, and bounces off chrome and plastic. I don't know the differences in our bodies anymore; Haven and I are one person, floating and falling on crests of melody. Magnetic, we part and join again and again. I'm not sure what's so funny, but I can't stop the laughter that joins the encompassing noise from the speakers.*

*I go deeper and higher all at once, flying on the feel of her, the twins' smiles, the mirage of the stage along that wall, calling to me. Strength rushes my body—I'm powerful here, in this room, ready for anything.*

*I am tickled with light and taste the keyboards, metallic and sweet. Skin is hot, electric velvet against my fingertips and yes, she is all I need. She and Alpha and Omega and my guitar, safe and full of happiness that doesn't die as soon as the speakers shut off.*

*Coherence is leaving, chased from my mind by the drug's relentless pursuit. For tonight, I surrender—dance harder, laugh louder. I was tired before but not now. Now I can take over the world.*

⊕

Son of a bitch, that hurt, even with the painkilling tracks just ending in my ears.

"Never thought I'd see the day, man," Scope says, starting to clean up the area around the chair in his studio. "Feel okay?"

Actually, it stings like hell. I finally found what I wanted, and now fresh chrome gleams on the back of my right hand.

"Be careful with it for a few hours. You know, no one's going to know what it means."

"I know what it means."

At a casual glance, it will probably look like nothing, just a strangely decorated circle. Anyone who has seen or read about such a thing will probably think it's a set of crosshairs from a gun. And I am making myself a target, but that's not what this is.

I spent an hour flipping through Johnny's old musical theory book this morning. Its pages are crisp and thin from age, its print is worn out in places from the touch of too many fingers, and its corners are curled like petals. I wasn't sure what I was looking for until I saw it.

A coda symbol, used to signify an ending. The final piece of a song that isn't like the verses and choruses before it.

"Ready?" Scope asks. He opened the studio just for me, and now we have to go.

"Yeah." I wince as I swipe my wrist to pay, and the beep feels like needles in my ears. We walk through the bustle of Saturday, making sure no one is looking before we duck into one of the tunnel entrances Pixel's told us about and follow yellow arrows to the club. Haven is waiting under the trapdoor, a few deliberate feet from the slimy walls.

"About time," she says, lowering her flashlight beam from our faces. It catches my hand for a split second on its way down and makes it to my knees before she jerks it back. "Anthem!"

Scope snickers. I look down at my new chrome, glowing against my skin. "Yeah."

"Let me see! What is it?" she asks, careful to hold my wrist, well away from the tender area. I explain while Scope climbs the old crates to the ceiling.

We hear voices as soon as we open the storage room door, and Haven smiles wryly at me. I didn't exactly take the time to introduce everyone after the last show. We were out of there, down in the tunnels, before the last note finished buzzing from the speakers.

"Hey," I say to the group assembled on the club's main floor. "Guys, this is Haven."

Most of them wave and give their names. Pixel and Yellow Guy smile at her. Mage surprises me, standing, grinning as he comes over to us.

"Haven," he says. "*The* Haven?"

I try to remember if I've ever told him her name. "Depends on who's asking," she says, metallic eyebrows arched.

He holds out his hand. "Mage."

A wide grin spreads to match his. "*The* Mage?"

"Depends on who's asking."

"Do you know what the hell is going on?" Scope whispers. I shake my head, staring at their clasped hands and perplexing delight.

"Mage and I are old friends, kinda," Haven says. "It's a hacker thing."

"No point in bragging if you don't tag your code," Mage says to me. "Course, she has a lot more reason to brag than I do."

"I get lucky," she says. Mage laughs.

"Haven't seen you around for a while."

"Been busy with something."

My mother's memory chip. Another wave of gratitude washes through me. "We should get to work," I say. The others are getting restless.

"Anthem's right," Haven says, looking around at everyone. Pixel, Yellow Guy, my band and Crave's, the three girls who go onstage first, and the duo who play after them. I can't remember all of their names even though I heard them five minutes ago. "We have to do it now. One more concert, and we tell them we've picked a day to attack. There were a thousand people in here last week. If we're smart, that's enough. We ask them to stick around after the show and assign them all a position."

"You solved our biggest problem?" Scope asks, looking smug. "I knew we needed you."

"Sort of. We don't need to know *who* they are, just where. Doors at the Corp are like doors everywhere, but I can hack in and put them on emergency lockdown. Standard security procedure. Trap them inside, then unlock as needed. Less chaos, meaning we won't need weapons." Haven looks at me. I've told her how I feel about that. "But thanks to Crave, we'll have them if we need them."

"I still say we storm in and open fire," Yellow Guy says. Haven scoffs.

"Do that, and they'll kill us all without a second thought. You think we can take them on by force alone? Not a chance. The Corp is ruthless," she mutters. "Believe me, I know."

We all do.

"Blindly storming headquarters, even with guns, isn't the answer," Haven insists. "You have to do it the right way. Look around here; almost all of you work for the Corp in one way or another.

They already think you're part of them. That you believe what they do, right? It's like using this place for the concerts. They don't look here because they don't expect it. All of you can walk into the building, and no one will suspect you. *Then* use the army you guys have already built up here."

*I overheard my father talking about it. They were discussing ways to get inside the groups.* I grip her hand tighter.

Yellow Guy stares at her through narrowed eyes.

"Tomorrow," agrees Pixel. "Just don't start a riot and destroy my club, okay?" He grins. "Save it for headquarters."

"We'll try."

"We're really doing this," Haven says quietly to me, inspecting the new chrome on my hand. Everyone's broken off into groups, talking amongst themselves.

Every cell in my body is taut, poised. A crossroad is coming; I can feel it.

I slip my arms around her waist. "Yeah, we are. Are you ready?"

She hears what I'm not saying. "I picked my side a long time ago," she says, leaning in to kiss me. If I were a better person, less weak, less selfish, I'd tell her I'm not worth going against her family. I have nothing really to offer her; I won't even live as long as almost any other guy she could choose. But her lips are against mine, we're tongue to tongue, and it's an excuse to stay quiet, keep her against me until the opportunity passes.

We go back to my place after the meeting breaks up and settle in to an afternoon with the twins that feels weirdly domestic now that I don't have to try not to touch her all the time. Alpha and Omega make up for the days they didn't get to see her. Jealousy nibbles at me, but it was my own fault. They'll spend tomorrow night with Fable, so we take extra time with dinner and bedtime stories, Haven making sure they brush their teeth while I feed my father and set up a few tracks for him.

Scope and Yellow Guy will understand why we're not at the club.

Rain is splattering the windows when we wake up and continues all morning, a soundscape for my restlessness. "Will you be here tomorrow, Haven?" Omega asks as she ties his shoelaces, his little face worried.

"I'll see what I can do," she says, smiling and kissing his forehead. Something in me relaxes on Omega's behalf. Alpha gives me a hug before grabbing her bag and taking Omega's hand to drag him out the door and downstairs to Fable's. We give them a few minutes head start, maybe a bit more, and venture out into the rain.

◐

We're only half an hour late to soundcheck.

"We'll have the apartment to ourselves tonight," I say, running my hand down her back. My father doesn't really count. I can hear the cacophony outside, but I'm only listening for her answer.

"Hmmm. Choice. You've got to get out there."

"Go with him for a sec?" I jerk my head toward Yellow Guy, already at the door, obviously waiting to see if I'd ask Haven to leave. She kisses my cheek, keeps hold of my hand until the last possible second, and takes his arm to lead him out into the club. I look at the others, take a deep breath, and exhale.

It's been too late to stop for a long time, but tonight still feels different. Tonight we ask for help, and when some of those people outside—the ones dancing, singing, and chanting with freedom they've never had anywhere else—go home, they'll be charged not just with the music they've heard tonight, but also a task for the days to come.

"Just another night, man," says Mage, clapping me on the shoulder.

"For Johnny," I say. I haven't stopped wishing he was here with us, and every time I think of him my anger at the Corp climbs another note on the scale.

"For Johnny," Phoenix agrees. She's glowing; the nudge she gives me is jerky and impatient. Besides me, I think she loves this the most of all of us. The ferocity of the music meets its match in her, and she relishes the fight. "Come on."

Six times I've walked out of this room, climbed the steps to the stage, and looked out on an ever-growing throng of people. I've smelled the sweet tang of sweat and perfume, been blinded by lights and chrome. Six times I've glanced at the others, in position behind their instruments, and stepped to the mic with my fingers already on guitar strings.

Tonight, I inspect the audience a little more closely than usual. For Haven, yeah, but I know she's there and just want to look at her for a second before I move on. Tango is on the balcony, purple hair taken out of its normal, severe knot so it can hang down over the railings. The sound implants in her hands are flashing in time with the noise. When we start to play, the streaks of light will go crazy. She waves, I smile back.

I catch a few comments from the crowd; people are wondering if I'll jump off the stage to go kiss some girl again this week. Tempting, but no. That has to wait.

Mage starts. I feel the thud in my feet. One, two, three, four . . .

Scope next. Glass bottles—each a different, perfect note—give the first hint of melody and the bodies begin to move. They know this one.

The xylophone joins in, Phoenix's arms a blur of accuracy.

Three more bars. Two. One.

My turn.

I'm home like I am in no other place except with Haven, and she's here with me, against the back wall, pink lips parted in readiness for the lyrics she's learned over the past week. In the DJ booth, Pixel controls spinning lights and turns the volume up just a little.

The drums are hammering in my head and the guitar is the sound of my fury, the wall of noise behind which I will protect everyone I love—Alpha, Omega, Haven, even my father for the time he has left. I'll vindicate Johnny, and a mother who played her violin in secret. My friends are with me and so are the hundreds of people out there, singing the song I give to them and throwing it back to my ears. Sweat beads on my eyelashes and turns my sight to neon rainbows as I stomp blindly around the stage, strings shrieking, aggressive and dramatic.

Final lyrics leave me in a growl, but I'm not done. "More?" I ask them. The screams are deafening. "If you want more, it's time to fight. Time to tell the Corp we're finished with letting them make us sick, *killing* us, with something that should feel like this." I hold up my guitar to more screams. "But we need your help." When I lift my hand again, just my hand this time, the new chrome shines. "This symbol means an ending. It's what I believe. What I know is right. We're going to end the Corp. Three days from now." Wednesday. Johnny's day.

Chants of *Fuck the Corp!* start again, familiar in this room to me by now, but stronger than ever. Enough talking. I can't resist the instrument in my hands, and I have them. They're not going anywhere.

I lose myself in the music, higher than I'd be on any track. This is *real*. Everything narrows to pinpoint focus: the sharp, wiry strings, the cool, textured metal of the mic against lips stinging from salt, the roar filling the room. I taste copper and dance faster around Scope and Phoenix, in time with Mage's speeding beat.

Sound stops and starts again, an ear-piercing feedback whine. It takes a second to register the screams above it. I play harder, thinking maybe I have gone deaf because I can barely hear my guitar.

The screams aren't for me. Not this time.

Panic.

I don't know where they came from, or exactly who sent them. I don't know how long they've been watching, but I can guess why they're taking action tonight. I know the feel of the stage as I'm forced to my knees and the stabs of pain that shoot up my legs.

I know that the thing against my head is the barrel of a gun.

Time stops. The gun is cold against my temple. I can feel it so clearly: the round muzzle, the hard, chilled metal, the steely menace. I don't understand how the hollow space in the middle can be so solid and bruising. How emptiness can make sweat bead fresh all over me, send my pulse into a panic, as if it's trying to squeeze as many heart-beats into my final moments as possible. The gun goes away, but I'm not being granted any favors. My guitar strap is pulled over my head. The breaking strings, splintering wood, and snapping metal are the shots that start the clock.

The gun comes back. Screams are everywhere as people shove their way to any possible escape route—down into the tunnels and through the old fire exit at the end of the hall, even to the now open door, right into the waiting arms of the guards who must be out there on the street.

I can't see Haven anywhere. Beside me, Scope is pushed down. A guard curses and there's a sickening crunch before Phoenix cries out in pain. Mage folds quietly, I think. I hope that's why I can't hear him.

Pixel's dragged from the DJ booth by his hair, black and green wound around a strong hand. Yellow Guy is pushed face-first into a speaker.

I still can't find Haven. Calling her name earns me a steel-toed kick that cracks at least one rib. Fiery tongues lick through me, feeding on the air in my lungs. Gasping, I can only watch through watering eyes at the unfolding scene. Where the fuck is she? My chest burns.

The club clears in minutes. I don't know exactly how many were here, let alone how many get out safely.

"On your feet, scum." The blue tubes tear from my head and neck jack. They crumple under the guard's purposeful boots and I'm shoved across the floor, past Pixel's chair below the scanner, into the night. It takes me a second to realize I'm even outside. The flashing lights of a dozen pods and the deafening sound from sirens . . . it's so much like the club.

I fall, bare skin scraping on asphalt. Everything . . . over. I just want to say good-bye to Haven. I need to see her.

"This is the one in charge. They want him in one piece." I'm pushed into a pod, doubling over from the agony in my rib cage. Cuffs bind my wrists. When I try to look out the window, my head is slammed against it and my vision goes black.

My consciousness flashes like a strobe light of awareness, illuminating enough to tell me where I'm going. Up, up into the middle of the Web, along neon-bathed threads to the giant glass spider in the center.

And I'm a fly.

Faces. Voices. Hard marble under my feet, then something softer. I see red that could be blood or could be . . .

"Scope!" I yell. A hand claps over my mouth, but not my eyes. I watch a struggling Scope being dragged through a door by two guards and then . . . blankness.

✛

I'm alone.

The cell is spartan, cold, designed to break me against rigid lines and sharp corners. There's a bed, but before the lock seals to separate me from the guards who brought me here, I've already decided I won't use it.

It's pretty much the only thing I'm sure of.

*The twins.* I curl my battered body in a corner. They're safe, for now, but knowing that only gives me time to think about what happened at the club. Fractured memories piece themselves together and I want to beat my head against the wall to smash them again.

Someone betrayed us, and now I'm trapped. Dead man rocking on the floor. I assume my friends are in other cells. That's the best option, and I don't want to consider the other ones.

We were so stupid. I was so naïve. I squeeze my eyes shut but can't make the faces go away. Everyone in the band. I don't think it was any of them. Tango, who I was so surprised to learn was coming to the concerts. Pixel, though I can't believe he'd hurt Scope like this, even if he wanted to hurt me for some reason I can't figure. Crave, who only would've had to mention it at work. Anyone else who was playing, Yellow Guy, Pixel's friends, or any of the hundreds of people there. The options are endless.

Hours pass, I think. My watch is gone, along with anything else I can call my own. My clothes must've been stripped off after I blacked out. I imagine someone pushing dead-weight limbs into this scratchy gray jumpsuit. There aren't any windows, so I can't judge time by daylight or lack of it.

It's bright. Fluorescents hum on the ceiling, and the flicker gives me a headache.

It's not the silence. Not the empty sonic space. It's the lights. Under them, my bruises turn livid and angry. The skin around my chrome implant stings. What a joke. Who the fuck did I think I was?

The crowd swims in front of me, hundreds of blurred faces. I wonder what happened to them all and I make myself stop before the guilt smothers me.

At some point I fall asleep, propped up against the wall. Dreams are rhythmic things that thump through my brain.

Noise jolts me awake and pain slashes through my side when I look for the source of the sound.

"Breakfast time, scum." An intercom crackles and a tray slides through a slot in the wall. Well, that answers one question, at least.

"Where are my friends?" I ask, unsure if the thing works both ways or if I'm audible if it does. My throat is full of glue because I don't even know who I'm asking about—who my friends are anymore.

Cruel, harsh laughter fills the cell.

The food is as gray and dead as the room. It tastes like nothing, though I'm sure it contains the exact amount of nutrients I need from a single meal. There's some reason they haven't turned me into an Exaur already, some reason they want me, like the guard said. I don't know what it is, but it's the same reason they're feeding me. They want me strong, alive. That alone is almost enough to push the plates away, but then I think of the twins.

Fable's mother will look after them. She and my mother were friends, years ago. Hopefully she'll check on my father, too.

*Please, please let my family be okay. Please tell me they won't go after little kids and a sick old man who knew nothing.* I don't ask through the intercom about them. I don't want to give anyone ideas.

Meals arrive on a schedule, so I can measure time. On the second day, long scratches, where I've clawed my skin during restless sleep, join the bruises.

Day three. I'm shaking. My legs won't hold me anymore, and it takes several tries to turn on the taps in the hygiene cube after I crawl there for water. My thoughts are ridiculous tangles. I see hazy images of the twins, Haven, and my mother with them, which can't be true.

I found her body myself. I remember the blood and my mind stains red.

It's obvious what they're doing. I've read about withdrawal, its suddenness more painful than the slow decline of tolerance. I try to fight it, but I'm only fighting myself. There's no audience to my gritted teeth and clenched fists and my limping pace around the cramped cell as I take breaths of processed, plastic air as deep as my ribs will let me.

✥

In a pool of vomit, I wake up on what could be day four or fourteen.

"Good morning."

I'm too weak to lift my head. I'm probably hallucinating anyway.

"You call yourself Anthem, don't you? Not the worst handle I've heard, if perhaps a little misleading. Come with us."

I love the way she says the last part, like I have a choice. I don't ask how she knows my name. Spiteful arms haul me to my feet, their owners exuding pleasure when I flinch from the grip on my bruises. A face, blurred and smiling with wide blandness, appears in front of me. I think maybe I've seen her before, but I think a lot of things right now and have faith in none of them. Dark hair, a Corp-approved suit . . . it's not as if these things make her unique.

"Who are you?" Only half the syllables make it out as sound.

"Citizen L5329." I decide to call her Ell because the numbers are swimming in a pool of confusion and don't add up to anything but fear.

"I'm fine right here." The guards tighten their hold as I try to break free. I bite through my tongue.

Ell clucks. "Lying is not a good start for us, Anthem. Cooperate, and you will have everything you want."

"I want to die." She asked for honesty. "You can do that. I know about your special tracks."

"Oh, don't be that way. We have discovered your talent now. You can be useful to us, and we can help you. Your record expunged, your family cared for . . ."

In the guards' steely grip, I sag a little. "Are they okay? Are my friends alive?" I whisper.

Ell smiles. "For the moment. Whether that continues to be the case is entirely up to you. Bring him."

Carpet burns my bare feet. Out of the cell, along a curved corridor. My captors seem to be trying to bump me into every available obstacle, but I don't give them the satisfaction of complaining about it. In the elevator, Ell pulls a tablet from her pocket, types a message that will speed along the Grid in a blip of light to its recipient. I know it's about me.

More dragging, more burning until I'm shoved into a chair with a force I'm surprised doesn't break more bones. Maybe it does and I'm just too numb. Rising bile stings my raw throat. I can feel that and hear one of the guards curse as the scant contents of my stomach hit his shoes.

"You little—"

"Go clean up," Ell orders him. He gives my arm a last, vicious pinch and I'm free again, if freedom can be measured in inches. Footsteps. A door closing. "Look around, Anthem," she says.

My neck screams when I raise my head, the skin around my jack taut and sore. There are instruments everywhere—guitars, drums, keyboards, a violin too warm and brown to be in this world, let alone this building. It belongs in dusty, candlelit memories. Blinking lights flash over recording equipment, microphones wait for voices.

And there is stillness. The mainframe's hum I can always hear at headquarters is gone. I ball my fists and grind my teeth almost to cracking point. I want to touch everything, so I don't. The moment I show weakness, they have me.

Not that they don't already.

"All of this can be yours," Ell says, flicking a switch that brightens the spotlights overhead. "*Look*, Anthem. Do not tell me you don't want to play them. Imagine what you could do in this room. Think of the music you can make, all with our blessing. We will give you everything you need. Anything you want. You can have a life you never imagined. You will be our newest celebrity."

I don't answer. I almost say yes. I'm so close I can feel the word stuck in my throat like a cough. A moment passes, and she calls the remaining guard forward again. "We'll have another chat tomorrow," Ell promises as I'm practically carried away.

Five, six, seven, eight. The days are all the same. The time I don't spend screaming or puking, I spend thinking. The twins, Haven, and my friends. I wonder if my father's even noticed I'm gone.

I scream some more. It hurts less than thinking.

Every day, I'm taken back down to the studio and the smooth instruments, a slick attempt at seduction.

Decisions rip me apart. Giving in means I can get back to the twins and make sure they're okay. Giving in means I can only make sure they're okay for now. It's one thing to know what faces them when they're older: the music, the addiction, the decline. . . . It's another thing to make the tracks that will do it to them.

And if they step out of line, it could be one of my songs that . . .

No.

This punishment is no accident. Killing or turning me into an Exaur would be the easy thing for everyone, but that doesn't teach me a lesson, does it? And whoever betrayed us knows me, of that I'm fucking positive.

A new, creative punishment. Just for us.

◆

On day nine, Ell is late. Maybe she's given up on me. Maybe I've missed my chance and the twins are . . . My father is . . .

"Good morning."

I exhale; the sound harmonizes with the swishing doors. She's alone; no guards flank her. From my corner, I wonder why, but I don't get up since she hasn't brought anyone to make me. "We have tried to be generous, Anthem," Ell says, "but the time has come for this to end."

Death. I wish.

"You are too talented to go to waste. With what our techs can do to your music, we will have more success than ever before. You simply must be made to understand this."

"You're asking me to kill them!" I say. Impassive, undisturbed by the most energetic she's seen me, Ell smiles. "To kill anyone who gets in your way!"

"Music enriches us, Anthem. It makes us all happier. Death is inevitable for all of us. Why not enjoy life on the way? Any problems the Corp might have with a given citizen are not your concern."

"You really think what you do is right?" Having everything to lose feels strangely the same as the reverse. I just want all of this to go away.

"The Corp has the Web's citizens' best interests at heart, always. I hoped it wouldn't come to this." Reaching into her pocket, Ell hands me her tablet—a more expensive, advanced one than mine, wherever it is now. Hers shows pictures and videos in full color. And suddenly I understand everything. Why she's known all along that she could break me whenever she felt like it. Why there are no guards. Why she was patient, at least in the beginning. It's because she knew before she came here in her fancy suit that the instant I saw the screen, I'd pull myself to unsteady feet.

The tablet is small, a few inches square, just enough to see what I'm supposed to. A video stream—live, if the time stamp is accurate and I've counted the days right. I feel myself unravel, inch by agonizing inch.

"You cannot trust anyone, Anthem," Ell says. "This is your only chance to take control of your fate, to protect your family and the people you love."

They're all good reasons, really the only ones I should need, but they aren't what drives me to surrender. I only know one thing that can—maybe—erase this kind of pain and if I go with Ell, they'll let me track again.

"Are you going to use my songs to murder people?"

"Tsk. Such an ugly word. You can relax; we have other plans for you."

Fine. I don't care what they are.

"I want to see my brother and sister," I say. "And you have to release my friends."

She nods. "It will all be taken care of."

Somewhere, buried in the depths of the mainframe, there's a track strong enough to erase the sight of Haven, sitting, relaxed, in a plush leather chair, and the sound of her voice coming from tiny speakers as I stare down at the tablet.

"You've done very well," says some guy in a suit who looks old enough to be her father.

He is. She smiles. "Thank you, Daddy. Boys are all the same. Too trusting."

If there isn't a track that strong, I'll make one.

# 0111010001710010101011

The headphones placed over my ears are soft, cushioned pillows that make me want to sleep, but there's so much pain. Torn skin and snapped ribs and my heart, a heavy, aching ball of lead in my chest.

Music, the resonance of carved wood that reminds me of the violin I never heard, the sunlight-gold sound of horns. A melody of caged birds who sing because it's all they know, because not to would mean death, swelling louder, stronger, until they are set free. It's been so long. The strings stitch me back together, the woodwinds blanket me in warmth. Numbness starts in my toes and climbs a ladder of muscle and bone and sinew.

Relief. Intense, blessed relief, and I smile. I missed this. Why was I ever fighting against the people who want me to feel this way? Clouds move in on my mind-sky—not the heavy ones that threaten rain, but dull, soft gray, tinged with pink. Overhead lights diffuse. My body hovers above a bed.

I can still think in fuzzy, abstract patterns. My lips won't cooperate; I need something stronger. The anesthetic is only skin-deep and Haven is still everywhere and nowhere, gone after she betrayed me.

Hands hold me down when I start to struggle against the tranquilizing effects of the drug. I have to find her. I'm fine, now. Nothing hurts anymore. I can find her and make her tell me why she did this. Make her pay.

See her again, one last time.

"There, that's much better, isn't it?"

Finding Ell, in her black suit, is easy in this blindingly white medical facility. I'm sure she can see both my answer and my reluctance to give it because it proves her point.

She smiles too much.

Thanks to the track, I'm not in any physical pain while a bunch of white-coated med-techs tend to my wounds, and my brain is the softly fogged park on a winter morning. Salve, thick and stinking, covers my cuts and scrapes. X-rays show my two fractured ribs are healing okay on their own. I float, letting the conversation between the techs wash over me. The instant I flinch from one of them, I'm given another track.

It's like water, and I've been so, so thirsty for days.

Someone dresses me in the nicest clothes I've ever owned, gentle against my battered, bandaged skin. They're even black. My feet are laced into soft leather shoes.

"Can you walk on your own?" Ell asks.

I don't know if I can, but I will.

I make it out into the parking lot, filled with rows and rows of white pods emblazoned with the Corp logo, before I stumble. A guard reaches for me and I shrug him off.

"Just lost my balance," I say. "I'm fine."

The guard in the entrance booth has pink hair in short, gelled spikes.

*They were discussing ways to get inside the groups. Like, catch them in the act.*

Onstage, where I was strongest, was where we were weakest.

Our vigilance was only for getting the next note perfect, remembering the next lyric. Pixel was too busy playing with light and volume, the crowd was too immersed in sound.

I'm led to a private trans-pod in one corner. No one handcuffs me after I'm helped carefully inside. I lean against the window, conscious enough to watch buildings I don't recognize slide past on one side, the upper end of the park on the other. I've never had a reason to come this far north before.

Beside me, Ell chatters about my new apartment. Apparently my family is already there, and a small part of me has to admire her, or whoever is giving her orders. They knew it was just a matter of time.

I'm weak, but I don't care. I just want not to think, and Ell seems happy to make my decisions for me.

The building I'm taken to is tall, smoked glass and steel, reeking of the intangible, static smell of credits. Guards surround but don't touch me, their attitudes transformed from menace to protection.

What was it Ell said? Their newest celebrity. Right. That's me. She taps out a hundred messages on her tablet, not stopping when we exit the pod and file into an elevator. "I've got someone coming to fix you up and make you look more like the star you are," she says brightly. "A few hours with her and you won't recognize yourself."

"I already don't," I say. She's not listening.

We step out on the twenty-seventh floor, a world away from my old place at the bottom of the Web. I follow Ell only because I don't know where I'm going. As soon as we stop at a thick wooden door and she's scanned her wrist, I push inside.

An impression of huge, white space hits me, but all I'm looking at are the two running figures.

"Alpha, Omega," I whisper, holding them so tightly my ribs scream. "You're okay."

"We missed you," Omega says, burying his face in my new sweater. "Where did you go? We thought you left us like Mama did, and Daddy didn't like moving here. I think it hurt him."

I can't say I'll *never* leave them. "I'm here. Are you sure you're all right? Both of you?"

"The food here is choice," says Alpha. My heart seizes. "Bee keeps making us cookies, but she never talks and we have to write things down for her on a tablet like you have."

"Really?" I force a smile, my lips crack. "Why don't you go get one for me?" I don't want to let them go, but they're unharmed. They even seem happy here, and I've wasted nine days of it.

I turn to Ell when we're alone again. "Bee?"

"Citizen B8773. Her crime was not serious. They have been well cared for. That will continue for as long as you cooperate."

This isn't exactly comforting. If her crime wasn't serious, it means they turned the woman into an Exaur for some minor infraction. "Okay." What else can I say? "My father?"

"Through there." She points to a door on the far side of the living room—a long way away. "A med-tech is with him. He'll have constant attention. When his time comes, we will ensure that it is painless."

The difference between the rich and the rest of us. Except that it's not *the rest of us* anymore, because here I am. The twins come back with treats held out in sticky hands, and their smiles are worth my hypocrisy.

". . . tomorrow at the studio," Ell is saying while I chew, and I use my old clubbing standby of nodding even though I haven't been paying attention. It's not as if the Corp is going to forget about me or let me forget about them, so it doesn't matter if I listen or not. I'll be taken wherever I need to go, told whatever I need to do, and this place is *huge*. I count four more doors down a hallway and see an arch that leads to a kitchen bigger than my old apartment. Everyone I know could fit around that dining table, and plush couches sit at angles to tall windows that overlook the park. With the twins holding on to me, I walk over to them.

At least the cherry blossoms are gone.

"Oh, excellent." Ell joins us. Her heels make no sound on the thick white carpet. "You will be making a television appearance this week. I wasn't sure we would be able to get you in at such short notice."

"I . . . what?"

"You won't be playing live, of course," she says, as if I'd expected to. My head is hurting again and I can't see any consoles. I don't want to leave the twins, anyway. Ell just keeps talking. "You'll be asked a few questions so the citizens can get to know you. How you came to be playing music, that kind of thing. We will have to think of something to call you, but that can wait for now."

Alpha's eyes go wide. "You play music, Ant?"

*Fuck.* "I will be," I tell her. "That's why we get to live here."

"Choice!"

I'm really going to have to get her to stop saying that.

"Of course, you approached the Corporation with your desire to be one of our musicians," Ell continues. "We were skeptical, naturally, as we always are. Everyone wants this"—she gestures around the blinding room—"but not everyone deserves it. You applied and were given access to instruments while we assessed your talent. You have given up your conduit job to pursue the thing you love. This also gives you more time with your brother and sister. You do not mention anyone else."

Yeah. That makes sense. "What about all the people who know . . . ?"

"You're a lesson, Anthem. Why do you think we only wanted you? Do you think anyone will argue publicly with the story? I have business to take care of, but I'll see you later. Guards will be posted outside the door; let them know if you need anything." Her eyes flick to the twins, and she lowers her voice. "There is a console in your bedroom. The last door down the hall."

I don't track as soon as she's gone. The air in my father's bedroom is already sick-stale, saturated with the aura of death. A lump of blankets on the bed rises and falls with wheezing breaths. I stretch out one shaking hand and pull it back.

"You must be Citizen N4—"

"Anthem," I interrupt the guy emerging from the room's private hygiene cube. Back home, we all shared one. Keeping my name is the smallest of victories. "How is he?" I ask the guy. Sallow-skinned, in his white uniform, he blends into the room.

"The move disturbed him, but he's stable again now. I'm J. Citizen J52229. The tech on the night shift is C1774."

"Okay, well, I . . ." Don't want to be in here. J reads it on my face.

"These things don't have to be your concern anymore. He will be fine with us," J says. There's something I'd like to think is sympathy in his tone, and in the faint smile he sends on the way to settling himself into a chair at my father's bedside and picking up a book.

Slowly, I lean in. "I know about the violin," I whisper. My father's breath hitches, just slightly, and settles back into its rattling rhythm. J watches both of us with curious eyes.

I'm out of there before he's found his page.

◈

The sky is a light shade of nothing on the other side of my bedroom window, blue masked by late-afternoon clouds. On either side of me the twins are still sleeping, cradled in feather-softness. The tightly controlled stretch I try is a mistake. Alpha shifts when I gasp in pain.

I need another hit, badly. Everything hurts and there was way too much pink in my dreams. Carefully, I untangle myself and cross the room to my new console, fully stocked with the latest and greatest tracks. I guess it doesn't matter anymore how much I spend on each one.

I can't believe she did this. To me, to us, to our friends, to Alpha and Omega.

I can't believe I fucking trusted her. I *know* she has Corp connections—she never hid that—and still I let myself fall for her kindness to me and to my family. And her killer legs.

So stupid.

This track isn't working.

A small hand grabs my shoulder. Quickly, I pull off the headphones and look down at Alpha's face, creased from the sheets. "Why are you crying?" she asks. "Are you sad?"

"No, Al, I'm fine. Come on, let's wake Omega or he'll be up all night." It's been years since either of them napped, but I guess some kind of Pavlovian response kicked in after the week's worth of stories they demanded after Ell left. Alpha runs back to the bed to jump on him, and I wipe my eyes.

Bee is a short, round woman, maybe in her thirties, who smiles broadly at the twins and nervously at me while she cooks. Omega reaches for a cookie when her back is turned, but before I can say anything, she's shaken a finger at him.

I wonder how long she's had to get used to being an Exaur.

Dinner is served on heavy dishes; the fork is thick and solid in my hand. I've never eaten red meat before and have to concentrate on not swallowing it all in a single bite.

We didn't have a doorbell at our old place; water spills into my plate and my lap, the glass shatters on the tiled kitchen floor. Bee shoos me away, pointing at the mess, then at herself.

This is just . . . weird.

The woman at the door introduces herself as Peacock as she breezes past me into the apartment, her hands full of bags and boxes. It's the most appropriate handle I've heard in a while. The upper-Web must have tricks we don't down in Two because swirling green and gold eyes are dyed into her blue hair, impressively detailed and disturbing. I feel as if I'm being watched even when she's looking out the windows.

I glance at the ceiling's corners. Maybe I am. I can't see any cameras, but that doesn't mean anything.

Peacock pulls a chair from the dining table and drags it across the living room. "Here, this has the best light," she says firmly. "Sit." The twins pile onto the couch to watch me for what feels like hours. When she's done, an artist's representation of me stares back from an ornate, gold-framed mirror on the wall. My hair, limp and greasy from my days in the cell, is restored to clean, bright spikes, a little shorter than before, with some kind of dry shampoo and gel that stings my nostrils. My eyes are encircled with black painted in a steadier hand than mine ever was. The blue lips make me feel a little like *Anthem* again.

I'm allowed to dress myself this time, putting on new clothes for the second time in hours. They're black, just like the ones I took off and almost everything I owned in my former life, but the resemblance stops at color. The pants are covered with pockets, the tight shirt is silky and fine. There was a mesh one, too, but Peacock didn't question me when I refused it.

"You should get some more chrome done. You totally have the

coloring for it," she says, covering my face with powder. Like my body hasn't taken enough damage already.

I hope Scope is okay. Maybe they'll let me see him if I keep cooperating. "No, thanks," I tell her. The symbol on the back of my hand catches the light and I shove my fist in one of my pockets.

"Excellent, you're ready," Ell says, walking in a few minutes after Peacock's left. So the doorbell is optional. Good to know. She's wearing a leather dress that on anyone else would be sexy, but on her looks as much like a uniform as the suit from earlier. I look at my feet and see a pair of boots on the floor. It takes me five minutes to do the heavy metal buckles up to my shins.

"I have to go out," I tell Alpha and Omega, crouching down so I'm level with their heavy-lidded eyes.

"With her?" Omega asks, staring at Ell. I wince because I know he's remembering Haven. I have no fucking idea how I'm going to explain her absence from our lives—again—and I'm waiting until they ask.

"Yes. I'll be back."

Alpha throws her arms around my neck. "Do you promise?"

"I promise."

"Don't worry," Ell says. "Your brother is very important now. We won't let anything happen to him."

"Go to bed, okay? I'll see you in the morning." Reluctantly, they head down the hall, both disappearing into a room with two small beds in it.

"Adorable, aren't they?" Ell muses when they're gone. I want to agree with her, but remember what she wants me to do to them— what I *will* do—and bite my tongue until I taste blood. "Let's go."

"Where?" I ask. "The studio?"

"Oh, no, not yet. It's been a long time since you were at a club.

We must get you back into the swing of things. Give you a little inspiration, no?"

What the hell. Maybe the club will have something better than the console did.

My life is now an endless cycle of elevators. Up and down the Corp, my new building, and the skyscraper Ell leads me into now with half a dozen guards following behind.

"Welcome to your new world, Anthem," Ell says, stepping out on the top floor. "And welcome to Sky-Club Six." She raises her wrist to the scanner and the high-frequency beep pierces my ears once, again when I lift my own hand. The guards follow us in, but I'm not paying attention to them now.

This place *can't* be for real. A mass of slick, polished, upper-Web types fill the revolving room. The glittering skyline outside is nothing to the one held in by the massive windows. Lights bounce from glass to metal to painted lips and back again, making spots dance in front of my eyes to the rhythm of bodies. Water bottles are lined up on a long, gleaming bar. Mirrored balls hang from the ceiling.

A guy dressed in black vinyl pulls a velvet cord to one side. Pixel's club doesn't even have a VIP section, and if it did I'd never have gone in it. For a moment, all I can do is stand and stare at the leather of the empty chairs, which would make me a hundred outfits back home, and the people in the occupied ones.

I can't even imagine the number of credits some of them have spent. A few are more chrome than flesh, and one heavily muscled guy has gone the more expensive route of ink tattoos that wind around his arms and flow up from the collar of his shirt. Most mesmerizing of all is the woman with the snake across her shoulders, its head weaving eerily to the rhythm.

Where I come from, cats are the only pets anyone has, though

Alpha tried to keep a cockroach for about a week once when she was younger. The few, more exotic creatures that survived the war have been endlessly cloned for the rich. There's no point in cloning people in an already overcrowded city, but animals don't take up as much space.

Ell jerks her head impatiently, and I force myself to follow her to a curved booth along the wall. She nudges me around the bench until I'm trapped between her and the captors-turned-bodyguards with us. A waitress—now I *know* I'm in a Sky-Club—appears, somehow managing to balance a tray of water bottles despite heels higher than the platforms of my new boots.

"The music," I say to Ell when the waitress is gone. She smiles at me in approval. It took me longer than it should have because there are so many other details to absorb.

"It's encoded," she assures me. "Just . . . not quite as much as you're accustomed to."

"Why not?" The answer comes to me before she's opened her mouth, but I let her confirm it anyway and use the time to get my reaction in check.

"People up here don't need the same encouragement to enjoy their lives." Her teeth glint under the lights. "And losing those lives too early would be tragic."

Breathe. In. Out. Remember the twins. Remember why I agreed to this. Still, the overrecycled plastic of the bottle buckles in my hand. "My mother was just . . . what? Expendable? My father?" Me, until they'd discovered I'm useful?

My bodyguards haven't completely left their captor personas at home. The atmosphere at the table shifts subtly.

"Settle down," Ell says. I almost have to give her credit. She doesn't justify or placate or even deny. *Settle down* is all I get. "It will work, just let yourself absorb it."

"People up here aren't addicted?"

Ell shakes her head. "Of course they are; we all are. This is the best feeling in the world, Anthem! Everyone tracks; the people up here simply prefer to do their harder drugs in private. No point in running the risk of embarrassing yourself, is there? And tracking in the privacy of one's home allows for greater judgment as to when to stop. I'm sure you never left a lower-Web club before it closed for the night, correct?"

Yeah, because once you're in, the music has you. I've never been strong enough to walk away while it's still playing. Something itches at the back of my mind, but Ell's right, it *is* starting to work, a breeze of high lapping at my skin, and I came here willingly because I don't want to think. I sit back, watch the people on the dance floor, and gently drift away.

I put a guitar down too carelessly and earn a sharp, brief scowl from Ell on the other side of a window.

This isn't right. The instruments are too perfect in my hands, the sound I pull from them too loud, and it's just me. With my ever-present audience of guards, of course, and Ell, who has dropped by to check on my progress like she has a dozen times a day for almost a week.

I pick up a different one and pluck out one of the old songs I played that night. . . .

I switch again.

It's not working. I feel like I'm trying to wrap my arms around a shadow after I've spent my life with the person who cast it.

Above me, a red light glows. I know Ell can hear. "I need my band," I tell her. If they'll play with me again. If they'll even speak to me now that I've sold out to the Corp.

Through the glass, she's quiet for several beats. One. Two. A silent rhythm I could string a melody along. Finally, she nods. "I will see what I can arrange," she says, looking at her watch and turning to my guards. "I have a meeting about our new project. Make sure he doesn't do anything foolish."

I go back to practicing. There are enough guitars here that I can keep one in every tuning I'll ever need. A deep turquoise electric is already my favorite, but at the end of each afternoon, I've ended up in a corner with a deep, mellow acoustic that sounds like honey from the bees kept at the North Edge farms. My first real day in here, Ell sent someone to teach me things I didn't know, about different kinds of pickups and distortion pedals and other fancy equipment we didn't have down in the warehouse.

Between songs, I hook myself up to the console so conveniently placed on the wall. I don't think I've really been sober since Ell took me to Sky-Club Six, but I long for the consuming, euphoric, hallucinogenic highs of Pixel's club.

I want to forget. I want to be numb.

At least I don't have to be scared anymore. They haven't gone to all this effort just to kill me now.

⊕

Ell probably won't let me go down to one of the lower Quadrants just to get a fix. She does keep her word about the band, though, so after the guards bring me lunch I spend a pod trip to Two with my stomach in knots.

I talked her out of bringing them to headquarters. Scope and Phoenix are both more likely to agree to something if they think they're making the choice for themselves.

Instead, I'm the one with the escort. As long as I behave, they will, too.

"Let me go in alone," I say when we've stopped outside the building where Scope lives with his mother and Pixel. Uncertainty twists three faces. "What, you think I'm going to run away? You have my family."

"One moment," says the one I think is in charge. The others watch him with a measure of respect, anyway. He pulls out a tablet and types a message. The reply comes a moment later in a synchronous *beep* and *buzz*. He nods.

Up four flights of stairs, along a vomit-colored hallway. The carpet is stained and scuffed. The original gray only peeks through at

185

haphazard intervals.

Bubbles of homesickness explode in my head. I lift my hand to knock and stand there, frozen, until courage thaws me out.

"Anthem." Pixel looks somehow surprised and not, all in the second after he opens the door. And more tired than I've ever seen him, his skin pale and his once vibrant hair dull around his face. The brightest thing about him is the hint of anger in his dark eyes.

"I didn't have a choice." It's the only thing I can say that matters right now.

The spark glows, then fizzles, leaving the irises a dull, sad brown. "I know. Saw you on TV. Nice band name." He can't blame me too much if he's teasing me.

"Fuck, don't remind me. And yeah, that was . . ." Ridiculous. Five minutes with a spokeswoman, regurgitating lies. Ell says they already want me back again. "Can I see him?"

"Come on in." I follow him into an empty living room, body wracked with the fever-chills of nostalgia. "Scope!" he calls.

The door to Scope's room stays closed. Maybe he knows it's me.

"How is he?"

"He's been tracking pretty heavy since we got out. Not that I blame him, guess I have, too. Maybe he didn't hear me." He crosses the room and opens the door, not bothering to knock, closing it again before I can glimpse anything inside.

Out the window, I look down at the roof of my pod. A few of the guards are on the sidewalk, leaning against the vehicle and staring up. One of them catches my eye and glances pointedly at his watch.

Whatever. They can wait.

"Hey," says Scope in barely a whisper. I turn so quickly something pops in my neck, and I rub it with my fingers, feeling the edge of my jack. Useless now. I'll never have to go down to the Energy Farm again. I wonder what happened to Tango.

"Hi." We stare at each other. I'm not sure which of us moves first, but suddenly we're in the middle of the room, hugging, our shoulders shaking in unison.

"Are you okay? Did they hurt you?"

"Not badly. You?" He pulls away, examining my face. His eyes widen. "The twins?"

"Okay. We're okay."

"What about Haven? Anthem? What, did they do something to her?"

"You don't know."

"We don't know much of anything," Pixel says from the bedroom doorway. "They had us. I spent days in a fucking cell trying to figure out who'd done it. Then, they just let us out. Took away the club, and the chrome studio, and I see guards all over the damn place, but they just let us go."

"They only wanted me," I say. "Leader of the rebellion, now the biggest sellout to the Corp. Of course, they don't want everyone *knowing* what I did, because that'd give people ideas. But for the ones who do . . . they let you go as soon as I caved."

"That's smarter than I give the Corp credit for," Scope says.

"Yeah, well, they had some help. Who's the smartest person we know?"

"No, shit," they both breathe at once. "*Haven*?"

I stare at my boots, too shiny in this dusty apartment. We all just stand in silence for a minute. I'm sure the guards are getting impatient. "I need your help," I say. "I can't do this alone, Scope. I don't know how to play alone."

"Anthem, I don't—"

"Look, I know what they're asking, okay? I can't see a way out of it. If nothing else, we can keep ourselves safe. And our families. The revolution"—I spit the word—"is over, but at least if we do this they won't target us with death tracks. You'll have credits again. Please."

Scope presses the heels of his hands to his eyes. "What are they going to do with our music?"

"Not *that*. I asked." Assuming Ell told me the truth.

"I guess we're used to each other," he says, nodding. "And if it's just normal drugs . . ." He looks at Pixel.

"I can get them to move you up the Web. And take care of your mother."

"We'll stay here," Pixel says firmly. "But the credits would come in handy, not gonna lie." His eyes flick to a closed door.

"You, too," I say, making a sudden decision. "We'll figure something out. They're not denying me much."

"Have you talked to the others?"

I give Scope a look. "You think I'd have asked them first?"

Something like a grin flashes across his face. "Just checking. Mage or Phoenix next?"

I've been tossing this back and forth all morning. "Phoenix. If anyone's going to say no, it's Mage. Strength in numbers and everything." I've thought *that* before.

"Good point."

The guards aren't the only ones waiting for us when we get outside. I stop dead, my eyes widening to stare at greasy streaks that hang around a nauseatingly matching face, the faded yellow of healing bruises.

"Hey, Anthem, Pixel." Yellow Guy says softly. "You guys okay?"

"Yeah," we say together. "You?"

"I'll live." He looks at Scope and swallows, Adam's apple bobbing in his throat. "I've, uh, been waiting for you to come out. Thought it would be better if we weren't, you know, inside." His hand lifts, as if magnetized to Scope's face, and he forces it down to ball in a fist at his side.

"C'mon," Pixel says, nudging me toward the pod. We climb in with two of the guards, the third waiting by the door. All of us watch them on the steps, the gestures and the moving mouths. Scope's face is falling, Yellow Guy's is full of regret.

The finality of the hug nearly makes me give up on all of this. How many lives have I ruined?

"Scope—" Pixel begins.

"I'm fine," Scope says, taking a seat beside me. "He was never part of the band, and he has his own family to worry about."

"He should blame me, not you," I say.

"Doesn't matter." He bites his lip and gazes out the window. "Let's go."

Twice more, I have to explain Haven's betrayal, my own stupidity by extension. The prospect of credits and being heard wins Phoenix over without much effort from me. I'm still not sure why she wasn't always legit—maybe she just liked the risk of what we were doing. Now, she'd rather play for the Corp than not at all. I'm right about Mage. Our combined forces aren't enough to sway him. I want to be frustrated by his refusal, but I think this tight, itchy feeling I have on the pod ride back to the Corp is envy.

The Corp's lobby is quiet in the middle of the day, only a receptionist covered in chrome sitting at the marble desk and a few milling suits glance up as we walk in. I don't think the guards can help surrounding us, protecting and preventing in equal measures, even though the others are here more willingly than I am, and I'm not going anywhere.

Up we slide, into the sky. None of the others have gone this far before. Faking confidence, I lead the way down the hall, pulling my sleeve back in anticipation of the scanner. Somewhere in the mainframe, a byte of memory records my entrance. Can't have anyone coming in here to mess with my stuff—before the Corp gets to, that is.

The memory of my first time in here is too clouded by pain and withdrawal to appreciate it. Now it's just laden with guilt that I *do* appreciate it.

"Go in there," I tell the guards who've followed us in, jerking my head to the control room. "We need the space to ourselves. And get some food sent up here."

I guess if I act the part, I can get away with it.

"Anthem, this place . . ." Scope is doing what I wanted to the first time, his fingers reaching for every instrument, trailing over wood and ivory and strings and brass.

"I know."

Phoenix is already behind a keyboard stack, hands flexing an inch above the keys. I saw that coming. Pixel examines the drums, knocking a cymbal, gripping it to stop the harsh *clang*. I shut my eyes against the instruments we've paid for in blood, a silent apology to Johnny on my lips.

We need to get started. Walking to the wall, I try to decide which guitar to play today. I haven't tested them all yet and wish I had more hands.

"Hell, yeah. *This* is mine." I look over my shoulder at Scope, who is at a computer filled with stored sound effects. I think of the breaking glass. That works, and it's the first time he's smiled since we left his apartment.

I pull a glittering purple electric down from its rack, missing my battered old one. This one is too smooth and slick to feel like I'm doing anything real.

*Metal, wood, and strings breaking. The crowd screaming. I'm calling Haven's name, looking everywhere for her.* Nauseated, I loop the strap over my head.

"What now?" Phoenix asks. Her impatience makes her hair dance like real fire beneath the lights. "I'm assuming a lot of our old stuff is off-limits."

I'm not so sure. I wouldn't put it past the Corp to encode songs about how despised they are. It's basically what they've done with me. And everything else I've written is about . . . But here, I have a choice.

"We need to practice," I say. "Pixel needs to learn. Maybe do some of Johnny's old stuff first since we know it the best." Scope opens his mouth. "We won't record them," I assure him, and he closes it again, nodding.

Pixel takes a seat behind the drum kit. "You remember the one we used to close with at the shows?" I ask.

He thinks for a moment, head beginning to nod as a rhythm runs through it. "Yeah, got it."

This is something we know. As soon as I strum my fingers across the strings, with most of my friends around me, it doesn't matter where we are. We could be in our basement or at Pixel's club or somewhere far, far from the Web where the Corp has no hold on us. It's not just sound. I feel it, see it, even taste it—the lyrics a favorite food I haven't eaten in too long. It's nowhere near perfect. Pixel might one day be as good as Mage, but our edges haven't smoothed out to fit his differently shaped piece into the puzzle yet. We stop and start, helping him as much as we can.

Guards come back with lunch and we fall on it like starving children. For the others, I guess that's not so far from the truth. I eat as much as they do, piling food I'm not hungry for on top of the break-fast Bee cooked for me. Wiping our fingers free of grease from the rich, delicious chicken, we attack the song over and over until Pixel loosens up and begins to trust his instincts.

I knew he'd have them. He recognized them in me.

"So what are we going to record?" Scope asks. Discounting Johnny's songs and almost all of my own, we don't have a lot to work with.

"I'll write new ones," I say. Pixel raises his eyebrows.

"Just like that?"

"Yeah. Phoenix, you might need to take more vocal parts. That okay?"

"Finally," she says without malice.

The guards are still in the control booth, mostly ignoring us. It's weird because it's only just occurring to me that they must hear unencoded music all the time. And not just these—we might be a bigger risk than most of the Corp's other bands, but I know for a fact that all of them get protection, too. After what Ell told me at the club, I shouldn't be surprised.

Assholes. Control, everywhere. The valued with money, the unimportant with drugs. The difference bothers me more than it should for reasons I still can't figure out.

Tired, we fool around a little longer in the studio, taking turns at the console on the wall. Ell shows up while Phoenix is experiment-ing with a harp, her eyes sharp above her too-smiling mouth and impeccable suit. I handle the introductions, she pretends to be inter-ested. I guess that's part of our deal, too. Pixel and Scope are still adamant about returning home, but Phoenix accepts Ell's offer of a new apartment. The two of them leave, followed soon after by the others and the guards who emerge to escort them down to Two.

I find what I need in a cabinet along the wall. The acoustic I choose—my favorite one—fits neatly into the case, and just to be safe I pick up a few extra strings and a handful of little triangular plectrums from a drawer. The one guard that I think is in charge watches me through the glass, but I figure if he was going to stop me, he'd have done it already. It's not like I can do anything illegal with it once I take it with me.

"Ant! You're home!" The twins accost me as soon as I walk through the door. I shouldn't be so gratified that they're happier to see me come back than they used to be.

"Hey," I say, putting down the guitar to hug them. "How was school?"

"I miss Fable," Omega says, scowling. "I want to go to school with him again."

I swallow. "You'll make new friends, okay? Give it a chance."

"What's that?" Alpha asks, pointing at the case.

"It's . . . uh . . . it's a guitar," I tell them both. "For making music."

"Really? Can we see it? Can we hear it?" they say in unison. "Please, Ant?"

"Not today." Their faces fall. "One day." Yeah, they'll hear my music one day, but if Ell finds out I've let them listen to unencoded stuff, I'm pretty sure our deal will be off.

What the hell am I doing?

Quiet snores fill my father's room. J the med-tech looks up from checking his pulse and gives me a sad kind of smile. No, no change. Not that I expected there to be, or not for the better. He's resting, which is enough.

This place is still so weird. I can't blame the strange, unsettled feeling I get here on the fact that it's only been a little while. For one thing, it seems much longer. For another, I *know* I'm never going to get used to Bee in the kitchen, handing out treats to Alpha and Omega and watching them when I'm not here. I'll never get used to the brightness or the space or the corner-to-corner slick perfection of it all. I won't get used to med-techs coming and going, though it's possible—definite, actually—that I won't have to inure myself to that.

The guitar safely hidden under my bed, I shower in my private hygiene cube and change into yet another outfit of the soft, finely woven clothes that fill my closet. Black, exaggerating my paleness in the mirror. My bruises are fading, albeit slowly, to nauseating yellow, putrid green.

Dinner with the twins makes me feel normal for the first time since Scope, Pixel, Phoenix, and I stopped playing in the studio. I get the same feeling I could be anywhere. We could be at our old kitchen table when I tell Alpha not to talk with her mouth full and persuade Omega to try food he distrusts because he's never seen it before.

Bee's a better cook than I am, but that's the only difference in a room awash with steam and grease.

That, and there's someone missing at the table.

Again and again, I pluck Haven's name from the strings, too softly to wake the twins through the thick walls of the rich or for C, the night-duty med-tech, to hear me. Bee I don't have to worry about.

Haven was happy with me. I know she was. I know the way the corners of her eyes wrinkle up when she's really smiling, not faking it for someone's benefit. I know the difference between her shoulders relaxed or rigid beneath my hands. I know the curve of her lips and what will bring light or tears to those green eyes.

The guitar goes back under my bed, and I walk to the console. Padded headphones go over my ears, menus scroll past at my touch.

I think she was happy.

I find a track, strong if the price is any indication, which it usually is. Another. Another. I set up a whole playlist of them and sit on the floor.

Maybe I just wanted her to be.

Drums *here*, my guitar just *there*. Phoenix's keyboards chime in *now*, and Scope offers some bizarre sound I can't identify but that fits seamlessly into the melody. Besides the computer, he's reassembled his whole collection of oddities and then some. Next to my foot sits a plastic bucket, a small rubber ball still rolling around in it from when Scope used them a minute ago.

Notes climb and return home—pounding, almost cold—inspired and embellished by the electronics we now have access to. Blinding lights sear my eyes. I close them, trying to go back to the basement, the club, and that feeling.

We're getting better. For a week we've done pretty much nothing but practice and sleep, calluses deepening on our hands and our voices roughening to hoarseness.

But better, yes. I'm almost ready to hand over a batch of songs, songs that will live on unburned pages I hand out to the band. Every night after I've tucked Alpha and Omega into bed, I've retreated to my room, fingers alternating between the strings and gripping a pencil to scrawl half-formed lyrics.

I can usually make good progress before Ell arrives to take us to one of the Sky-Clubs. Six is my favorite so far, where the spinning dance floor makes me feel like I'm flying. The rest of the band is always in the trans-pod when my guards and I get downstairs, legs jerking impatiently for the music. Peacock worked her magic on them, too. We all look like we fit in now, perfect upper-Web citizens. The others agree the eyes in Peacock's hair are creepy. We dance or sit in the VIP section for hours, absorbing the mild hit, go home, sleep, wake up, and head back to the studio.

Like Johnny depended on all of us to fill in empty space, there's only so far I can get on my own. Now I need Scope, Phoenix, and Pixel to make the songs better than they are in my head. We're only safe as long as we keep making music they want to use.

The door opens and closes again. I smell flowers with a stinging, toxic edge to the petals. Ell's perfume. She still drops by a few times a day to check we have everything we need, suggest—but not order—more TV appearances, and speak to the guards. I'm not worried about what they tell her; we're behaving ourselves—practicing, tracking, and stopping those only to eat. Food is delivered at times which seem completely random until I check a clock.

I'm the one out of sync.

My hands keep moving, and the others catch up after the briefest of pauses. Ell can see for herself that we've been playing. No reason for her to report otherwise to whomever she answers to. No reason to hurt my family.

No reason to order a death track for me.

"Excellent," she says at the end of the song, her teeth bright under the studio spotlights. "I'm glad you've all been working hard, but practice is over for today. You're coming with me."

This is new. My hand tightens around the fretboard. "Where?"

"Just to a little gathering of important people who should meet our newest wunderkinds." She turns and pulls open the door again, not telling us to follow. But then, she doesn't need to.

Every day, my gut twinges when the elevator drops past the floor on which I was kept prisoner for nine days. A glance at the others tells me their thoughts are in the same bright, square, claustrophobic space.

Darkness would've been okay. Light is the terrifying thing to people who've lived in fear of exposure.

We step out of the pod in front of a water bar and walk into a sea of upper-Web people, shiny and black and neon with latex and rubber. Soft, ambient music that sounds like blue skies comes from speakers in the corners.

Everyone in here is completely blissed out, as Haven would say.

Ell puts us in front of a hundred interested faces. I won't remember any of their codes, and I don't care, so I don't try. A few of them are other musicians, people I recognize from TV. Ell's wrong; I have nothing in common with them. As soon as I can, I step away from her, grab a water bottle from a tray held by a passing waiter, and stand as close as I can to the source of the sound.

"You're N4003, aren't you?" I open my eyes and see a beautiful woman in front of me. Chrome forms devil horns at her temples, holding back a halo of curly, scarlet hair. Interesting, but I'm already bored and don't really know why we're here. Leave us in the studio. That's what they want from us, after all.

"Yeah."

She holds out a soft-looking hand edged with sharp nails in wicked red. I take it because I can't figure out a way not to. "Citizen F9023."

I remember hands like this. I drop it as if the crimson was actually hot enough to scald.

"So, you're a musician. Tell me about it."

The edge of the speaker digs into my back. "What do you want to know?"

"It must be fascinating," she says. I can see every crease of her slick lips and the black discs of her dilated pupils. "To be there at the beginning, working with the raw material, knowing how powerful your music will become."

"I try not to think about it."

"Such a shame. Power is very sexy."

I'm not an idiot, but I can't do this. I inch farther away, trying to climb into the peaceful melody in my ears, let it wash me down a river to somewhere else. I just feel like I'm drowning. "Excuse me," I say, looking for a way past her lethally spiked boots. She holds her ground. "Excuse me," I say again.

"Don't be like that." Breath washes over my neck. "Citizen L5329 told me you could use some company."

*Really.* Now I am burning. A gulp of water does nothing to wash away the acid on my tongue. I push past the woman and over to Ell. "I'm leaving."

Ell turns away from some guy in a suit. "We just got here. I think we'll stay for a little while longer, don't you?" Her eyes narrow. I stare into them for as long as I can and look around the room for Scope, Pixel, or even Phoenix. Someone to be on my side. They've blended into the party. Everyone here is dressed in black, accentuated with vibrant colors.

"Yeah," I say. "No. I'm getting out of here."

The smile still fixed on her face, Ell grabs my arm, nails digging into flesh through my shirt. "Stay, *Anthem*."

I snap. From the beginning, she's used every weapon Haven gave her, pretended to be friendly, pretended to have my best interests at heart. Using my name, the thing I chose for myself, the *only* thing I have that's really my own anymore, is too much, and she knows it.

It's why she's still smiling.

"You're making a scene," she hisses, eyes darting between me and the people who have stopped talking to stare at us. "Do I need to remind you why that is a bad idea?"

Part of my shirt stays in her hand when I rip my arm away. Fuck it. I have a closetful, now, thanks to her. Thanks to Haven. Thanks to the Corp wanting to make an example of me. The bodies that don't get out of my way to the door in time are pushed aside. I don't give a shit.

"Bad reaction," Ell says, too loudly, as a tray of bottles crashes to the floor. "I'll help him."

For the briefest of seconds, I remember freedom. Fresh air fills my lungs, tinged with the promise of rain. My reasons for agreeing to this are as distant as the land on the other side of the river. I can't forget Haven. Nothing makes it hurt less. The twins are in trouble no matter what I do.

"Restrain him," Ell calls over my head to the guards by our pod, right where we left it. She snaps her fingers. "Gag him, too. I don't feel like listening. You three, go in and watch the rest of them."

They follow her orders quickly and efficiently and take me down on the sidewalk. My pants rip at one knee and I taste cement. It's almost impressive, except I'm the one bound, hands behind my back, and thrown into the pod, a thick strip of rubber over my tongue. None of them pay any attention to my struggles on the way to head-quarters. The suits and the receptionist in the lobby keep their heads purposefully bent over tablets and keyboards.

The guards drop me in a chair in an office on the ground floor. The mainframe hums in my teeth. Hands hold my shoulders, another pair yanks headphones off the wall and clamps them over my ears.

*Don't Please, don't.* I scream and fight against my restraints. I've heard about what it sounds like. For as long as the person can hear, anyway. A split second feels like forever while I wait to hear an ear-splitting whine. They say it takes days for the pain to fade. Weeks for the sound to stop ricocheting around inside your head. My own sudden detox is still fresh in my mind. I can't go through that again.

I hold my breath, hoping it's the other kind.

A guitar, just like any of mine. My heart sinks and a slow, lilting drumbeat rises above it. The singer joins in, her voice climbing the crescendo built by the instruments; my anger dilutes with every note.

"Now, do we have a problem?" Ell asks, one of the guards clumsily hanging the headset back up.

I'm still gagged, and a little calmer, but I refuse to shake my head. Sighing, Ell motions for me to be freed.

"What the hell do you want from me?" I ask, able to speak again. "What the fuck was that? That woman?"

"I merely thought you might desire some company. If you'd prefer a man, that can certainly be arranged. Nothing is beyond your reach if you cooperate."

Haven really did tell them everything about me. Is she still talking, or has she served her purpose and returned to the luxurious life she was born to? "No!" Maybe. No. It's too soon. "Why are you treating me like this? I break the law, *your* laws, try to stop you, and I get a studio and an apartment and more credits than I could ever spend. What *is* this?"

Ell gazes at me for a long time. "You are inconveniently curious," she says. "But perhaps it is time for you to know certain things. Come with me."

Everyone who visits headquarters knows where the sound labs are, even if, like me, they've never been in one. When we step out of the elevator, I see that every lab is protected. Every twenty feet a guard stands in front of the seam between frosted, sliding doors, a scanner blinking a few feet from their left shoulder. I count at least a dozen on the outer wall before it curves out of sight completely, all sucking power from the mainframe behind the inner one.

"Citizen." The guard's salute isn't for me. Ell nods and steps to the side to swipe her wrist. The doors part instantly. She motions for me to follow her inside, our escort lingering out in the hall.

I'd expected it to be bigger. More impressive or terrifying somehow. But it's just a room, white like most of the ones in the Corp, a lone guy sitting at a bank of computers and equipment I can't name. Headphones litter the desk, and knobs and switches are everywhere. The place has an enclosed, soundproof quality that yanks at my eardrums.

The tech greets Ell. Every part of his body twitches, no two in time, as he immediately launches into the progress he's making on the track currently up on his monitors. A hallucinogen, nothing new. She lets him talk until his eyebrows and fingers have slowed to a less manic pace, then holds up a hand. Pulled out of his little world, he notices me and looks curiously at Ell.

"This is Citizen N4003," she tells him. "His songs are the ones you will be working on for our little experiment. He'd like to know more about it."

Excitement adds a sudden bloom of color to his pasty face. "One of President Z's most *genius* ideas," he says. "We've been working on the beginnings of the technology for a while, but it's all starting to come together now. Tell me, do you know how music works? Oh, it's so amazing . . ."

This guy needs a downer track. "Works? You mean, how the tracks work?"

"No, no." He shakes his head. "I mean music itself. What we've always known. You see, the human brain's response to sound is an incredible thing. Listen to a song you like, and it will make you happy. Listen to one you hate, and it will make you angry and irritable. It can even make you feel lonely. Even if you *want* to love the song in question, your brain will decide for you."

"Okay," I say slowly, looking at Ell. I'm sure he's right, but it feels wrong. I know the way I feel when I play. That shouldn't be reduced to this. To nothing but science. The same way we're reduced to numbers and codes, chips and usefulness.

"We are well into the process of customization," the tech continues. "Tracks tailored for each Citizen's specific brain chemistry. It's all on file, you know. Because of the memory chips. And we've been studying overdose cases, learning about what makes a track more invasive to a given brain. And with that, with that we can do anything. We will truly get inside every citizen's head. Body, too, if we want."

"Precisely," Ell agrees. "Pull up what we have for N4003," she orders the tech. I start to back away in the small room, but there's nowhere to go. Monitors flash, taken over by peaks and troughs of sound waves. Ell glances toward the doors as she hands me a set of headphones and I put them on.

A small choice. For some reason, it means something.

I see her lips move, the tech nod in response. A song I've heard before begins to play. A favorite from Pixel's old club. The throbbing techno beat kicks in and my stomach, full from lunch just before Ell turned up to take us away, is suddenly empty and growling. Saliva pools on my tongue as I think of greasy, spiced chicken, fine bread, chocolate cake. It's not what I ate two hours ago, but it's what I want right now. For five minutes I feel as if I haven't eaten in days.

I pull the headphones off when the track is over and stare at Ell. "You're going to tell people what to think. Brainwash us." I'm not hungry anymore. My stomach threatens to reject the food already in there.

She smiles widely. "Your intelligence is not as inconvenient. Well done, Anthem. It won't be necessary any longer to merely use the tracks to keep citizens subdued. Drugs will once again be merely for fun, just as they used to be. With this, we will be able to control what every inhabitant of the Web thinks, feels, and desires. No more rebellions like your little attempt. Advantageous marriages created without the irritating need for people to fall in love of their own volition. People placed in the jobs we wish them to have. Your friend Phoenix, for example, really should have been a guard. And, as you know, if we simply need to dispose of anyone for some reason, the guards will no longer be required to find them."

"You can't . . . You can't do this."

"Oh, I believe you'll find we can. As he said, we are perfecting the capacity to target one person, and one person only, with any track we wish. There have been a few hiccups, but those are behind us. Tests in recent months have been executed extremely well."

*Johnny.* "But it only lasted for the length of the track."

Ell shrugs. "It was a light dose. I don't want you distracted. You are due to record soon."

She was right, that last day in the cell. Death is inevitable, and knowing about those tracks was bad enough. This is worse. "Why does this even matter? You can just order people to do what you want. Stop them from doing anything you *don't* want. Our deaths aren't enough for you? You have to take our lives as well?" The small room echoes dully.

"Ah, but they *remember* being controlled by force, and resentment is such an unpleasant thing, don't you agree? Really, do you think we aren't aware of the feelings some citizens have about us? Surely you have wondered why we only wanted you. Our focus was not the other bands, or your audience. We will have them all soon enough. There's no reason to alienate them in the meantime. Already they are grateful for the Corp's generosity in not punishing them. Soon, they will have no reason, no *ability*, to ever think the things that led them to follow you in the first place."

I look around for a chair, but the only one is behind the frantically grinning tech. My teeth grind together, and I try to keep the strength in my legs. "You still haven't told me why you need me."

Ell pats me on the shoulder. "People enjoy your music, Anthem. The rawness of it is appealing to them. News of what you were doing spread far more quickly than we anticipated, thanks to your talent. We had to catch you sooner than we'd planned, though naturally it worked out for the best. People *wanted* to hear you, even without the benefit of encoding. Equivalent experiments with other Corp musicians have not shown such results. By applying our new discoveries to your songs, we can ensure a greater success rate than we might otherwise have hoped for. Brains will not reject the music you have to offer. Citizens will come willingly into the new age of the Web. Now, shall we?" She motions to the door and guides me out, into the elevator, down to a waiting driver. I let her usher me into a pod and take my seat, staring out the window, not seeing anything. The door slamming sounds far away.

Dazed, I'm surprised to find myself outside my apartment when we pull to a stop. As soon as I see Alpha and Omega, I'm sure Ell just wanted to remind me of what I have to lose by even trying to say no. I hold their small bodies in my arms and battle my thoughts.

What will they become? What will the Corp force them to do when they're older, after they've been exposed?

All evening, I argue with myself over telling the others. I think I'd want to know, if I were them. I *did* want to know, though I'm reconsidering that now and wish I knew where to find a memory-erasing track.

Back and forth. Eventually I'm so dissociated from the argument I forget, for a moment, that I'm involved in this at all.

I'm not sure I trust Ell's word that they didn't have anything to do with it beyond the obvious. The end result would have been the same either way, I guess.

Whether it was painless, like she promised it would be, I have no idea. Hopefully more so than my mother's, at least.

J seems genuinely sorry when he swears he left my father for only a few minutes. I tell him it's okay.

Or it is until I have to talk to the twins. They're at school. Maybe my father knew that when he got to the console and found what he needed—his last act of kindness, though it's been so long I can't remember what the one before this was. I'm half-dressed for a day in the studio. We're supposed to record our first song today.

Too many people walk in and out of this too-large apartment while I sit on a too-comfortable couch, wondering what the fuck I'm doing. Voices ask me questions and I answer without thinking. Knowing. Caring.

The only thing I'm sure I insist on is that my father's chip, once removed, is taken down to the Citizen Remembrance Center in Two. He should be with my mother, even though he died in Quadrant One.

A stretcher carves two perfect lines in the thick carpet. I stare at them until they wriggle like that snake at the club.

Someone'll have to fix that.

He's been gone for a long time. We were just fooled into thinking he wasn't by the continued presence of his body. I'm not sure why I feel so much more alone now. Things really aren't any different.

Yells break through the fog. Can't everyone just be quiet? My bare feet are numb and I walk unsteadily toward the kitchen; the voices get louder.

No. Just one voice.

Bee, her whole body radiating fear, cowers under the onslaught of the guard. I don't know him; he's not one of mine. She doesn't need to be able to hear his shouts about his dislike of the sandwich she made.

This is all so pointless and fucking stupid.

"Get out," I growl. He tries to wrench his arm from my unexpected grip, but I hold on.

"Let go, scum. You think because you're a musician now, you get to order me around?"

"Get. Out." I shove him away. Bee glances between the two of us, her eyes wide and confused.

"You haven't heard the last of this," he says, nostrils flaring. "And she never heard it at all." He laughs at himself as he strides through the archway.

I'm not expecting it, so the sudden presence of Bee's arms around me is a surprise that makes me stagger back a little. Hurt crumples her mouth, and I rush to right myself and hug her back. I try to put into it everything I can't say out loud and which feels weird to type into a tablet for her. Thanks for looking after the twins, for the cups of peppermint tea to soothe my throat when I get home every day, for this moment. No one's hugged me like this since my mother died. Since months before that, really. Then the lesions took over and she stopped recognizing me.

When I pull back, my eyes are wet. Bee's sad smile is blurred, fragmented, smashed crystal under the kitchen lights. She points at the fridge, and I shake my head. No, I'm not hungry.

I know where to go if I want to be, though . . .

Shit. I can't think about that right now.

A blue-uniformed woman is pulling the sheets off my father's bed when I walk past the open door. Soon to be another empty room in this ridiculous place. Alpha and Omega are still insisting on sharing the one with the two small beds in it.

Telling them isn't going to be any easier this time than it was five years ago. A hand squeezes my heart, rips it out of my chest, and pushes me to sag against the wall. I wish Haven were here. She was so good when they first learned about the music.

No one stops my stagger to my room. Death is an everyday thing, my part in the necessary routine already done.

New track symbols flash on the console screen after I punch the Corp logo away with faint satisfaction. I'm tempted to try them, but they're all cheap, weaker than what I want—need—right now. Piles of credits sit in my account, more than I earned in my years as a conduit. Might as well use them for something.

It's not like at Pixel's club. I'm not transported into memory, but a stronger, healthier version of my father invades my thoughts. Tall, straight-backed, and dark-haired before he started to stoop and fade. I remember him in his uniform, the nights he wasn't around because he was on patrol.

We all do what we need to do. I hold out a lingering hope that he was never cruel, though I won't ever know for sure. If he was, the Corp will edit his chip accordingly.

Dazed and blank, I check my watch when the track is over. I still have hours before the twins get home. Ell told me to stay here, but disobeying her is tempting. I could walk in the park with the guards a short distance behind me. I'm just looking around for my boots when the door opens and I glance up, expecting Bee or one of the countless people here I don't know.

"Anthem," Scope says, crossing the room to me. I hold on to him for longer than I did with Bee in the kitchen. Two more pairs of arms join in, awkward because we're all different heights. It works somehow. "We came as soon as Ell told us."

I think she gets a weird pleasure from doing things I don't expect, and I'm too grateful to question this one.

"You okay, man?" Pixel asks, backing away to sit on my bed. Phoenix joins him, but Scope stays with me, my fingers curled into the hem of his shirt.

I nod. "Yeah. We all knew it was coming."

"That doesn't actually make it much better," Phoenix says. "It's just something people say."

"Really. I'm fine."

They stay with me for hours; the four of us sit around my room and eat the food Bee brings us. Even the peppermint tea tastes like sawdust. Ell's apparently given us all a few days off; I'm not expected back in the studio until Friday. She probably thinks that's generous. I'm trying to figure out how I'll get through until then. In the corner of my eye, the Corp logo bounces around the console screen.

I guess that's how.

Tight anxiety corkscrews into my muscles. The twins will be back soon. I don't think they're going to be as receptive to the explanation of permanent sleep as they once were. And my father wasn't completely gone then, so he helped when they became afraid of bedtime.

"We should go," Pixel says, his eyes on my twitching foot. My hand won't unclench from around Scope's.

"Stay?" I ask in a whisper the others choose to ignore. He smiles softly and squeezes my fingers. He's been through hell, too, but glimpses of his old self have been shining through and right now I need them.

The people are gone. There's just Bee in the kitchen when I go out into the living room to wait, leaving Scope in my bedroom to track for a while.

"Ant!" Alpha runs through the door, her bag swinging from her arm. Omega follows, more controlled. Panicked, frozen, I watch their faces as I struggle with words I immediately know I don't need. They both stop, looking around me to the open door behind my back.

Every day since we moved here, I've taken them in to see him, paused with my hand on the knob before opening it and quietly reminded them to be gentle with him.

I turn to look at the stripped bed and the empty chair beside it that will never hold J or C again. They're smart kids. They know. I almost leave it there and let their minds absorb the truth for them- selves, waiting for whatever reaction there's going to be.

"This morning . . ." I stop and start again. "After you left for school . . ."

"He's dead, isn't he?" Omega says, with the calm of the accepting.

"Yeah," I say. "Yes, he is. Come here."

I take them both to the couch. Alpha sniffles quietly into my shoulder, Omega is too still.

"Are you going to die, Ant?" Alpha asks, pulling her face from my damp shirt to look me in the eyes because she's too smart and she doesn't want me to lie.

"One day," I say, forcing the words out. "I don't know when. Nobody does. I won't live as long as other people do."

"Why not?"

"The job I used to have . . . it made me very tired." It's enough of an explanation to make sense to Alpha.

"Is that why you don't do it anymore? Is that why you make music now and we live here?"

I clear my throat. "Yeah, kind of. There will always be people who care about you, though, okay? To help look after you if you need it."

Omega stiffens. "Like who?" There's a trace of something in his voice. Anger? Pain? Both are more than I can really feel right now.

"Like Scope," I tell him, tightening my arm around his shoulders. "And his brother. Fable and his mother. Even Bee." I know she loves them already, and wonder if she has kids of her own or if she became an Exaur young enough that it made her decide not to.

"Haven doesn't love us anymore," Alpha says, almost accusing. I can feel my stomach in my toes. "She left us, too."

*Not just you.* "I'm sure Haven still loves both of you," I say, averting my eyes from Alpha's. I have no faith she ever did. Hurting me I can understand, if she had a goal to achieve, but I'll never forgive her for *this*. "Haven is mad at me, not you."

"Why?" Omega asks.

I shake my head and kiss both of them on theirs. "I don't know. I wish I did."

Bee comes in, her instincts another sense that was heightened after the loss of one. Or maybe she's always been like this. She hugs the twins, too, and leads them into the kitchen. For a few minutes I sit, trying to compose myself. The black curtain on the TV screen doesn't help. President Z is talking about the opening of a new Sky-Club, but in my head, all I can hear is what she wants me to do. The way the twitchy, manic tech is going to alter the song I'm supposed to record on Friday, and every one after that. They've got me until the day I die.

It's been a long time since Scope sat at a dinner table with us. Haven came into the picture, then Yellow Guy, and we stopped spending so much time together. I'm reminded why we've been friends since we were younger than Alpha and Omega are now. Bee piles his plate with food, but the sight of the twins and me not eating takes his appetite, too.

I need a hit—as many as I can stand before I pass out. The club is out of the question tonight, and the console will be better, anyway. Stronger. More effective, I hope. Everything about my life is reversed up here.

There's pretty much nothing I wouldn't give to be back in my old place, my father alive—sort of—on the couch, me playing in the warehouse basement, the twins happy and with their friends, or asleep while I'm out clubbing with Haven and Scope. Even if some of that was a lie, it's preferable to this truth. Pretty much nothing I wouldn't do, but the two things I won't surrender are curled in new pajamas on their beds, waiting for me to tell them a story. Routine. Life as normal, except I don't know what to say. Eventually, when they're almost asleep on their own, I fall back on the old standby of life outside the Web, a history so old it's reformed to imagination, not anything real anymore.

"Thanks for staying," I say to Scope, quietly in my now hushed apartment. Bee is in her own room, the twins are in theirs, and the med-techs are gone for good.

"Sure." There's nothing easy about the smile he gives me. I think that makes me appreciate it more.

"Track?" I hold out a pair of headphones. He nods, climbs off my bed, and comes to me. Together we set up a list that should get us high for hours.

I still haven't told him or the others about what the Corp is going to do. Ell's conviction that what the Corp's planning is right has left me no confidence in my own decisions.

Scope slides to the floor, his back to the wall and his hand reaching for mine to pull me down. Our shoulders touch and it's the first time I've felt warm since the twins left me on the couch. The music starts, an eclectic mix of everything I like—soft, velvet-toned guitars and hard, glass-shattering keyboards. Drums like the intangible pulse of the earth, or the footsteps of a monster. I only care about strength.

We sit there for ages. Bright colors climb from dark shadows in my white room, shifting, separating, coalescing in front of my eyes. They wipe my mind blank until they're all I can see: the blue halo around a mirror that sucks a little more of me into it every time I look inside, the ghostly yellow of a lamp's remembered light. Red, streaks of it that splay across my shoulder.

His skin is warm, the muscles and tendons beneath it firm. With the hand not holding his, I pull my own headphones off, then Scope's. He gazes at me through blinking eyes and says nothing as I stand and lead him to the bed.

The sheets are cool; a rush of lavender wafts up when we sit down on the edge. It feels as if only minutes have passed since the last time we did this. Scope's fingers rise and stroke over my jawline. This time, the smile isn't forced.

Pink clashes with red in my head, and I force it away.

His mouth is softer than it should be after kissing so many. Maybe mine remembers that I was one of the first. Sparks tingle in my fingers and toes. Life, finally, to erase this day of death. I hold on to his lip with my teeth, unwilling to let him go, for this moment to fall in pieces around us. But we need to breathe, more proof of life, and he uses the distance to pull my shirt over my head, then rid himself of his own.

We're lying down, chest to chest, familiar, but so different to the last . . .

*No. Not her. Not now.* I kiss him again and try to think of nothing but *these* lips, *this* tongue, *these* arms clasped around my back.

I pull away. "I'm sorry," I whisper. "I can't do this."

Scope finds my eyes in the dimness, his own sad and sure. Carefully, he tucks a strand of hair behind my ear. "I know," he says. "Come on, let's go to sleep."

My throat burns. I scream through the fire. Help. Please. Someone, anyone, help me.

*We're in the studio. A red light blinks above my head. I close my eyes and don't think about the fact that we're recording. Pixel pounds his drums, never sounding better than he does today. Phoenix's keyboards are perfect, exactly as we've practiced for weeks. Scope, most faithful of us all to the people we used to be, makes music from objects that have never been instruments.*

*Guards in the control booth watch, less bored now that we're actually doing something. Moving forward. Celebrating their Corp with lyrics it sickened me to write and scrapes my throat to sing. But the guitar feels incredible in my hands. I try to forget everything except that.*

*We don't get it the first time. Nerves place Phoenix's hands on the wrong keys at the last minute, though she'll never admit it.*

*We keep going, over and over. Bathe our skin in sweat. Get it perfect, each note precise and howling. No one will have any reason to find fault. This is the best we can do. All I can offer.*

*The red light blinks out and I drop my guitar. I feel the curious stares of the others as I walk to the console on the wall without looking back. I know. They don't. I need whatever I can get that'll stop me from thinking about what that song is about to become. Even as I prod the screen, it is zooming along the Grid, right into the computer in that lab, right into fidgeting, impatient hands.*

Please. Help. Water. Anything. My fist connects with something I'm sure is flesh. A curse, but it might be my own.

*The first minute of the track is so perfectly mind-numbing. But then the breath freezes in my chest and icicles of pain start to scrape through my veins. The earthquake is inside me now and I slam to the floor, teeth rattling, back arching.*

*"He's OD'ing!" I hear. Someone calls for the guards. Heavy footsteps sound; strong arms carry me away.*

*The bed is hard, slippery plastic, wrong. I can't move my arms or legs anymore. Cold steel bites at my wrists and ankles. Cool, pure oxygen floods my open mouth. What happened to my old gas mask? What happened to my old life?*

*Headphones. No. No. My neck turns and twists away. They're what started this. Help me.*

*Static. A mechanical buzz, or the thud of a head held for too long underwater. By inches, my body relaxes in its restraints, the pain fading as the white noise begins to work. It blows through my brain, a gusting wind flaying my neural pathways clean.*

*I'm so tired. Please, just let me sleep.*

⊕

This bed is soft, the room strange.

"What?" I didn't mean that. Words jumble in my brain. Someone in a white coat slams water bottles down. It hurts, the noise and the white coat and the lights. I was in a fight, but I don't know if I won or lost. Her hands are deep brown. Nice. I look at those instead. "Why?"

No. Damn it.

"I'm surprised you're even alive." She turns to face me. Pretty. Skinny fingers lift my wrist, her nails digging in. She reaches for headphones and I don't trust my words. Bombs go off in my shaking head. She glares at me and places them over my ears. Strange, electronic music filters into my head. It must do what it's supposed to, because I only have to listen to one before she leaves me.

"Where am I?" I ask when she returns with a tray. Figures that even patients here would get better stuff than I ever ate down in the Energy Farm. My tongue is furred, eyeballs dry, the pain is mostly gone.

"Headquarters OD station," she says eventually. Clipped. Cold, but her voice is rich and warm. I wonder if she can sing. "Feeling better?"

Doesn't say much for her self-confidence. I nod. Ow. "I guess so. What day is it?"

"Monday. You were in bad shape when you were brought in. It will take a little while to reorient yourself."

"I need to get out of here." The twins, the band . . . I try to sit up. The room orbits around the middle of my brain.

"Not possible. You need to eat, and you should track some more. We'll keep you overnight for observation to make sure you're all right after that. Don't want this happening again, do we?"

I'm not too out of it to recognize sarcasm.

"No." I try to shake my head and regret it. "No more tracks."

She ignores this. "I know who you are, you know."

"I've been on TV. Everyone knows who I am." Maybe hiding out here in the OD station for as long as I can isn't a terrible idea. "Hey." I jerk away from the unmerciful light she's shining in my eyes.

"Not what I mean," she says, her voice lowering so it won't carry out the open doors. "You're Anthem." Finally, she looks at me, her face tight. "I saw you play. Word got around."

Oh. Yeah, it did. Not that it mattered in the end. We were betrayed by our own. By *my* own. But it explains why she hates me.

"Traitor," she hisses. "We thought you were going to make a

difference. Hmmm, your heart rate is a little high. Here."

I don't lift my hands to take the offered headphones.

This is different than other OD stations I've been in. Down in Two, we're all together in one big room, machines bleeping, techs scurrying back and forth between patients. We watch each other through the eyes of shared experience.

Here, I'm alone. The room is small, just big enough for the bed, a chair, and a counter above a line of cupboards along one wall. The chair confuses me; it's waiting for a visitor who wouldn't be allowed back home.

None come, thankfully. Not even Ell. Phoenix, Pixel, and Scope are probably busy, or Ell forbade them from coming. It's kind of difficult to face Scope right now, anyway. I definitely don't want the twins to see me like this, skin ashen and leaking cold sweat. It was so fucking stupid, OD'ing when they need me now more than ever. I knew I was tracking too much between recordings in the studio while I was doing it. I knew I shouldn't go for so many strong ones.

The console is within easy reach; the careening logo makes the backs of my eyes ache and I don't look away. Metal bars on either side of me are cool under my white-knuckled grip. I shouldn't . . .

Antidote has scoured my brain, cleared it like hot, minty steam rising into clogged sinuses. One won't hurt. I was fine after the track the tech gave me. Of course, I don't want medication this time.

I've failed. At everything. Revenge for Johnny, putting a stop to the Corp, protecting the twins, and keeping my promise to my mother—and *that* was all for nothing. I'm just a puppet now, an addict and a dealer against my will. The worst kind of hypocrite, because the twins are happy and I love all my new guitars, and I wish, more than anything, that Haven was still mine.

I wish they'd just killed me, like they did to Johnny.

Maybe I should try—not here, because station consoles ration tracks. I know that from personal experience. But at home, in my room, I'll have all the freedom I need to choose song after song until my brain shuts down. Late at night, when no one will come looking for me in time.

I don't even know if it's possible to do it on purpose, not unless you're already so far gone, like my father was, that all it takes is a little push. Maybe your body fights if it's not ready. Or your mind does.

No. The twins need me.

"Oh, good," my tech says, walking into the room and seeing the headphones in my hands.

I put the headphones back on the console. "It wasn't my choice," I say. "You don't have to believe that, but it's true."

Her eyes thaw slightly. She waits until the doors swish shut. "They got to you. After they caught you. All that stuff you said in the news interview about deciding to go legit was a lie."

"Smart. You must be a med-tech or something."

She fights a smile and turns serious. "I thought they'd kill you, or make you an Exaur. I wasn't expecting to see you carried in here after an OD. I didn't expect to see you working for them. So, when they brought you in, I thought maybe you'd traded somehow."

So that's where the surprise came from. "I did trade, just not by choice. You work for them, too."

"Being a med-tech is all I ever wanted. So I guess I didn't have a choice, either. It's not all giving med-tracks to people and curing ODs."

"What's your code?" I ask.

"You can call me Isis."

"Okay. You were there. The last night."

Isis puts the tray down on a cart, like the ones we had in the

Energy Farm, and wheels my food over to me: chicken, vegetables, potatoes. My mouth waters and my stomach churns. "From the second time, actually. I'd never heard music like that," she says. "So real."

It was. I let myself remember it, just for a second. The studio is amazing, but it doesn't compare. Every note there vibrates with the knowledge of what will be done to it later. "What happened to everyone?"

She briefly closes her deep-set eyes. "We escaped through the tunnels. I was terrified at the thought of what they'd do to me if they found me. We thought the guards would come after us, but they didn't, so we just . . . ran."

"They wanted me." I say. "I'm glad you got out." That's one less death or injury I'm responsible for.

Finally, Isis smiles. Faintly, but it's there. "Press that blue button if you need anything," she says, backing up until the doors open and holding my gaze with her steady one. "You're not alone, *Anthem*."

$\oplus$

Ell brings the band to visit in the morning. I'm really not in Two anymore. Isis slips from the room as soon as they come in, her hardened eyes lingering a moment too long on Ell.

*I'm not alone.* I want to trust Isis with a spark of hope from the same fire that word, revolution, came from. But it's pointless—sympathy for what I think doesn't matter much if I'm not doing anything about it anymore.

Phoenix and Pixel fidget around the room for a few minutes after asking me how I am. Tired, mostly. The ache in my bones is beginning to fade, but my head is still wrapped in a strap of pressure that tightens when I think too hard. Scope hangs around for a little while after the two of them disappear, Phoenix to touch up her makeup and Pixel to wait in the hall . . . or so he says. He wasn't exactly subtle about checking out Isis.

Scope tells me he's been checking on the twins when not busy with Corp stuff. It makes me want to kiss him again, and for once I'm grateful for Ell's presence. I've made enough mistakes twice. I reach out to grab his hand, and he squeezes back. We're okay.

Not once have they blamed me for Haven, even though they should. I completely freaked out on Scope for telling his boyfriend our secret, and the whole time we were being watched by the person I love. Loved.

Ell's taking them to another party today, but I don't have to be there. A guard will be sent to escort me home. I don't even try to feign disappointment. I just want to see the twins again.

"How's the track going?" I ask because I'm a masochist. I don't remember what it's like to not hurt somehow.

"It's being mixed now," she says. She glances at Scope and back at me. I give the tiniest shake of my head. "The sound techs are very impressed; everyone loves it. We will let you know when we've decided how we're going to encode it."

"Um. Great." I'm impressed. I've never been that good a liar.

"We got to hear it, Anthem," Scope says. "It's awesome. You've never sounded better."

Yeah, that's comforting. "Cool," I say, forcing a smile.

"We should let Anthem rest," Ell tells Scope. "You'll all be back in the studio tomorrow."

I track when they leave—not heavily, but enough to take the edge off. The coda symbol on the back of my hand catches the light as I tap the console screen, and I wish chrome removal wasn't so painful. It might be worth it anyway to get rid of this meaningless thing.

I kill time by thinking about Haven. Or the time kills me. Every expression she ever showed me plays itself out on my eyelids. I was so sure I knew her. Ghost-tears wet my hands as I remember holding her crying face in the middle of a crowd. Ell isn't the best liar I know. She could take lessons from Haven.

Maybe she is. Haven could be in a Corp office right now, sitting in a comfortable leather chair and laughing about how she fooled all of us.

She was always so beautiful when she laughed.

Over my protests, Isis insists on bringing me lunch. I can't look at her without thinking of what she said. I don't believe everyone in the Web wants the Corp destroyed, but I'm sure there are more than I ever used to think. They'll find someone else. Someone who can face trying again.

*You're not alone, Anthem.*

Maybe not, but I am trapped and broken.

The guard who comes for me is one of the ones I had before. He's alone, and for a crazy second, I wonder if he'd take a bribe and get me a death track. Fuck knows I have the credits for it. Weakened by my OD and everything else, I'm not any kind of a threat. Isis shoos him out while I change out of this thin gown and put on the same clothes I was wearing in the studio, fresh with the scent of soap.

We're in the elevator, my eyes on the gun over his shoulder. A *beep* carves through the thick silence. He tightens his grip on the black metal grip with one hand and takes his tablet out with the other. He curses and presses the button for a floor higher than the one we just left, daring me with his eyes to comment.

What's the point? It won't get me home to the twins any faster.

"Stay here," he orders, stopping in a hallway a little different than other ones I've seen. Flowers sit in tall urns at even intervals. Mirrors and paintings line black marble walls.

I hold up my hands. "Not going anywhere." He scrutinizes me for a moment and nods. I don't catch what's on the other side of the door he slips through, opening it just enough for his beefy body to edge through. No sound comes from inside, but that means nothing in this place. They could be yelling, for all I know.

Okay, I lied. I step a few feet away to a space where I can lean against the wall. Whether it will be enough of an offense for him to say something depends on his mood, but I'm probably fine. I'm still a musician, after all. Preferential treatment.

I wonder what he's doing in there. I want to get home. I put my hands in my pockets; a pang of unjustified disappointment stabs at me when I don't find a square of chocolate in there from Alpha. Those days are over. It's not a special gift anymore.

Down the hall, a door opens. The unexpected sound catches my ears, then my eyes a second later. Surprise turns uneasy by an instinct I don't have time to identify. I've never seen Yellow Guy in a suit before. He can change out of the baggy clothes with their neon-yellow accents, but the sharp silk tie is his favorite color, perfectly hued to match the streaks in his slicked-back hair.

"Hey," I say when he's within a few feet of me. He looks up, and his body jerks slightly. A tight smile spreads his lips.

"Anthem." I'm attuned to sound. The vibrato in his voice shakes alarm bells in my aching head. What's he doing up here? "How goes it?"

"Fine," I say slowly. He's *nervous*. He's surprised to see me, but not that I'm alive, with my ability to hear intact, because he's seen me since the raid. On his own terms. He's not angry, like Isis was, at my supposed selling out to the Corp. "You?"

His confidence falters minutely, but I'm watching for it. "I—" he looks back the way he came, contracting pupils measuring distance. He's the Corp sellout. It's all over his greasy hair and pressed suit. Just like the ones I used to ride the elevator with.

Rage begins to simmer in my muscles, rapidly reaching scalding heat. The truth is clear—the first pure, ringing notes of a song that clue to the melody. "It was you," I say flatly, through clenched teeth. "It was you the whole time."

A humid pause settles over us. I wait for him to deny it, to say something. I wait for too long, and then . . . I'm not waiting anymore. Adrenaline replaces the strength lost by my OD and I slam him against the wall.

"You *asshole*." I can't breathe. "*Why*?"

"You were breaking the law," he says thinly, grinning.

"You used Scope. You used all of us."

His eyes glint. "Price of business, Anthem. Scope was an easy target. He knows everyone. Hell, he's fucked everyone. I thought he'd know any gossip, but I got luckier than I imagined."

"Your OD. Did you fake that?" My head pounds and my heart races like it did in the studio before I was carried out.

"No. Your club tracks are stronger down in Two. Wasn't used to it. But it worked out. Totally . . . worth it."

Air leaves my lungs in burning pants. I was right about being wrong, but in the wrong way. . . . Oh, *fuck it*. I pull one hand back, my eyes on the bridge of his reddening nose. The *snap* echoes along marble.

"You wanted me to think it was Haven," I hiss at his falling body. "You made them arrest you, too. And not her. You made them hurt you so we wouldn't question it when we saw you again."

Gasping, liquid laughter. "You really made that too easy for me. I could tell you didn't trust her, not completely."

"Where is she?" Oh, fuck. *Haven*. "Is she alive?" Not betrayer. Betrayed. And this isn't spitting in a guard's face. I don't know if her family, her name, would've been enough to get her out of this.

He shrugs. A mouthful of sticky red blood spatters the floor and

I think of windshields. "She's alive. I have no idea where, though. I doubt she'd want to see you again, anyway. I made sure she knows you thought it was her."

My insides crumble to ash. "Scope loved you. He defended you."

"His mistake. But if it makes you feel any better, I had some help with that."

It takes a second to figure out what he means, but when the truth comes it flashes so brightly it almost blinds me. "You son of a bitch. The tracks. That's why he was different. You *made* him fall for you?"

"Nice try, but no, that part was all him. We just used them to keep him from questioning too much."

I taste blood.

"What was Johnny? Collateral damage? You got him out of the way because you knew I'd start the concerts if it was up to me. Get as many people as possible to like my music *before* they unveiled their new experiment. I watched him *die*." Spots dance in front of my eyes, my pulse roars in my ears. I'm done. They're not going to get away with this. My shattered pieces reform, glued together by anger.

He smiles again, teeth stained red. Blood-flowers bloom on his tie, the edges round and uneven. "You're smarter than you look. They seemed as good a way as any to test how *specific* we could be. Oh, we could have just quietly gotten rid of Johnny, made it less obvious like we did with the others, but I wanted you to figure it out. I wanted you mad."

My boot crashes into his chest, and he curls up, crying out. "You got your wish," I spit.

Hands clamp around my arms. I can't reach Yellow Guy with my feet anymore. "Do we have a problem, Citizen?"

From the floor, Yellow Guy shakes his head. "He's . . . just angry

... that I dumped his friend. Nothing to worry ... about. Just escort him ... somewhere else. Don't mention this to anyone. And send for a med-tech." He waves a yellow-nailed hand.

Doubt relaxes the guard's hold on me, but he doesn't let go completely. "Are you sure?"

"Do as I say," Yellow Guy orders. The guard pulls me away with a vicious jerk, dragging me down the hall and into the elevator before he lets me go to sag against the wall. My knuckles hurt. Everything hurts, and I was so wrong about Haven. I should have trusted her. And myself.

They used one of the mind-control tracks on her before making that video, making her believe anything, do anything, say anything for long enough to convince me. Maybe they still are, or they've wiped her memory, and that's why she's stayed away from me. Or Yellow Guy is right.

I open my mouth to demand to be taken to Ell and change my mind. She was wrong. I can trust people, just not her. I press my lips together. I need time to think, and I need to see the twins.

It might be the last time I ever do, after I'm finished with Ell. The thought yanks my lungs into my mouth.

We're always under guard. I can't remember the last time I was awake and alone for more than twenty feet. Lurking on the other side of doors, of glass, casting shadows that seep into the room. I'm pretty sure I have to be careful about what I say and do in my apartment. Phoenix's new place is probably the same. Where there aren't guards, there's Ell, with her snapping fingers and heels. I have no good excuse for visiting Scope and Pixel down in Two when I see them almost every day up here.

I spend the pod ride trying to calm myself. I should've killed that fucker with my bare hands.

No. I need to be smart. Maybe for the first time since this whole mess began . . . or longer than that.

Haven was killing herself for me. The itch that began the first night Ell took me to Sky-Club Six has finally been scratched by something that asshole said, and my mind is finally clear enough to understand what bothered me so much. She could have stayed in the upper-Web, Sky-Clubbing to mild tracks that wouldn't invade her brain so much. Instead, she used the stronger tracks she'd have gotten from her console at home, *and* came down to Two to see me almost every night.

I want to blame my willingness to believe that it was her on the nine days I spent in the cell while they broke me with silence and lights and slick promises.

I want a lot of things.

Choruses of "Ant!" chime through the apartment as soon as I open the door, still lowering my wrist from the scanner. The guard takes his place in the hall, feet spread, hands behind his back. I shut the door on him.

"Hey, you two," I croak. "I missed you." Anger steps back, just a little, to lurk in the shadows.

"That lady with too many teeth said you were sick. Are you better now?"

"Much. Have you been good for Bee?"

They don't quite meet my eyes when they say they have been. Strangely, it's comforting. Getting into trouble was so much simpler when I was a kid.

"We wanted to see you," Omega says, tugging on the hand I punched Yellow Guy with, not noticing my wince. Good. "But Teeth-Lady said we couldn't."

I try to smile. "I was asleep the whole time. It would've been pretty boring for you." I can't confront Ell. Not yet. I can't leave them. Can't give this up. And there's more than that, too. "Are there any cookies, or have you eaten them all?"

They drag me to the kitchen, and Bee turns from the counter as soon as we enter. I still don't know how she does that. A smile deepens the creases in her face, and she beckons me over to pat me on the shoulder, examining my eyes for a long moment before she nods.

"*Thank you*," I mouth. Her smile widens.

Through the evening, my mind is a puzzle with mismatched pieces I need to fit together, all in shades of violent red. Protect the twins. Find Haven. Cause Yellow Guy pain that will make a broken nose seem like nothing. Stop the Corp.

I've never been so glad to OD. Now, I can think again. My skin tingles and my head hurts, but I leave the headphones hanging lonely on their hook. Not tonight.

The twins are doing well with their homework since Bee is better at math than I am. Whatever I do, I'm saving her as well.

Bedtime stories roll automatically off my tongue, the same ones I've always told them, ones my mother told me and I don't need to think about to repeat.

I feel like I'm back in the basement again, after Johnny's death. They're going to pay. For all of it.

The console screen glares seductively at me. I ignore it and keep pacing around the room, bare feet whispering on the thick carpet. My temples throb and I press my palms to them to hold my thoughts in so I can sift through memories fuzzed by rage and fear and too many tracks.

We were set up, and we played—literally—into the Corp's hands. I wonder if Yellow Guy got a promotion for a job well done.

*"All of you can walk into the building, and no one will suspect you.*

Then *use the army you guys have already built up here."*

Haven was right the whole time, and we're deeper inside the Corp now than ever. Spoiled musicians, their hold on us enough to make them believe we won't fight back. Maybe not the last people they'd expect, or there wouldn't be guards outside my door, but close.

Dusky shades of early sunrise paint the sky over the park, coating the cherry trees in false pink. I have a plan now.

It's time to live up to my name.

✧

A handful of guards look up, the window between the studio and the control room rattling in its frame. "I want to take my brother and sister to visit our parents in Quadrant Two's CRC this afternoon," I say, lowering my hand and turning to the others. "You guys want to go?" We all have family in there.

Scope's eyes narrow. I don't blink. *Please, get this. It's the only idea I have. Trust me.* "Yeah," he says, loud enough for his voice to breach the barrier.

"Sure."

"Sounds good," Pixel adds.

The chief guard nods. "I'll arrange it," he says, pulling out his tablet.

"Thanks." I pick up my guitar again. "You guys ready?"

They're all watching me. I strum the opening notes of the song we're rehearsing and avoid Scope's eyes. I'm dreading the moment when I have to tell him the truth, but there's no way out of it. The strings dig into my fingers, and I grit my teeth.

Normal. Just act normal.

Ell's visit this morning nearly undid me. The room got smaller, my breathing got harder, and my fingernails left deep dents in my palms. She'll be the first to regret everything she's done. I gripped my guitar, tempted by its solid weight and her fragile skull until she left again.

Pixel starts in with the drums. Music. This is normal. Right now, right here, I know who I am. My body moves without conscious orders from my brain, a link to melody and rhythm that runs in my blood.

Low, rumbling, sensuous and deadly, like that snake from the club is coiled in my veins.

If I get my way and we can make it work, soon everyone who wants to will be able to feel this. Phoenix's keyboards chime in; she's done something different with them, created a ghostly sound like a gale blowing through power lines. Nice. Scope loops a sample of rain against glass around the rest of us.

I sing my voice to shreds. When the others need a break, I follow them to the console and find the mildest tracks I can.

◈

Scope, Pixel, and Phoenix stay in the pod while I go up to my apartment to get the twins. Their excitement for going *home* stings. They insist on taking Bee's cookies down for the others. Phoenix's awkwardness with them almost makes me smile for real.

The front of the Citizen Remembrance Center glows welcoming green. For a moment, I hold a fragment of hope in my hand that Haven will be in the lobby, gazing at the artwork, waiting for me.

"A little respect?" I say to the two guards who've accompanied us here. "It's not your parents in there."

They stop and exchange glances. "You have one hour."

My watch catches the sun. I pull back my sleeve to expose my chip. Scope keeps hold of Alpha and Omega for me, and we file inside, up the stairs to the third floor. I scan the ceiling, looking for halos of light. One, along a stack in the middle. Okay. I lead everyone down to my mother's locker, set up the chip in a viewer for the twins, and find a long memory that will keep them busy for a little while.

I wish they could see everything, like I have.

"Come on," I say to Pixel, Scope, and Phoenix. We crowd into a corner.

"What's going on?" Scope asks. "Why did you need to get us alone?"

"We won't be overheard here, but keep your voice down. We don't have a lot of time. Scope, I . . . I learned something yesterday."

Phoenix and Pixel lean in closer. Scope eyes me warily. "What?"

*He needs to know.* "It wasn't Haven who told the Corp about us. It was . . . *him.*" Scope stares at me, comprehension sinking in the second before he punches the wall, an inch from my head, as the other two gasp. I hear his knuckles crack. Alpha's head peers around the stack, and I smile reassuringly at her. "Go back to Omega, okay?"

"Slimy little fucker," Pixel hisses when Alpha's gone. "How do you know?"

"I ran into him," I say, grabbing Scope's hand to stop him from doing it again. "All dressed up in a suit, coming out of one of the offices. He didn't even try to weasel out of it."

"I'm gonna kill him."

"He's not our biggest problem right now. There's something I haven't told you guys."

"What?" Phoenix asks, tight-lipped. I don't blame her.

I take a deep breath. "The stuff we've been recording . . . it's not for normal tracks. Not like we know. And it's not for killing tracks, either." I lower my voice further, to a whisper, and explain everything I learned in the sound lab and from Yellow Guy. The special, person-specific encoding. The mind and body control. I tell them Johnny's death was on Yellow Guy's orders, to get him out of the way. And probably on Haven, to make her act the way they wanted so they could shatter me into malleable pieces. Why they wanted me in the first place. What Yellow Guy did to Scope.

"Holy shit."

I look at Pixel. "Yeah." The rage is getting hotter again. I clench my free hand and try to hold myself together.

"I don't believe this," Phoenix says, turning away for a second and raking her fingers through her wild hair.

"He wouldn't make this up," Scope tells her, his voice cracking. I look at him gratefully—not just for knowing that, but for his certainty that I wouldn't hurt him this way unless I had to.

"No, okay, maybe not," she admits. "But what the fuck difference does it make? They own us now. It doesn't matter who ratted us out. We're stuck because of him." She jerks her chin at me.

"That's not fair," Pixel says, grabbing her shoulder. "You know what they did."

She sags. "I know. But there's still nothing we can do about it."

I've been so blind. Until this moment, I hadn't guessed just how much the Corp had broken the rest of them. "Yes, there is."

Footsteps echo on marble. My heart stops until I see that it's just Omega, approaching with his lip between his teeth. "It's over, Ant," he says. Panic turns my skin cold and then warm again, when I realize he just means the memory. Quickly, I take him back to the viewer

234

and find something else for him and Alpha to watch.

"What do you mean?" Scope asks, back in our dim corner. "What can we do?"

"Haven . . ." I pause. It still hurts to say her name, in a different way. "Do you remember what she said at that meeting in the club?" Just a day before my world imploded. "We're inside now. They've given us everything we need to get rid of them, almost. We just need some help."

"Mage. He's our best shot at finding Haven. And Crave. He wasn't there that night, they probably don't know about him." I just have to hope Yellow Guy and the Corp were too focused on me. "Tango, too, I think. My old tech from the Energy Farm."

"Anthem," Phoenix says slowly, "just what exactly are you thinking about?"

I smile. A grim, determined thing. "Giving them a taste of their own medicine. Literally."

The club is bathed in chemical light, false rainbows to replace the ones so rarely seen outside. Music thumps and vinyl is a thousand black mirrors painted on moving bodies. I weave through the crowd, just high enough to relax, not so spaced that I can't think.

A woman stops me, throws the garland of purple feathers in her hands around my neck to pull me in so I can hear her whisper-shout above the pulsing sound. Yeah, yeah, they've all seen me on TV. I smile and duck out of her hold.

Phoenix is surrounded by upper-Web guys, the ones I always imagined were waiting for Haven when she got sick of me. I push away the thought that maybe she went back to them. Maybe I've lost my chance. Scope is alone at a table with his eyes closed, studiously ignoring the admiring eyes of mistaken women and men who are just out of luck. It's going to be a long time before he trusts himself again.

Pixel is dancing with Isis. We'd teased him about inviting her, just for the relief of a lighthearted moment, but it's good. She's one of us.

"Hey," I say to Ell, passing her one of the water bottles I'd gone to pick up from the bar. She had offered to send for a waiter, but it was a good excuse to get away from her for a second. My hands hurt from holding in my anger, faking that everything's okay.

"I have a surprise for you," she says, setting her drink down on the table. "A reward, you might say."

She has nothing I want. "Oh yeah?"

"You've been incredibly cooperative, for the most part." I try not to laugh and wait for her to go on. "Of course, you know the plans we have for your tracks, but I thought you might like to hear one . . . as you're used to. Almost."

A tiny spark flares in my chest, but I keep my expression unchanged. "I wanted to talk to you about that, actually," I say, my jaw aching. "I have an idea for a new song. I think you could do amazing things with it."

"But?"

"I need another drummer. For a fuller sound."

She nods. "We can find you one," she says, and I shake my head.

"I want my old one. I think I can convince him, now that he's had a chance to, you know, cool off. After everything." Mage any cooler would be frozen.

Ell smiles widely. *Teeth-Lady.* If this works, I can protect the twins not just for now, but forever. "You may do what you like, Anthem. Let a guard know if you would like him brought to head-quarters, or you may go to Two and fetch him. Just take security for your safety, of course."

Of course.

"Also, I want to see the sound tech again. I have some questions."

"He is at your disposal. Are you ready for your surprise?"

I ball my fists under the table. "Sure."

Ell pulls out her tablet, typing without looking at the screen, her eyes on the DJ-comp booth across the room.

I inhale. The spark bursts into flame.

It's me. And Pixel and Scope and Phoenix. I know exactly where each instrument comes in, the instant my voice begins, but this isn't like hearing an old favorite burned into memory by repetition on a console or at a club. This is *me.* The music speaks to my brain, entering my ears in a way that is less listening than homecoming.

Searching the dance floor, I find the others again. They've

stopped moving, are statues in a sea of motion, all staring at me, openmouthed.

Ell leans over. "You see? This is one of the things that gave us the idea in the first place. It likes you, Anthem. Your music *knows* you. It is the same for all our musicians. We simply had to learn how to expand the effect."

I grit my teeth. She's not stealing this moment from me with a reminder of what they're going to do. They're not going to get the chance.

I'm taking this. She's right; it is a reward, just not for what she thinks.

It's the closest I've come to being back in Pixel's club in weeks. Or our old basement. The strength, the power. The whine of my guitar wraps six strings of my own soul around me, ties me up, and keeps me whole.

I haven't been tracking much, counting on the Corp not to watch my usage as closely as they do lower-Quadrant people. The melody pulls me in and I'm *falling, sinking, spiraling into myself. Sharp beams of neon morph to formless clouds, into the faces of my parents, who died the sick, shameful, lonely deaths that were expected of them. The twins, who need me.*

*The brightest color is hot pink. Somewhere, sometime, Haven will hear this and laugh.*

*Phoenix is dancing again, her hair fire on an oil slick of black, whirling, grinning as her keyboards return to her. Pixel and Isis are knotted into one, their bodies moving to his own cascading drumbeat. Scope smiles for the first time since I told him the truth, a real smile that draws the gathered crowd closer to him.*

*The Corp is strong, benevolent. They want the best for us. Warmth spreads through my chest, my skin tingles, and the colors*

EMMA TREVAYNE

*swim. I move my hands, watching the trails of light my fingers leave behind. So pretty. Everything tickles and I giggle at how amazing it all is.*

*No. NO. This is what they want me to think, using my words, my music to control my mind. I wrote it; I must believe it. But these strings are lies, not logic, I know that. I know it.*

*I orbit around sense and strength for the final verse. My knuckles are white as I grip what I am sure of. The coda begins, harsh and needy, begging not to go, instrumental feet planted firmly in refusal. It ends with a final, sudden crash and my brain* is my own again, the high receding to what is normal for a Sky-Club.

Focused. Direct. Music meant for me. Ell looks too fucking pleased with herself, clearly misjudging my spreading, satisfied grin.

"Clever, isn't it?" she asks.

I nod. Clever, useful, ammunition, whatever. Because I'm sure now, more than I was before, that what I'm about to try will work. And they're not going to know what hit them.

✛

"Hey, man."

Mage's ashen pallor is emphasized by the whites of his widened eyes. "Can I come in?" I ask, looking past him to the empty living room. He steps back to let me through. The last time I was here, it was like walking into an escaped demon-child of the mainframe. Wires glowed everywhere, lights flashed, monitors flickered. The lock snaps, and his strong, drummer's hands motion to a sagging couch that used to be covered in circuit boards and cable-ganglia. The room is nearly empty now. "I need your help." The music at the club last night confirmed my suspicions, but I can't do it without Mage.

He shakes his head. "Look, I know you're in a rough situation, but—"

"Not that. I mean, yes, I need you to play with us, but not like that. Not just that."

Limp dreadlocks weave through his fingers. "Gonna have to explain a little more."

"They're going to try to control our minds, Mage. Not like with the normal drugs, but brainwashing. Completely removing the ability to think for ourselves. You, me, everyone if they want to. I've seen their labs. I've had it done to me. We've got to stop them. This isn't just about killing people anymore, and I know this doesn't sound as bad as that, but—"

"I get why it's worse. Rather be dead than that. Not like this is much of a life"—he gestures around the room—"but at least it's mine."

"Yeah, exactly."

I'm impressed by how well he takes it. Then again, it's difficult to be surprised at the lengths the Corp will go to, especially down here. My time in the upper-Web made me forget a little, but now I remember. "Didn't go so well the last time we tried to fight against the Corp," he says finally.

"I know how to do it this time." I think.

I was the wrong person to lead an army. The wrong face for a revolution of the masses. I'm the right person for this, even if I wish it were someone else's responsibility. For generations people of the Web have had chances, I'm sure of it. I can't be the first. But I'm the only one with Alpha and Omega to protect. I'll die trying if I have to.

I don't want to think about how realistic that possibility actually is.

"So you need me to . . . what? Drumroll the end of the world?"

A smile cracks my lips. "I need you to get into the mainframe. To code. And I need you to find Haven for me."

"I thought she was . . . ?"

So did I. *Haven, I'm so sorry.* "It was that bastard boyfriend of Scope's."

Mage nods. "That makes more sense. She was so into you, I couldn't believe . . . but what can I do, man? They're not watching me anymore, but I lost my job as a coder. Said I was a *security risk*. I work at the depot now. Want some apples? Fresh from Hydro-Farm Four."

"You're telling me you need to be legit to get in to the network?"

A dry laugh barks from his throat. "Point. But they took all my gear."

"Can you do it if you have the equipment?"

He eyes me doubtfully—at my ability, not his. "Find her? Yeah, probably. The scanner hub is pretty open. You know her code?"

I tell him what it is. "That's step one."

"And step two?"

Inhale. Exhale. "They get in to our minds through our chips. We can get into theirs the same way if we find the right information. Haven knows how. She's . . . good with memory chips. She hacked the system and accessed my mother's. *All* of it. The Board and President Z, their info is going to be more well-protected than someone who's dead, but it's got to be possible. We find them, maybe the sound techs, everyone who ever thought this was a good idea and had a part in it. I'll write songs and we'll encode them. Control their minds for long enough to get them out of the way and take over. Then we destroy the tracks. Not just ours, every single fucking one of them."

He's quiet for a long time. I struggle from the sunken cushions to pace the room. Outside the window, a guard-turned-pod-driver is waiting for me on the street, more patiently than his kind used to.

"What happens to everyone else?"

"How do you mean?"

"Say we do what you just said. Overthrow the Corp, put them all in cells or whatever. Make it all stop. Even if we don't think about the fact that we'll be doing the wrong thing—maybe for the right reasons—the Web is full of addicts, Anthem. You gonna force withdrawal for everyone? You have any idea what that'll do?"

The shaking. The puking. Crawling around my cell, wanting to die. "You have a better plan?"

"I'm not saying the Corp's right, okay? Not by a long shot, and you've always had a point about using their weapons against them. If nothing else those are the only weapons we've got, so fine. But if you want to force your way on everyone, you're almost as wrong. Taking away the choice? Not your decision to make, man."

"Will you help me find her or not?" We can worry about all the other shit later.

"Yeah, I'll try."

"Thanks."

I feel more like two totally different people than I ever have. It's not just a matter of washing my makeup off and making breakfast for the twins anymore. Not that I do the latter much these days. Mage whistles as he climbs into the pod ahead of me, fingers running over spongy seats then reaching out to touch the console screen. The logo fades and a message appears that instructs him to swipe his ID chip. I tell him to track if he wants, and he shakes his head. That might explain the pallor. I'm not sure how concerned the Corp are these days with making sure everyone tracks enough, not with what they have planned.

"Depot Two," I tell the driver. He turns to look at me, eyebrows raised. "What? He works there. We're just dropping him off." Mage's shoulders shake with silent laughter as he stares out the window.

The ride to the depot is short, just long enough for me to watch my old neighborhood slip past, familiar faces trudging well-worn streets. We pull to a stop, and I take a deep breath, telling the guard I'm going inside to buy something. He just shrugs. I've become boring.

Good.

It takes a second after I open the door for the noise of vendors to die down. Shouts advertising their wares bounce to a stop on the tiled floor. My head is suddenly heavy, harder to hold up and look these people in the eye. Word has definitely spread in the month or so that I've been gone.

"Sellout," hisses a guy who came to at least one of the concerts. My father used to like his cheeses. Agreement swells like the slow, steady intro to a song that will explode when you least expect it.

"Tell me what you wouldn't do to save your family," I challenge him. "And that goes for everyone here," I say, looking around the room. "You know me. Knew my parents. Know my little brother and sister. Tell me what I should have done."

Silence. I haven't changed their minds. These are people who have spent their lives backing down from those with power, and now I'm one of them.

"I'm not here to make trouble for any of you. I just need Imp."

A head rises above the floury counter of a bread stall as Imp steps onto the stool he keeps there. What he lacks in height, he makes up for in width. Mage follows me and a hundred pairs of eyes follow both of us.

"Anthem," Imp says. His voice has been high and reedy as long as I can remember, but hearing it now brings me back to when I was shorter than he is, holding my mother's hand as she bought loaves for the week. I lean over, close as I can get to his ear, splintered wood digging into my ribs. I think he remembers, too. His face is a little less guarded than some of the others who are still watching us.

"Mage needs some gear."

Imp scrutinizes me, and I hold up my hands. No, this isn't some kind of trap. "Come with me." He doesn't bother to open the hatch in the counter, just ducks a little and shuffles out from under it. He waddles to the back of the depot, through a door that's supposed to be kept locked, down to a labyrinthine basement and into a room that reminds me of a cross between our old rehearsal space and the storage room in Pixel's club.

There are no water bottles on these shelves. Imp turns to us and waits.

"A computer, to start with." I say. "I don't know what else. Mage?"

"A de-commed console," Mage tells him. Every few years, the Corp upgrades them. The old ones are supposed to be recycled. Not all of them make it. "Six rogue tablets."

I didn't even think of that, and I hope his optimism that we need six untraceable communication devices, not five, is justified.

"This is going to cost," Imp squeaks. I shake my head.

"Doesn't matter."

Mage wanders along the shelves, grabbing cables, circuit boards, and other stuff I wouldn't know the uses for. "Can you get a clean memory chip?" he asks Imp. "And an ID chip, too. Gonna need to know how they work," he says to me.

Imp tilts his head. I know he's curious, but he's not in the right business for asking questions. "ID, yes. Not cheap, but there are a few floating around. Memory . . ."

"Not important," I say. I think Haven has one. Either that, or she never needed one to figure them out.

"Scanner?" I look at Imp. He takes me to a corner where a reclaimed scanner is blinking on the wall, most of its tracing functions disabled. The credits it takes from my account will appear to remain there, ghost-digits I can't spend but will look normal to the spying eyes of any overattentive Corp suit angling for a raise. Imp types in an amount that makes my stomach clench.

I tell him to double it and scan my wrist.

"I need four of those tablets now," I say. Imp nods and goes to a shelf to pick them up. "And something to hide them in." I check the number of the one on the top of the stack and give it to Mage so he can let me know as soon as he finds anything.

"Anthem. The rumors about the tracks they're using to kill . . ."

Imp breaks the law every time he brings someone down to this room. "They're true," I say. "Give Mage everything he needs."

A minute later I'm out of the depot, back under the indifferent charge of my guard. The loaf of bread showing out of the bag in my hand doesn't look hollow. "My brother and sister miss it." I explain.

In my conduit days, I read a lot of books about what people before the war thought life would be like on earth now. I envy the ones who didn't see what was coming, and wish they were right about a lot of it. I'd like to be one of those automaton robots right now, going through the motions of home, putting the twins to bed, hitting the club, and walking into the studio in the morning without imagining every one of Mage's illegal keystrokes, praying he's close to finding Haven.

Thinking about what I'll do if he can't.

I hand the rogue tablets out to the others. The guard in

the control booth doesn't even look up. We've become boring, well-behaved, good little citizens. Half the time there isn't anyone in there at all, just the twitchy sound tech. Life's not any fun if they don't get to point a gun at someone at least once a day, I guess. Even Ell's visits have dwindled. She's probably busy overseeing the Corp's new experiment.

On second thought, I don't want to be a robot.

I saw Mage on Tuesday. Friday morning, a guitar string snaps, but I ignore the long welt on my hand and reach for the tablet that's been silent for three days, until now. The rest of them know I'm waiting and haven't tabbed me because they're not cruel. I have to wake up the guard and feign nonchalance as I tell him we need to go pick up our other drummer. The kit is there next to Pixel's, ready and waiting.

I barely wait for Mage to open the door. "You found her?"

A strangled sound squeezes from his throat. He coughs. "Yeah. But Anth—"

"Where is she?"

He points at his bedroom. I don't remember crossing the floor or turning the handle. All I know is seeing her, sitting curled around a pillow in her lap.

"Haven," I breathe. Suddenly she's in my arms, her own wrapping tightly enough around my neck to choke. I'm home. We're both safe, at least for this moment. I'm not even conscious of the words I'm whispering in her ear, over and over, until I realize she's not responding to them.

"I'm so sorry," I tell her. "Did they hurt you? Are you okay?"

No answer. Fear bubbles, bright and hot and angry, in the pit of my stomach. I pull back a few inches and cup her face in my hands. "Can you hear me?" I ask.

Her eyes close; twin tears break the dam of her lashes to run down her cheeks.

I'm going to destroy them all.

# 0110010101251001100110

"Who did this to you?" I demand. The dumbest thing I can do right now, probably. The only sign that I said anything is the stuttered flicker of her sound implants. She just shakes her head and grimaces.

They say the pain takes weeks to subside. I tense my arms and try to hold my anger away from my hands so I don't hurt her.

"I found her through Exaur records," Mage says from the doorway. "I looked other places first—scanners she might've hit at clubs and whatever—no joy. I didn't want to think it, but . . ."

"Thanks," I say hoarsely. "Did it say who?"

"Just the med-tech who did it. Nothing about orders or whatever."

"Can I have your tablet?" Mine is sitting on top of my guitar where I dropped them both in the studio.

He brings it to me and closes the door on his way out. I spend too long figuring out what to say first.

`I'm sorry._`

Haven reads the screen and presses her body closer to mine, her hand lifting to take it from me. Pink nails click for a moment, loud because I'm listening for both of us. `You thought it was me, didn't you?_`

I can't bring myself to type it out and nod against her instead, waiting for her to climb from my lap or hit me or something else that would be completely justified. Sadness rises in the heat from her skin. `They wanted you to. I know that's why they filmed me._`

`That doesn't make it better._`

`It makes it forgivable._`

That's an argument I'll have with myself later. `Who did this to you?_` I ask again.

She takes the tablet from me and holds it for a while. `Direct orders from President Z._` Rage builds in me with each stumbled-over letter. `It was decided that a person . . . in my position . . . should know better._`

My nostrils flare, my pulse pounds heavy, and I bite back a scream. They're so convinced they own her that they don't even care if she hates them forever, or if they hurt her. No brainwashing tracks for her. They wanted to punish. They *wanted* to cause her pain, and her family couldn't save her this time. They made it worse. I wonder if they even tried to stop it, if they were given the chance. Haven puts the tablet down and slides her hand across my chest to rest over my heart. I close my eyes and steal the warmth of her touch through my shirt.

"Anthem," she rasps. My eyes snap open again. A lot of Exaurs give up speech, though the ability for it stays intact. She sounds like she's just woken up, throat raw and dry, and she stares at me, the pure green intensified by worry. "I wanted to hate you," she says, and I cringe. "But I missed you too much."

I will never deserve this girl, but I'm too selfish to not try. I want to tell her I know exactly what she means. More than anything, I want to erase that fear in her eyes.

It's like . . . I can't even think. Her lips are so soft, wet from fresh tears. I hold her as close as I can, spelling words on her tongue with my own. Promising that what happened to her might change everything to the world outside but nothing, *nothing* between us. Gasps slide down my throat like food I've craved that no other flavor could satisfy. Fingers play around the edge of my neck jack, a reminder of who I used to be—and which I'm going to need, one last time. She was there for that, and she's here now, and I'm not letting her go again.

We come up for air only when oxygen deprivation demands it and Haven presses her face into my neck, breathing me in. I shift enough to pick up Mage's tablet again, rest it on one knee and type, awkward and single-handed, so I don't have to let her go. She lifts her head to read the message when I tap her shoulder, and a slow, fierce, determined smile spreads across her face.

Not without my help._ It makes me smile, too. They've taken her hearing, but they haven't taken *her*. Together, we'll finish what we started.

She wants to see the twins but understands why she can't, not yet, and asks about my father. I swallow the lump in my throat once to speak, again when I remember I don't have to.

"It'll be okay," Mage says a minute later, grasping my arm and pulling me down the stairs, away from her. "She knows where to meet us, and her new tab number's in that one."

"Vortex," I tell the guard, jerking my thumb at Mage. "Have to get this one some new clothes." I take my seat, and Mage's tablet buzzes in my hand.

They took her straight from that leather chair in that comfortable office to the same medical facility in which I was treated after I finally caved. We must have missed each other by minutes. Maybe we were even there at the same time. I swallow stinging acid. It took four guards to hold her down, her drug-induced complacent happiness replaced by screams and terror.

My tabs asking about the pain and her weeks of withdrawal go ignored, answered instead by questions of her own. More fuel for the fire inside.

Phoenix, Pixel, and Scope beat us to the Vortex, their pod idling outside a row of stores.

"Fashion consultant," Phoenix says at our guard's raised eyebrows. "You think these guys know anything? Mage, you look like hell."

"Good to see you too, girl," he says, hugging her in the middle of the neon-bathed sidewalk. The others exchange high fives with him, and we turn to face the two scowling uniforms.

"Uh, yeah, this is gonna take a while," Phoenix says. "Obviously. I mean, look at him."

I wait, breath held. My fingers twitch, still warm from Haven's skin but cooling too quickly.

"I'm not here to watch a bunch of fucking kids play dress up," my guard mutters under his breath. "We'll be in there." He points to a water bar on the corner.

"We'll find you when we're done," I say. "C'mon, guys."

Inside a store filled with racks of leather and vinyl, I toss one of everything in Mage's size onto the counter and pay, not meeting the bewildered eyes of the employee. Pixel turns from the window, thumb up.

"Good to go."

Mage leads us out, around the corner into an alley that smells of rot and rain. Tendrils of light from the signs on the street stretch into its mouth and we run beyond their reach, down to the iron disc set into the ground that Pixel promised was here. I land in the tunnel below and take off, following the directions Mage calls from somewhere behind me.

"Wait!" Mage says and I stop, lungs burning. A glow of green light beckons ahead. Once, twice he flicks a flashlight on and off; its beam bounces off a far wall. "Be bad to sneak up and scare her."

"Thanks," I say, my throat dry.

"Mage, what—?" Pixel starts. I don't hear the rest because I'm moving again, into the alcove where Mage has set up the gear we bought. Monitors glow, and a rainbow tangle of fiber-optic cables streaks across the floor. Everything hums, not as strong as the mainframe, but enough that it raises the skin on my arms. A nest of blankets is piled along one wall with a pillow on top of them.

"Haven!" Scope yells, voice echoing up slimed brick. He rushes past me, picks her up, and swings her around. Holding her so close, he can't see the pain on her face. Phoenix is busy hugging Mage. But Pixel notices. His eyes follow me as I pull Scope away and put my arm around her shoulders.

"Haven? How are you?" Pixel asks, nearing her. She does a good job of pretending, watching his lips and forcing a smile, but not good enough. The concentration is evident as she tries to figure out what he said. He looks at me. "No way."

I nod.

"What?" Phoenix and Scope ask together. Pixel is more gentle with her than Scope was; I release her into his arms and he kisses her cheek.

"She can't hear you," I say. "She's an . . . She can't hear you." Their mouths drop open into shocked silence.

It makes Haven's scratchy voice louder. "The first person to treat me like some kind of delicate princess is going to regret it," she says. "I may be deaf, but my eyes and my brain are working just fine. I've had weeks to cry and break shit. I'm done now. That goes for you, too, Anthem." She squeezes my hand for a second, and my stomach unknots. I was right. They haven't taken her.

"Always knew I liked you." Phoenix grins. Haven seems to get the sentiment and smiles back, a real one this time.

"Pixel?" I offer Mage's tablet to him, my glance cutting briefly to Haven. He shakes his head and pulls out his own, ready to tell her what I say.

"I need to get Tango. We'll need power. And we're going to need Crave, too. Mage, you have to get the Board's codes and talk to the sound tech."

"No sweat."

"Haven's going to help with the memory chip stuff." Pixel's fingers blur across the tablet screen; Haven looks at it and nods at Mage.

"The Board," says Scope. "Who else?"

"President Z." Haven nods again. "The rest of us are going back in the studio, and I'm going on TV."

"Anthem, wait," Haven says. We all look at her, and the ghostly light of the monitors plays across the crease between her chrome eyebrows. "Mage told me what you're planning, and I think there's a problem. I think it's not going to work."

I curse my small, involuntary spasm of irritation and look at her. "Why not?"

Pixel's fingers tap on the tablet; Haven reads the message and takes a deep breath. "You guys want to use their new tracks to control their minds long enough to lock them up, get them out of headquarters, whatever. And that might work, except"—she closes her eyes — "the Board, the President, they're not like normal people, like us. They're *part* of the mainframe. Do you remember when I told you that the system has intense security on it?" she asks, opening her eyes again to meet mine.

I nod, confused.

"*They're* the security. Their chips. The system communicates directly with their minds. Nothing gets changed without their authorization, or not much, anyway. Small stuff, sure, but everything that keeps the Web running—food, water, power—depends on their authorization. Anyone who takes over won't have even one of the right chips, let alone all ten of them. The only way you could make it work is if you controlled their minds *forever*, kept them agreeing to whatever it is the new leader wants. And isn't that exactly what we're fighting against?"

Yes. Exactly that.

I face the wall, knotting my hair in my fingers. Shit.

"Ask her if there's a way around it," Mage tells Pixel. More tapping, then heavy silence. I recognize the pattern of Scope's breathing and hear Phoenix toeing the dirt with her pointed boots.

"I think there is," Haven says. I turn back to face her and see nothing but calm resignation from her. "I need to check a few things. But if I'm right, we're going to have to kill them."

$\oplus$

The elevator sinks. Down. Down.

Haven spent all weekend at a computer. She's sure now, and I'm done not trusting her. The plan doesn't have to change, not that much. We still make a song and encode it. I still go on TV and call for rebellion, counting on the ensuing chaos to cover our movements. Mage has been tracing and spreading messages in the system; the concerts are still being talked about. The anger at the Corp is still there, simmering, waiting for a tiny bit more heat. We still trap the President and the Board like rats and make them track, but they need to die so we can get the chips out of their heads. I close my eyes, picture Johnny's face, and think of the gruesome symmetry of what we're going to do. I'm the one who has to change. My friends do.

There's no chance of doing this peacefully anymore, and I guess there never really was. The fact that our original rebellion was always doomed to fail, even without Yellow Guy, isn't much of a comfort.

Alone, I step out into the wide expanse of the Energy Farm. I never thought this place would play a part in *saving* my life.

It's not nostalgia I feel when I pass my old cubicle, but it's something. Nothing was simple then, but it was complex in a different way. I thought I knew what was coming. I prepared for it as much as I could.

I hope I'm not as wrong now as I was then.

I hope . . . I hope . . . It's one thing the Corp didn't take from me, at least not recently, because I haven't had any for a long time. Grim satisfaction fills me. Credits, guitars, and supposed safety. With those things they've been generous, but I'm sure hope was the last thing they wanted to give.

Tough shit.

"Anthem!" Tango hisses, her purple hair not exactly preceding her from a cubicle, but it's the most dominant thing I see. "What are you doing down here?"

"Looking for you."

She searches my face for a minute, then drags me to a cubicle in an empty sector. I see the chair and the looped cable with the plug at one end. My spine tingles.

"You shouldn't be here."

"I know. I'm glad you're okay."

Her shoulders soften a little. "What's wrong?"

Everything. But maybe nothing soon. I take out my tablet, write a message, and show it to her. Her eyes widen.

"Is it possible?" I ask.

Energy is banked all the time. It's one of

the ways they make themselves live longer than the rest of us. Energy drained by tracking is replaced by . . . you guys._

"How are your brother and sister?" she asks aloud.

I stare at her. They have neck jacks?_ My own was implanted when I was hired as a conduit. Three weeks of healing later, I came to work here. It's a sign of shame. "Good. They love their new school."

Not on their necks._

I grit my teeth. Figures. I wasn't just powering all the blinding neon, all the mind-bending music. I was powering *them*.

What happens when they use it?_

"We should meet up at a Sky-Club sometime." Nothing. Their account level just drops. It's not allotted to the main Grid, so it doesn't show up on usage meters. You think they want everyone knowing about it? We only know because we get instructions on when to siphon more off and which account to send it to._

Okay. "Sounds good," I tell her. "I should go, before . . ." I know how closely techs and conduits are watched and listened to around here.

"What are you planning?" she whispers. I shake my head.

Not now. But I might need your help._ I wouldn't if we had our generators back, but I'm sure those are long gone, destroyed in the raid on the club. Imp didn't have any for us.

Her lips twist, and her eyes dart around.

Think about it?_ I ask. "Tab me, we'll meet up." Sighing, she nods. She sees what the Corp does to us more clearly than a lot of other citizens do, but I don't blame her for remembering what happened the last time, just like Mage.

One down. One to go. Getting to Crave will be harder, and I can't go to the guard station under the pretext of visiting an old friend. We never learned his code, and I don't know anything about him other than that he's stationed—or was—in Three. Finding him won't be simple, but at least there will be traces somewhere for Mage and Haven to find.

Anyway, there's someplace important I have to be.

◈

Haven answers the door of the address she tabbed me, every light I can see giving a last, unified flash before returning to their normal states of on or off. I don't know if all Exaurs have the systems installed, or if Haven's family, though they hadn't saved her from this, had at least made sure she was as comfortable as possible. She's in my arms before I can say anything. Words don't matter now, and not because she can't hear them.

She smells delicious. I keep my face in the fruit-scented skin of her neck as her legs wrap around my waist. No idea where I'm going, I stumble in and out of a living room and a tiny hygiene cube before I find the one small bedroom, dark—curtains shut against the afternoon.

There's a console on the wall. The accidental blow I land with my shoulder is the most use it'll ever see. A sound, muffled and strangled, escapes against her and she pulls away to look at me; a playful smile is the only reassurance that makes sense right now.

Legs, skin, fingers fumbling to reveal more of both until it's just us. Her body is the warmest instrument and our breaths synchronize to something more harmonious than music. We say nothing and so I hear everything—a hitch here, a whimper there that curls warmth in my belly.

*It's really pink in here,* I think as she half sleeps on my chest. She's been here long enough to make her mark on it. I wonder if it was her decision, if she was unable to face the parents who couldn't protect her or whether their shame forced her out. Even if it was the latter, I doubt it took much to make her go. I want to bring her home with me and see the expressions on the twins' faces as I walk through the door with her, but if I had a credit for every bad idea . . .

I guess I do. At least they're being put to good use now.

Haven shifts, lifting her hand to draw a lazy question mark on my stomach. We don't even need our tablets. We'll survive this. I nod and she slips from the bed. I watch her and get up only when she's slipped a shirt over her head and left the room.

The console beckons. I grit my teeth and look away. Not here.

"Tell me how it'll work," I say around a mouthful of my sandwich. My brain's been stuck on a *we're going to have to kill them* loop. Haven slips her tablet into my hand, and I repeat myself. I don't know if I have it in me.

"You guys get the chips. The system checks in on the members twice a day, so if we don't want to trigger a mass shutdown, we need to get them all between those two points. Once I have the actual chips, I can use them to trick the mainframe into thinking the owners are still alive."

You're sure?_

"Positive. I told you, each one is password-protected, and the people who have them don't know what it is. There's no way to get it out of them except to get it *out* of them. The passwords are installed on the chips when a Board member or the President steps into the job, and nothing in the mainframe runs without them. The system communicates with the chips, and if it doesn't get a signal from one, like if someone dies, the whole thing shuts down. To reactivate it you have to implant the chip into a new person *and* physically jack everyone else in while the system does a security check. It's the only way."

The tablet screen is blank, waiting for words I don't want to type. Why didn't you tell us before, at the club? The first time?_

"I hoped"—she swallows—"I hoped that they'd realize what they've been doing is wrong, when we went to take the Corp." She points a pink-nailed finger at her ear and shakes her head, lips pressed tightly together.

I put my plate on the table and lean back into the couch, one arm around her. Do I want to know how you know all this?_

Haven tilts her head to smile wryly up at me. "We don't talk about that."

No, we don't. Pinpoints of detail from the room gather to form a fuzzy picture of a life I don't know much about. Books—mostly stuff from just before the war with their spines faded and cracked—are arranged alphabetically on white shelves that meld into the walls. A glass bowl I once watched her buy from a store in the Vortex sits on the windowsill, a single pink flower floating in it. Cheap, long-dead fiber-optic tubes splay over another table, as if she had them out recently. I wasn't ashamed when I gave them to her, but now heat crawls over my skin. She kept them, brought them here even while I was sure of her betrayal.

One kiss turns into ten, but I really do need to leave.

Quadrant Four is maybe the best preserved of them all. Old buildings outnumber new and steel staircases cling to their sides—

sharp-edged parasites with claws hooked into weathered brick. The clamor of my steps is swallowed by Web noise and I sneak, unnoticed, away from Haven's apartment and the guard still waiting in my pod out front.

It's afternoon. Just in time for patrol shift change. I leave Four and aim for the blinding lights competing against the shadow of headquarters. The Vortex spins my head and spits me out on the other side, a few minutes away from Quadrant Three. I find the low, flat-roofed guard station, surrounded by patrol-pods, and slip into an alley across the street to wait.

# 1111011100261001111001

Got Crave._

Simultaneously, every tablet in the studio apart from my own emits a sharp buzz and the others pull them from pockets and bags. Pixel and Scope grin, Mage nods because he already knew, and Phoenix purses her lips as she taps out a response. He can do it?_

Yeah._ Not easily. We'll have to get into the armory at night after clearing it of the guards who are stationed to protect it around the clock—and getting rid of our own. When I climbed back into Haven's apartment it was empty. She had already gone to join Mage in the tunnels to hack into the mainframe and figure out the best way to create a diversion. Honestly, the two of them could probably get us in without Crave's help, but I need him to tell us what we're looking for. I know nothing about guns.

I didn't relax until Haven tabbed me to tell me she made it to Mage safely. Speeding pods . . . Exaurs . . . A rain of blood . . .

I force the slippery, many-legged thought back into its box. She's fine. Alone in the tunnels now, but fine. "Okay, one more time," I say out loud, my hands hovering over strings. It's a song the guard in the control booth has heard us practice a hundred times. Nothing out of the ordinary. The twitchy sound tech has joined him today. It's impossible to tell whether he's bobbing his head in time to the rhythm while we play or if he'd be doing it regardless.

With two drum kits, it's like clouds have descended into the studio and we're trapped inside a storm; crashes of thunder are set to perfect time and *there*, at the crucial moment of critical mass, the cymbals are metallic lightning.

I leave my voice packed away. Phoenix and I will record in one of the isolation booths later, when I can hear myself think. It's better to get the instruments right first, anyway, before I have to sicken myself with more singing of the Corp's praises. It's nice, novel, to be able to focus on nothing but the guitar, the bite of the wires into my fingers, my toes kicking at distortion pedals.

This one will go out to the Board members.

"Damn it!"

"It's okay." I smile at Phoenix, who is examining a broken nail.

"Maybe if you didn't hit it like its personally offended you . . . ," Mage tells her. She gives him the finger.

"Again," I say.

I know as soon as we hit the sweet spot, an intangible instant when the music gains control of fluttering wings to take real flight—soaring, swooping, diving and rising in the small studio. No single one of us is in control. The wall of sound is its own thing—lifted, weight shared, by five pairs of hands. I shake hair from closed eyes just because I need to move. If I let the pressure build and build and keep it in my hands, in the guitar, I'll explode. We carve out places for the verses, the chorus repetitions, and the coda. We line the edges of each sonic space with rhythm and melody and stand Scope's sharp samples at each corner.

I don't open my eyes again until we've finished, the final chord still echoing around the room. The guard still looks apathetic and it pisses me off. One of those types who just tracks because he has to, but doesn't know what any kind of music is really *for*. I'd love to shake him, tell him to listen and feel and let it take over. The sound tech gets it. He's staring at us with his eyes wide and milky; his hands dance over the control board by instinct, almost without looking. I guess we all have our instrument of choice.

Mage catches the slight incline of my head and follows my lead into the control room. "Can we get some food, please?" I ask the guard. Nicely. Good little citizens.

He snorts. "Babysitting a bunch of noisy kids. Do I look like a fucking servant? Sure. Anything for the *stars*."

Mage and I wait until the door closes behind him.

"Can you work with that?" I ask the tech. He nods furiously.

"L5329 and the Board and President Z will all be thrilled. It's even better than the first one you guys gave to me. L5329 said you got to hear it. Did you like it? This one is going to be amazing; I can't wait to get it upstairs. When do you want to do vocals? Today?"

"After lunch." Mage's lips are white with the effort of holding in his laugh. This guy and Mage in the same room is kind of weird. Maybe they'll counteract each other and cancel each other out.

"Yo, man, tell me more about this stuff?" Mage asks. "I used to be a coder, before I came to do this, so this kinda thing interests me."

"You really should see the computer side of it, then, you know? To really understand. And we always need more sound techs, people who really get the coding side and the music side. I should show you. Come with me."

Behind the tech's back, I give Mage a thumbs-up. The guy is talking nonstop about equalizer levels and chip codes and the auditory cortex and waveforms. Interesting, and knowing how this works is key. Mage grins lazily, opening the door for them both.

"That was easy." Phoenix smirks.

"It's going to get harder." Like the sound storm, critical mass is coming.

"You'd think you'd be less of a downer now that you've got your girl back."

Scope and Pixel laugh. I glare.

The chrome on the back of my hand gleams in the studio spotlights.

We're wiping our fingers free of the last streaks of grease when Mage and the sound tech get back. The tech joins the guard in the control room, and Mage comes in to grab a piece of chicken. He catches my attention and unfurls his palm under the pretense of grabbing the food. A small black object rests within it—a portable hard drive. The thing disappears into his pocket before he takes lunch and sits on a nearby chair to eat. I wonder if it feels heavy, the technology of death.

Mage's theft calms my stomach and relaxes my voice when I step into the vocal booth with Phoenix to record the lyrics, the nauseating, Corp-friendly message made bearable by the knowledge of what we're going to do with them. We get them laid down while the others track, their eyes glazing over, bodies relaxing against the nearest firm surface. I itch to do it, too. Between sending the twins off to school and coming here, I haven't tracked since this morning. A tightrope is strung across my brain from addiction to lucidity. I have to track enough to stand in the middle without falling.

"Next one?" I ask, stepping out of the booth and breaking Scope, Pixel, and Mage from their reveries. The smiles are too slack, agreements too drawled.

I clench my jaw. "Let's do it, then." I take down the turquoise guitar and shuffle my pedals as far across the room from the console as the tethering cables will allow.

Four pairs of eyes hit my face at once when I strum the opening chords. We haven't played this since our time at the club.

"Anthem?" Phoenix asks.

"Trust me."

✥

"That's what I think it is?" The question's been burning a hole through the tip of my tongue for hours.

"Yup." He holds up the tiny hard drive he stole and forces the word out through clenched teeth. "All we need to make one of their death songs is right here." The beam of his flashlight guides our way through the tunnels. "Dude's so busy moving he doesn't notice when anyone else does. Asked him to show it to me on the screen, copied it over when he wasn't looking."

"That's skill, man."

Scope's right. Mage just made things a lot easier. *Too easy*, says the voice in my head. It shouldn't be this easy. I ignore it. They've taken my parents, irrevocably hurt Haven, and killed Johnny. I'll take luck if it's offered.

"Okay, so we have the code, but we don't have the songs we just recorded," Phoenix says.

"Anthem's girl's got us covered." Mage flashes the light to warn her, and we round the corner into the alcove. Haven's waiting and I don't think she realizes what the sight of her does to me as she sits, smiling, in a leather chair. I pull her to her feet and wrap my arms around her. This is what's real.

Phoenix gags, a speck of normalcy, and I smile.

"You got it," Haven says, taking the little stick from Mage. "Choice." She sits back down and plugs it into the computer. A block of code that makes no sense to me scrolls down a screen like a blizzard against a black sky. Scope and I stand behind her, watching, until Mage taps me on the shoulder.

"Ready?"

I swallow heavily. "Yeah."

He's set up the de-commed console in a corner; a pair of old headphones hangs from it. In one hand is another, even smaller black object. In another is a knife. I push up my right sleeve and take a few deep breaths before I sit on the floor. Haven swivels her chair, face lit green and painful. I shake my head. *Don't watch.* She grimaces, nods, and turns back to the monitors. Pixel takes Scope's place near Haven, and Scope comes to kneel next to me, fingers wrapping around my left ones. "You sure we have to do it this way?" he asks.

"They don't work outside a body, man, or people would be stealing chips from corpses and charging credits to dead guys. Haven can hack in and alter the one Anthem's already got, but do we want the Corp noticing that someone with a master ID chip is coming and going where Anthem's supposed to be? We can get to where we've gotta go with ours, but Anthem's going after the *President*, man."

"Yeah, okay."

Phoenix and Mage start to argue over which one of them has steadier hands. I don't care. I just want to get it over with. Sweat turns my skin cold.

"Anything special you want?" Phoenix asks, giving me the headphones. I shake my head.

"Whatever. Something strong. Upper-Web strong."

"You got it." She taps at the console screen. I cover my ears and get the briefest moment of realization that I know this song; I used to throw myself into dancing to it at a club not far from where I'm sitting. Drums thump and a guitar begins, overlaid by hypnotic, rhythmic keyboards. The pull of the drug is heavier even than the way it sounded then, encoded for lower-Web scum like us. Meant for a perfect high in the privacy of lush apartments.

*I'm deep in a sunlit ocean, bathed in green, swimming. I didn't know I could do that. I've just read about it, the cool waters turning darker and darker the farther you go. Now I must be on the ocean floor because everything is black, sand and silt shifting beneath me and something—some wild sea plant—is wrapping itself around my wrist. I try to pull away, but it tightens, holding me fast, trapping me. No, stop. Let me go! I don't like that.*

*Pain, so much pain, as a sharp-toothed creature bites into my skin, the water around us and the plant staining, blossoming with my blood. A tooth, square and hard-edged, digs below my torn veins, lodges itself close to my bones. Again and again I try to drag myself away. My mouth and lungs fill with water as I try to scream, and I just choke, cough, gasp. My pulse is a wild drum beat, and I need help, please, I'm drowning. I can't see the light anymore, it's too deep and I'm trapped.*

*The plant tightens even more, winding itself in thick, flat straps around me, and then there is the snap of scissors, which don't belong here, down in the sea, and someone is rescuing me, cutting the plant, and pulling me up, up, out of the water so I can breathe again.*

My face is wet from the sea. I tug my hand from Scope's and wipe my eyes and cheeks with my sleeve.

"You okay, man?"

My eyes find Mage's in the murk. "Yeah." I don't even want to think what the fuck that would've felt like without a painkilling track. The edges of my brain are fuzzy, but too much of it is thinking clearly already. I look down at my right arm, now sheathed in white gauze, hiding the newly implanted chip that will get me through any door. "You sure this'll work?" Please, tell me I didn't just go through that for nothing.

"It'll work."

I breathe deeply. Air. Not water. "Okay." Scope is watching me carefully as Phoenix wipes blood from the knife.

"So who is he pretending to be with that thing?" Phoenix asks. "A guard?"

"That's the beauty of it. Not that I'm claiming credit—Haven over there's a genius. All the ID chips are the same to look at; it's just what's on them that's different for all of us. Haven put on an access code for a senior guard and inserted it into employee records, but it's not a real person. Nothing else is on there. Long as you use that chip and not your normal one, you aren't anyone, man," Mage says to me. "You're a ghost. Pale enough for it, too." He grins.

"Thanks." I try to smile, but it feels like someone's holding my wrist over an open flame.

"Come on," Scope says, helping me to my feet. I sway a little. "Let's get to the fun part."

Haven stands when she senses us behind her and pushes me down into her chair with a fierce expression on her face. I'm about to protest, but she sits on my lap and gets back to work.

Okay, I can live with this.

Equalizers and sound waves cover most of the monitors. A few others are scanning dizzying lines of code I can only half see because of Haven's elaborate hair.

One by one, nine numbers begin to replace the streaming code on one of the screens. I don't know which is which, don't even know what any of them look like, but I know who all of them are. President Z and the nine Board members who do her bidding. I angle my head, not to see the monitor more clearly, but to watch Haven's profile. I don't know if she'll tell me whether one of those nine is her father if I ask. Given what we're about to do, I'm not sure I want to know. Her expression of concentration doesn't change. These are the brain codes that will tie each memory chip to a specifically encoded track. A minute later, the contents of their ID chips dump onto the screen.

Haven makes a noise of approval and quickly types something, and the screen changes back to more code.

"How are we going to make sure that they listen to the one we want them to?" Scope asks. "I mean, yeah, it's guaranteed they're gonna track, and they have to scan their chips to unlock the console, but we can't replace all of the options. That'd take forever."

I look at Mage. "It won't matter what they choose. The one we alter is what'll play. They won't have time to realize it's the wrong thing." Johnny had no time.

"We're ready," Haven says. My arms tighten around her; the burn at my wrist intensifies. I'm glad she still uses her voice.

Mage leans over and types something on a second keyboard. "This is the first song we recorded today," he says. Rows of sound waves switch places with something else to show up on a monitor in the center of the bank. "We're using that for most of 'em, right, Anthem?"

I nod. He knows what I want to do with the last one. I told them all on our way through the tunnels.

He presses a few keys and a small window pops up. He points to a line of white letters and numbers.

I don't know Mage's citizen code. I know Scope's, but only because we've been friends for years. I've never asked for Phoenix's, or Pixel's, but I will never forget Johnny's. Everything else fades to white fog on the edges of my eyes as I focus on the J1942 in the middle. My mouth turns sour.

Haven follows his finger and nods. I wish she'd had a chance to meet him, but it was my own stupidity that prevented it. She replaces his code with one of the ones from the list she pulls up again.

It's almost . . . simple, though there's no chance I could do it on my own. I watch as codes are switched around, altered, and embedded into the song we spent all morning perfecting. A red line crawls slowly across a monitor, counting off percentages, fraction by fraction. When it hits the other side, it blinks and disappears.

A song a few hours ago. A weapon now.

Something's wrong.

Dust motes of stillness float through the air as soon as I open the door, lit by sun spilling through the huge windows.

"Alpha? Omega?" I call. Maybe they're just not home from school yet. But they *should* be, and the alarm in my voice is a sign from every cell in my body that it knows this. "Peacock?" I'm supposed to go on TV in a few hours.

"Bee?" Fear makes me stupid. There's no answer.

Door handles chip plaster as I race down the hall, looking in every room. This is more than the quiet of an empty apartment. It's the terrifying silence of space that should be inhabited and isn't. I turn back, promising myself they're in the kitchen. Of course they are. I don't know why I didn't check there first. And for some reason, the twins are just too focused on something to have heard me come in. Maybe Bee has just finished baking more cookies. Maybe they're doing homework.

I stop dead in the archway.

Oh, shit. I run to Bee, drop to the floor beside the fridge, and make my hands work enough to unbind her wrists and pull the gag from her mouth. Fucking bastards. Gagging her and leaving her here for me to find. Her screams would've been the last thing she had.

"Where are they?" I ask, my voice rising, as if that will make some kind of difference. Bee shakes her head, her pupils dilated by terror and her fingers going to the deep, angry welts left on her fleshy arms by the ropes.

My pulse speeds and breathing stops. Spots from the bright kitchen lights turn my vision to an electric snowfall.

I know who took them and don't need the confirmation on Bee's tablet screen I see when I make myself focus.

Ell is a dead woman. And she's going to know it, very, very soon. Another thing to add to the list of stuff I've been wrong about. I will *kill* her if she hurts them, and revenge is all the reason I'll need.

I take Bee's tablet and type out instructions for her as clearly as I can. I've never known the exact address. If they haven't fixed the hole in the fence, she'll be safe there. I was going to take her and the twins myself tomorrow. From my own, I send identical messages to Haven and Mage, telling them what I need. A different one to Pixel, Scope, and Phoenix.

There's only one place Ell would go. Her precious Corp.

I only needed another day, maybe two. My guard tries to stop me outside the door. I don't wait to watch him buckle to the floor or see his face start to bleed.

Any luck we had is gone. Air tears from my lungs and flays my nostrils. Shards of agony stab at my chest. I double over and force myself up again to keep going down the stairs, outside, and down the sidewalk running the length of the park.

It's there, looming and black, a threat made of glass. Buildings dodge and weave in front of it, but I don't let it out of my sight. My pocket buzzes over and over. I don't stop to look. I don't need to see the messages yet. I need to find the twins.

How the fuck did she know?

My thoughts race faster than my feet. The others are answering their messages and in any case these tablets are rogue. The power suck down in the tunnels? No, if they knew where we were, they'd have the others by now. We said nothing suspicious to any of the guards or to the sound tech.

I stumble and right myself. Why isn't it getting any closer? Blood drips down from under my sleeve, my hammering pulse breaking the barriers of gauze.

If I can't save them, this has all been pointless. I should let myself fall right here. The stabbing is getting more insistent, and all of this was for them.

All I can see is black. Shouts and curses bounce off me. I shove bodies out of the way. I must be getting closer. More people. The noise of the Vortex.

I don't stop until I'm in danger of slamming into smoked glass. Smashing one window isn't enough. I pull out my tablet and wipe blood from the screen so I can read.

`Level 3. Office 317. Ready if you need it. Others on the way. Be careful, okay? I love you._`

`Stay where you are._` Fuck, I hope she listens.

The receptionist is still bored, painting her nails a shade of yellow. I want to knock the bottle from her hand. No one gives me more than a passing glance as I run into the elevator and press buttons that don't respond fast enough.

I don't know what I'm doing. My body moves without me. I'm in front of doors, gasping and biting back screams. I scan my new chip and it slides open.

"Anthem," Ell says, sugar-laced and dangerous. "How nice of you to join us."

It's not a big room. The same sucking, soundproof quality of so many other Corp offices pervades it. White, everywhere. Clinical and hostile. For the smallest second I'm confused by the lack of guards. And then I'm not. I should have expected this from her. There are no guards because Ell doesn't need them.

The console on the wall glows the blue of being in use.

Alpha and Omega are attached to it.

"You're dead." I race across the room, trying to get past her. Through blurred eyes, I see silver motion. A knife flicking open.

"Always pays to have insurance policies," she says. She's glowing—teeth gleaming, face bright. "You are too late, little Anthem."

I look at the twins. Their eyelids are closed, and peaceful smiles are on their faces. As I watch, Omega laughs at whatever it is the track is making him see.

"The first track is the most addictive," Ell says. "You know that, of course. They've had, oh, three or four now. I imagine they're on quite a trip. Don't they look happy?"

"Let. Them. Go."

Ell shakes her head. "Oh, no, I don't think so. You have never been as hungry for fame as some of our other musicians, so it was curious that you asked to go on TV. I wondered if perhaps you were going to try something, maybe tell the citizens what we have planned. It seemed prudent to protect ourselves from that, wouldn't you agree?"

"I haven't said anything yet."

Alpha giggles. I try to breathe and blink away the haze behind my eyes. A steady flow of blood falls to the floor from my wrist.

"Yet. Of course. You have been *remarkably* well-behaved. Suspicious in itself, I think."

I say nothing.

"I decided you shouldn't be given any more time," Ell continues. "If we had continued on our path, you might have come up with some way to prevent it in time to protect them. But you know there is no reversing this. Not even white noise will completely erase the lingering effects. You come out of an OD recovered, but not cured of the addiction. Should you still desire to do your interview—that is, if you still have anything to say—you can now be completely certain that I have no qualms about punishment. Say anything, Anthem, and you know exactly how far I will go."

"You crazy bitch," I hiss. Failure strips strength from my muscles. I force myself to take another step toward her and silver flashes again.

"I learned from the very best." Ell smiles. "You could say President Z is something of a mentor to me. Took me under her wing long ago."

"You're both dead," I say. My eyes flicker between the knife and the twins. I'm no good to them dead. I'm not much good to them alive.

It would be easy, so easy to fall on that blade. The twins might not even see. I take another step.

"Good boy. Just give in. Life is so much easier that way. Let us decide what's best for you." Suddenly, Ell's face splits into her widest grin yet. "Excellent. Guard, remove him until I'm finished here."

I spin, ready to fight. The black uniform against the white hurts my eyes. A hand is pressing the button to keep the doors locked open. I don't care that they have guns and a knife. No one is taking me out of this room.

And then Ell isn't the only one smiling. Crave looks me straight in the eye and strides past, his gun out, to push Ell against the wall with a slam that breaks through the headphones into the twins' ears. In unison, their eyes open wide, confused, pupils blown. I run to them, pull the headphones off, and gather them in my arms. My right arm holding Alpha nearly gives out. Both are barely conscious. A heavy dose, so soon . . . I hold them tighter.

"Citizen!" Ell gasps. "What do you think you're doing?"

Crave smiles slowly. "Protecting the Web. Exactly as I swore to."

Ell tries to shout, but Crave has his forearm against her throat. Her shoes clatter on the floor as she tries to kick him.

The pain in my arm is nauseating. I try to think through the warm, sticky, thick feeling. Try to decide what to do next. Crave shouldn't be the one to kill her, and I don't want to do it in front of the twins. Remembering even a fraction of that would be too much. As it is they're scared—hearts hammering against my chest—and disoriented. Omega blindly reaches in the general direction of the console, trying to get the headphones back. I step away with them and will myself not to puke.

"Anthem." A familiar voice. A soft hand is on my shoulder. I let Phoenix pry Alpha from me, and Pixel takes Omega. Pixel looks at me in question. I don't know. I can't think.

"Isis," I whisper finally. "Get Isis. Take Crave and go in his pod. Down to the warehouse. Bee's there already. Maybe they can . . ." There's nothing they can do. The twins' minds will always know the drug. The itch of addiction, however faint, will be there forever. They'll never be satisfied without it. "I'll be there soon."

"Mage and Haven say the track's ready for her," he whispers to me. "Scope, stay with him."

Crave lets go of Ell; her wheezy breaths fill the room. As soon as his hands are off her, she tries to move, her foot trips over one of her fallen shoes. A loud crack tumbles into the soundproof abyss, and the wall six inches from her head explodes from the force of the bullet. Ell freezes and Crave presses his gun into my hand. "All yours."

Scope follows them and stands by the doors to wait. Fear paints Ell's face. It's a good look for her, and I let myself enjoy it for a second.

"I underestimated you," Ell says. She doesn't quite hide the tremor in her voice.

Fine. She can think that if she wants.

"You've poisoned my little brother and sister." My legs are working fine now. With every step I take, her eyes widen further. "You let me think the girl I love betrayed me, just so you could use me. You performed experiments on my friends."

"This has all been President Z's brainchild, but I was instrumental in its execution."

The bitch is *proud* of herself.

I laugh. Sharp. Not funny. But laugh nonetheless. "That's truer than you know. You weren't the only one paying attention." Her arm flinches under my hand. I push her over to the console. "Do you remember what you *tested* on my friend who died?"

"It won't work on me." Ell smirks. "It was attuned to him. Every such test has been specifically designed for the citizen in question."

"Yeah." I nod. "Exactly. You screwed up. If you'd left my brother and sister alone, I would've let you live. I don't need to kill you to make things right, just your precious President and her board."

"You can't kill them. You need the Board and President Z to run the mainframe. They're . . . connected. Without them, everything will shut down. No food, no water, no music. Is that what you want, Anthem? To kill the Web?"

She's good. Haven's better. "I don't need them. I need their chips."

The muscles I grip turn slack. Her fight melts like wax, and I shove her harder than I need to against the wall. More plaster falls from the bullet hole. "I guess I should say thanks," I say. "I wasn't sure I could do it before. Didn't know if I had it in me. You know what? I do."

"Anthem," Scope says, a low-pitched warning. "We don't have a lot of time."

He's right. There are other places I need to be. Ell, sensing my distraction, claws and kicks at me. With Scope's help, I force her wrist across the scanner; the logo that returned shortly after I unhooked the twins disappears again. I select the song and pin the headphones over her ears as she struggles against us.

It's over in seconds, just like with Johnny. She's there, and then she's gone, the life sucked out like a conduit machine on overdrive. Scope helps me do what we need to and we slip between closing doors with an inch to spare, my bloody handprint left on the *lock* button inside.

Ell is important. It's not going to be long before someone goes looking for her, or for Crave's absence—and his missing pod—to be noticed. We find the nearest hygiene cube and clean up as much as we can. Scope checks his tablet, and a minute amount of tension leaves me. The twins are safe in the old warehouse basement—for now. We split up in the hall, Scope back to our station in the tunnels, me for the little used stairs down to the Energy Farm.

◈

Tiredness is already infused into my bones, but there's no other way for this, and Tango, with her vibrant violet hair, is easy to find.

We have nine to kill, less any who happen to track of their own volition in the next couple of hours. But most upper-Web types, especially Corp people, wait for evening. We're figuring about five minutes for each, enough time to get into the consoles and get the tracks playing in their heads. Plus enough power to run everything we'll need to pull this off.

One year off for one year on . . . at normal drainage levels. Who knows what this will do to me? I sit in the chair for almost an hour, long enough to store the energy we need.

I'm exhausted when Tango de-jacks me. "Get out of here if you can," I tell her. "Please. You don't want to be here."

Her eyes dart around the Energy Farm. "Okay. Good luck, Anthem."

The man with the bionic arm looks at me in surprise when I walk—stumble—into the store. Yeah, I know. It's been a while. He takes out a bottle of grape juice and averts his eyes from the crust of blood around my wrist when I take it from him and scan my real ID chip. It's not much, but the sugar will help a little.

Withdrawal nibbles at my skin. I've barely tracked today, just a few times this morning and the one to kill the pain of the new implant—not that it helped much. The twins' faces, blurred and hazy-eyed, float in front of me.

The withdrawal can kill me if it wants. I will never track again. I finish my juice, throw the bottle into a container outside for plastics to be recycled, and head back into headquarters. Level five. Corp TV.

"Citizen, this is a restricted area. You can't come in here." A young guy sits at a reception desk a lot like the one downstairs, watching the door through beady eyes.

*Fake it.* "I'm N4003," I tell him, brushing my hair from my forehead with my left hand, the right buried in my pocket. "You guys have been asking for another interview with me for weeks and I finally agreed to arrange this. Of course, if you don't want one anymore . . ."

His face morphs into awe. "Oh, wow! I'm so sorry, Citizen. Yes, of course. We'll get you on primetime. Excuse me."

I fall against the desk when he's out of sight. By the time he gets back I'm just leaning on it, wearing an expression that could pass for conceited boredom. He helps me to a room obviously equipped for making sure no one goes out on Corp TV looking anything but beautiful, and his enthusiasm covers my near inability to walk. I'm put in a chair in front of the mirror and asked to wait. "It will only be a minute, Citizen." I grab a wet cloth from the counter and clean off the back of my right hand.

"Anthem?" I raise my eyes and see Peacock behind me in the reflection.

"Hi." How can she be so calm? Oh. No one knows about Ell yet. A smile stretches her blue-green lips.

"What *have* you been doing to yourself?" she asks. "You're a complete mess. Good thing you've got me." I watch the eerie eyes in her hair as she rummages in drawers and boxes and turns back with a handful of stuff. The eyes are still staring at me, through the mirror now. I shift and look away. She does her thing, cleaning and drawing and smearing and brushing.

I think of the twins. I should be with them, but leaving this half-finished would be worse than never having started it at all. It's too late to think maybe that would've been the best plan. Pixel and Phoenix have left them in the warehouse with Bee and Isis. Two women—one an Exaur—and two little kids. I need to get to them before anyone else does. I don't know whether Yellow Guy told Ell or whoever he reports to about our secret practice space, but I know he will when he learns what's going on, if given the chance.

"All done," Peacock says cheerfully. I look almost like myself. She's covered the dark circles under my eyes. My hair is clean, spiked, the blue streaks refreshed to match my lips and eyelids. Black lines rest against my lashes. "You want new clothes?"

I shake my head. She gave me these weeks ago. The tears and ragged seams from today make me *feel* like myself. Maybe, if I get out of this alive, I'll mend them with uneven stitches, over and over again, until they fall apart completely.

The room fills suddenly with people; every pair of eyes is on me in a way that makes me wish Peacock and her weird hair hadn't faded into the background. Someone clips a tiny microphone to a rent in my shirt, another examines Peacock's handiwork.

I recognize only one: the spokeswoman usually on the news in the evenings. The last time I was on TV as Ell's barely known puppet, it was in the afternoon. I wonder if she'll speak to me with the same enthusiasm she musters for hydroponics and new music developments.

She does. It hurts my ears.

"Is there anything particular you want to say, Citizen N4003?" she asks. This close, her voice is a feedback whine, dissonant and ugly. "Do you have news about new tracks? Or would you like to encourage more Citizens to follow your footsteps in creating our wonderful music?"

"Both, I guess," I tell her. She starts to vibrate like a tablet filled with messages.

"Right this way then!"

I push myself from the chair, follow her clicking heels out of the room and down a hallway. The crowd of people around us steals all the breathable air. Spots dance across my vision.

The TV studio is blinding. Not as white as the Corp offices or the medical facility, but the lights make up for it. Cameras meld into triangles of shadow in front of the stage.

Someone begins to count down from five. I could almost be getting ready to sing.

"We have a very special guest with us today, Citizens! Our latest musical sensation has just dropped by to share some good news with all of you, so I hope you're listening closely! Put down those headphones! Tracking can wait a few more minutes. N4003, what do you have to say to the Web?"

I take a shallow breath—the most I can manage—and look straight into the camera. "Some of you know me already. Not as N4003, but by my other name. Some of you have seen me play with my band, heard what *real* music is." Beside me, the spokeswoman gasps quietly, that fake, plastic smile stuck on her face. "If you've seen me, some of you might believe the lies that were spread about me, that I chose to turn legit. They. Were. Lies."

A ripple of noise spreads through the studio. I hear tablets buzz. I imagine the running footsteps of guards coming closer.

"The Corp threatened my family and hurt the people I love to get me to work with them. They wanted me to help make a new kind of track. One that will control our minds and take away the few choices they've allowed us to have." I stand on shaky feet and walk toward the camera. Around me, the TV crew have turned to statues, paralyzed and mesmerized. I was counting on that, but I'm sure it won't last much longer. "If you know this"—I hold up my hand to show the clean, bright, sparkling chrome coda symbol—"it once meant something to you. It still means something to me."

I close my eyes. *Mage, Haven, you better have meant it when you said you were ready.*

"And it's time to fight for it. Now."

I open my eyes to pitch darkness.

For one brief, blissful second, there is silence. Shock fills the room, a weighted, almost tangible presence gathers and intensifies.

"Get him!"

Something heavy crashes to the floor. I run as chaos erupts behind me, and the pandemonium is a musical thing. It should be discordant, disorganized noise—everyone for themselves—but it's not. The stomping feet, the waving arms, and the voices shouting to be heard . . .

The glowing blue tubes in my hair cast just enough light for me to see a few inches in front of me. Someone tries to grab my arm and is either pulled back or swallowed by the crush, I'm not sure which. Getting out of here is the only thing that matters.

There's no way of knowing how many guards we managed to trap in the elevators as they tried to come up here to stop me. Enough to make a dent, I hope. That was the plan. I push, pull, and punch my way through the door, and run down the hall to the stairs.

Some of those people back there are on my side. Not all. I wasn't going to stop to count.

In the stairwell, I yank the tubes from my neck jack and drop them. The gun Crave gave me I take in my right hand—even injured, I'm probably a better shot with it than my left, which I use to hold the flashlight to get through the tunnels.

A stampede is coming closer—people from upper floors, trying to get out, but anyone whose door was shut is trapped until Mage or Haven goes into the scanner hub to override.

I barely make it down. At every step, every turn, my body begs to give up.

The lobby is empty, a ghostly glass and marble tomb. One of the windows explodes into a shower of skittering, glinting shards. It wasn't the one I was aiming for, but I guess it doesn't matter. Anyone not stuck somewhere can follow me out.

Or come in. The streets are flooding with people—the only source of noise and life in the Vortex. Dead neon signs hang like sound implants in a quiet room, still and black against the skin-colored sky of early sunset.

Hundreds surge around me. Rage. Excitement. The energy is beautiful and terrifying. I did this. Already it feels like it was someone else who gave them what they wanted. Nearby, more glass breaks with a crack like lightning. A guy grabs my arm; recognition is clear on his face, but I shake him off and push my way against the current, my head down. Everything hurts.

I steal a pod, hardly waiting for the door to open at the swipe of my master chip to jump in the driver's seat. I force it south through a swarm of pods and people with whatever weapons they were able to find. All heading to the Corp. To fight. I press my foot more firmly down on the accelerator and let the auto navigation systems keep me from hitting anything too important.

I'll be back there soon.

I leave the engine running and the door open, the pod half on the curb. My clothes rip as I push through the fence and race into the warehouse. "Are they okay?" I ask, practically throwing myself through the trapdoor and barely touching the ladder on my way down. Isis's face emerges from the darkness.

"Sleeping," she says softly. "Anthem, I don't know what—"

"I know there's nothing you can do. Just . . . make sure they come out of it?" They're going to be terrified and I can't stop it. As I reach for my tablet to tell the others to go on without me, Isis touches my arm.

"They're safe here, Anthem. I'll look after them. Go."

I find them first, curled up against Bee in a corner, the old scrap of cloth Johnny used to wrap his guitar laid over them. Their bodies are relaxed and their hair is tangled, faces softened by sleep except for a furrow between Omega's brows—the sign of a forming headache. The image follows me through the old, almost-rusted door I nearly have to wrench off its screaming hinges to enter the network of tunnels. My tablet screen glows. A moment later it vibrates in my hand; a map draws itself in streaks of blue.

Even so, it takes me too long to reach the others. Every fifty feet I have to stop and catch my breath. When I finally see the hazy green light, I close my eyes and stumble forward into waiting arms. Haven and Mage catch me and drag me to the soft nest of blankets and pillows.

"What's happening?" I ask. Haven holds a bottle to my lips, and sweet, sticky juice pours down my throat until I cough. "What's happening?" I try again.

"Pixel, Scope, and Phoenix just left. Crave opened up the

armory in Three, letting people just help themselves. Too late for anything else now."

"You have enough power?"

"We're gonna have to. I'm not letting you drain out any more, even if we had the equipment here. You look half-dead as it is."

"It wasn't that much."

He raises his eyebrows. "On top of being in the studio all day, coming down here, back to your place, running to headquarters, killing someone . . ."

I wave a hand to stop him. "I need to get back out there."

Mage laughs. "Not yet. She's trapped, Anthem. Not going anywhere, trust me. And we're intercepting all her tabs, so she can't call for help. Drink. And eat this." He tosses me a huge slab of chocolate. Haven pushes me until I lie down on the pillows, my head tilted just enough to see the screens that are running on *me* now. Mage cut power to the main Grid, but we still need some for what we're doing, and now every light, every flash, is a second of my own life gone.

"Member Seven is tracking," Mage says, turning to the bank of blinking monitors and picking up his tablet. None of us are breathing and it makes the tunnel feel airless. I tighten my grip on Haven's hand. I don't know exactly where Scope is; I don't know how many interminable minutes it will take him to get to the guy's office and make sure the track has worked.

I picture my friends entering rooms, looking at consoles and corpses and removing chips with bloody hands. They've all told me they can handle it; I have to believe them. Phoenix was insulted I asked, and it's too late to back out now. Soon it'll be my turn, but the energy suck of providing the power has exhausted me, and I need to recover. I eat the chocolate, gulp down grape juice, and will my body to be strong.

The silence presses in. Even now, I wish I could track.

Never again.

Come on. *Come on.*

The tablet vibrates.

"Got him," Mage says. One Board member down. A tiny draft from somewhere fills my lungs with oxygen again. Eight more, plus President Z, who's the reason I am down here in the musty dark with Haven's head against my shoulder, sucking down juice.

"This is it," Haven whispers. I squeeze her hand, divided. My stomach flips between relief and horror. It's working.

A light, where there wasn't one a second ago, flares to life on one of the monitors. Another member is at a console. The tablet goes off again.

"Phoenix got Four." The image of Phoenix with a gun slides easily into my tired brain. She won't use it if she doesn't have to, but we're still killing. We'll have to live with that if we survive. I hope we can.

I need to get up there. My legs jerk and Haven holds me down. *I should be paying attention to* her. Listening for a change in her breathing, seeing if I can feel her muscles tense when a certain Board member is tracking or about to. I open my mouth to say something and close it again.

One. Eight. Nine. Our tablets buzz, a hive of electronic bees.

Two. Three. Pixel and Phoenix are going after the last two. Scope'll be back here soon with the chips he's collected.

It's time for me to leave. Mage hands me a knife. This time, Haven lets me stand. I pull her toward me and kiss her. Not goodbye. No. I'm coming back.

My tablet buzzes twice in quick succession; one of them is a map from Mage. Haven kisses me again, hard and bruising and terrified, and pushes me away.

Dirt from the tunnel floor sprays up from my feet. I follow the map, deep into the maze below the Vortex. The exit is above an old, broken ladder I'm not sure will hold me, but it got the others out. I stop long enough to type out a message, but don't press SEND. The ladder creaks and drops an inch when I step on the bottom rung. My stomach goes with it. I keep climbing until I can reach the ceiling, use all my strength to shove the metal circle out of my way. On the first try it rocks back; I hear every one of the fingers on my right hand snap. My screams echo down the endless tunnels.

Sharp steel digs into my thighs as I cling to the ladder with my legs and try again.

Smoke chokes me and clouds my eyes with stinging fog. I pull myself up onto the street, into raging fire. Tears stream down my face, adding to the blindness. I have no idea where the fuck I am.

"Let's get those evil bastards!" Dozens of voices echo the first. "Fuck the Corp!" I flatten myself against an abandoned pod and fall into step at the back of the mob. We run through clogged streets and dodge down hidden alleys when bullets whistle overhead. I trip over a falling body with no time for thanks or regret. Suddenly the smoke is hard and sharp; my scalp opens and a single rivulet of blood drips down my neck. I run my unbroken hand through my hair and examine what I find.

Dark glass.

I break away from the crowd and bite through my lip as I wrap my fingers around the gun. Inside headquarters it's less smoky, but loud enough to blunt every one of my senses.

"That's him! Anthem!" The sound of my name hammers into my brain. No idea if it's friend or enemy. I don't stop. A foot away, marble cracks.

The stairs are empty. Everyone is trapped in the lobby or is out in the street. Fighting a war I started and now have to end, twenty-four floors into the sky. I pause at the bottom, but staring up isn't going to make them easier to climb. I fill my lungs and run.

I think I can feel my leg muscles shredding. Air comes in ragged gasps and leaves before I can absorb much of it. Halfway, I stop and check that the pain in my side isn't a bullet wound, almost wishing it were. It might be a good excuse to stop. I hear the cacophony of destruction on every floor I pass, imprisoned Corp suits trying to break free. I keep going before one of them succeeds.

On my knees, leaning against my one good hand, I pull myself up the final flight. A single guard is waiting for me—a last shred of loyalty to the woman behind the door. It's my scream, I think, that throws him off. The heat haze from a bullet brushes my ear as I finish pulling the trigger with my mangled fingers. Blood sprays from the front of his uniform and he looks down, almost curious, before his eyes roll back in his head and he thuds to the floor.

*It was him or me.* I force back the urge to puke and look at my tablet, focusing until the screen stops swimming.

The message I typed while in the tunnel is still waiting, blinking. My hand shakes over the SEND button. N o w . _

A second passes. Another. Another. I watch the doors for any sign of movement and the scanner for a glimmer of life that comes just in time to pour ice on the boiling fear that there's none of my energy left.

The scanner blinks—a red eye—and beeps once. I open the door and stop, my feet trapped in heavy carpet.

What strikes me most isn't the woman in the chair; I was expecting that. I was prepared for the plush office, which is filled with electronics coming to life with the power Mage just restored, and the tall windows with their view over the Web. The video camera in one corner next to a black screen on a wheeled frame isn't a surprise, either, or the thing that looks almost like a smaller, sleeker conduit machine. Thanks to Tango, I can guess what that's for.

The woman was waiting for me. Smiling. Expecting me, too.

Behind the wide expanse of desk, above the console on the wall, is a portrait. A stern-faced man and the woman in front of me stand within the frame on either side of what can only be their daughter, who looks happy unless you know every nuance of her face, every expression she's capable of.

And I do.

President Z is Haven's mother.

# 01100110012910111110111

"Well, well," she says. "You must be Anthem."

I don't try to unstick my tongue from the roof of my mouth. My eyes are still flicking between the olive skin so like Haven's and the green eyes that are a few shades darker—though that might just be the concentrated evil of the brain behind them—and the painting. Old sound implants are quiet and dark on the backs of her hands. Her hair is Haven's shade of black, long and smooth, without the brightness of added neon or the wild sculpture of braids and artful tangles threaded with fiber-optic tubes. All those would have been there once. Green, I think, judging from her suit and her makeup.

"My daughter is irritatingly fond of you," President Z continues. "She always was completely useless. No ambition. No sense of what she could be if only she appreciated the opportunities available to her."

I raise the gun, my peripheral vision staining red. "You turned your own daughter into an Exaur," I grit out. "To punish *me*?"

She laughs. "Oh, no. Not you. Her. She could have had everything. Succeeded me. Used her—not inconsiderable—computer talents to further the Corp, and what does she do instead? Befriends conduit scum from the lower Web. And she helped you with your ridiculous rebellion. Frankly, I am surprised she kept this secret, but I think"—she tilts her head, examining me—"that you truly didn't know."

"If you were my mother, I wouldn't admit it either," I toss back. I don't think it was only the secrecy laws that made Haven hide this from me. President Z laughs again.

"Perhaps you are made for each other. Defiant and idealistic. A dangerous combination. Tell me, Anthem, do you really believe things will change? I am sure by now you have killed my Board, my husband, and my most trusted advisors. My dearest L5329, who was there for me in all the ways my daughter was not. But I wasn't the first to hold this position, to do the things I do. If you think I will be the last, you are a dreamer befitting your musician's soul."

"I don't care about the Web," I spit. It's more of a lie than it used to be. Her lips twitch in a way that makes my chest tight. So she and Haven are not completely different. "I just want my family to be safe."

"Work with me," she says. "I will guarantee that no harm will ever come to those you care about."

"No *more* harm, right? Sorry, I made that mistake once already."

She shrugs. "I tried. Someone will take my place and repair the damage you've caused. You will have no friends in a position to help you when that day comes."

I walk forward. Slow. Deliberate. "You wanted to control our minds."

Long-fingered hands spread in the air. "The happiness of the Web has always been my primary concern. If citizens need assistance with that, it is my job to provide it, is it not?"

I wonder how this woman could have given birth to someone as sane and kind as Haven. "Has it ever occurred to you that they're miserable *because* of the things you've done?"

"I did not start this."

*No, but you've tried to make sure it will never end.* "You're right. It's in my soul. Just like it's in thousands of others who never get the chance to see it for what it is. Thousands more who know, but have to hide." My mother, in a cramped, drafty room, playing a violin. "No more." The gun is aimed at her face, an offer of a kind death I have no intention of giving. My gaze goes to the headphones hanging from the console. "Put them on."

"Cooperate with me." No begging. Just calm self-assurance. "I was never musical. I have relied on others for that. You can lead us into a new age. My right-hand man."

"You're crazy. Just like your protégée. Put them on." Another step forward. Haven gets her fearlessness from this woman. I close my eyes, just for a second, and picture Haven's face. I get my fearlessness from *her*.

"I ask again, do you truly think killing me will make a difference? I know who you are, Anthem. Even if you never track again, you have perhaps another ten years, and then you too will die. Possibly you will maintain order in that time, but I do not think you have any designs on the kind of power I have enjoyed. Someone must step in to fill the void. Maybe they will respect what you have done here, or at least your ability to do it. They will not want to give you a reason to repeat your success, but after you're gone, things will change. The *Anthem* will fade from memory and go the way of all forgotten lyrics. The cycle will begin anew."

"Maybe," I agree. I round the desk, the gun's aim not leaving the spot between her eyes. "But it'll be without you. If you had never made more tracks, never tried to do what you have with them, never drained a conduit for the Grid or to make yourself live longer . . ." My breath comes in sharp pants as I pull the headphones down and tap the console screen with my broken fingers. Pain brings bile to my throat. "If you had never done those things, and if I didn't need to kill you, I would still do *this* for what you did to *her*."

Only when her ears are covered does she start to struggle; she tries to knock the gun away and push her chair back. I keep hold, a fistful of hair clenched in my hand above her ear.

Like with Ell, it doesn't take long. I can't hear the song, but I know every second of it. Even just the memory takes me back to the basement, to that first moment of singing and playing after a week without it. I saved this one for her.

A last apology to Johnny. His final vindication. Her struggle changes from me to death and her mouth opens in a silent scream, her body jerking as if electrified.

And then . . . nothing. I feel the moment her mind becomes the black screen she used to hide behind.

It's time to go, move, get the fuck out of here. Survive. I can't think about what this means right now. Later I can wonder if knowing would've changed anything.

I hold her ear with my broken fingers and fumble for the knife in my pocket. Skin and cartilage fall away. Warm blood oozes onto my hand, making my fingers slip in their search for the implant that contains so much evil. I dig, get leverage, and dislodge the chip with only a little resistance.

It looks just like any of the others I've seen. I'm not sure why I expected it to be different.

Muscle memory takes me down the stairs. Even if the elevators worked right now, I've had enough of them for whatever short lifetime remains for me. Maybe the ten years President Z guessed. Maybe less. I've drained a lot of my own life for this.

Glass, marble, and plaster rain everywhere in a storm of terrible, entrancing, destructive beauty. I want to sink down and just watch while the wall cracks under my back, sleep as the Corp crumbles to dust and takes me with it.

I keep running. Down. Out. Bodies cover the street as if a mythical heaven has cast them there. One guard falls at the hands of another and I can't stop to find out if the winner's on our side. I race around the curve of the fractured building to the front. It's still there, gouged and scarred, but standing. Clawing, scrabbling, trying not to scream, I pull myself onto the statue, raise my hands, and look down at the gathering mass of people.

"Stop!" I shout. No one hears me above the clamor. "Stop!" I try again. I slam the handle of my gun down on solid iron. A ringing echo spreads out and faces look up, the sound's unexpectedness more effective than its volume. "President Z is dead. It's over." Shock paints every face I can see. I want to sleep forever. A flash of speeding pink breaks through the crowd, then green, flaming orange, and dark dreadlocks. Someone—not one of my friends—calls something and it grows to a chant I can't hear, just noise. I jump down, fall against Haven, and feel three other pairs of arms wrap around us. I let myself stay there for as long as I can before I have to break away. "Help me," I say to my friends.

Bolts creak and metal whines. Soon it is more than the five of us, the collected weight of thousands leaning, pushing. The statue rocks on its pedestal and hangs in the air for a forever-second.

It falls. The crash is the most beautiful music I've ever heard.

✦

We push our way through the crowd, hands grabbing at my clothes and my hair until we find a spot away from the riotous celebrations breaking out behind us.

"Where's Scope?"

"He said there was something he had to take care of when he dropped off the chips," Pixel says. "He'll meet us back down there."

I look back at the joyful mass of people. It won't last. A broken city sprawls around us, and someone will have to fix it. Someone will have to lead it. President Z was right about that. Haven's face is streaked, her clothing torn, and the air around us is thick with cheers. It's not the time to talk.

"You have them?" I ask her. She pats the bright pink bag hanging from her shoulder.

"We need to get to a CRC and the warehouse." The twins. I pray Isis and Bee kept them safe—and themselves, too.

Pixel glances at my hand and winces. "I'll drive. Mage, you and Phoenix go make sure we have, what, another few minutes of power?"

"I don't need long," Haven says, nodding.

We steal a pod. Pixel climbs into the driver's seat, and I collapse into the one right behind him as he navigates slowly around the wreckage. Warmth covers my hand, Haven's fingers linking with my unbroken ones. Night has fallen, but everywhere it's as if the city is just waking up. Word's traveled fast, and some of those who hid in their apartments during the fight emerge to stare in the direction of headquarters. Others stay indoors, opening windows seconds before consoles smash to shards on the sidewalk.

After a while I close my eyes and rest on Haven's shoulder; her arms around me are comforting and safe. I have a million things to say to her; all of them can wait for quiet and stillness and until my hands don't hurt so much.

"I'll wait here," Pixel says outside the CRC, crossing his arms and leaning against the outside of the pod. His body blocks the Corp logo. Mage answers my tab quickly, though this one is less urgent, turning the scanner on so I can open the door. More stairs. It's easier with Haven's help, but it's still a struggle to climb, my legs screaming with every step.

She unravels wires and opens her computer on top of the nearest viewer. Once again the Grid blooms to life in front of us, flickering now. The energy I banked is running out.

"Inherited memory," Haven says, typing rapidly, the list of files rendered by the hologram scrolling up to infinity. "Passed down by every president and board member to his or her successor since the Corp formed. No knowledge is ever lost. Nothing's ever forgotten."

I believed her when she first told us, that day in the tunnel, but seeing it for myself—and knowing what I know now—makes it different.

You were next._

She glances at the tablet screen and nods, eyes wet. "They wanted me to be. We fought about it all the time. It changes you," she says. "Even if you could go back and take out all the stuff that isn't yours . . . you'd never be the same. They never were." Her eyes shimmer in the lights from the viewer. "It wasn't even like you were killing people, Anthem. More like unplugging machines. There was nothing left of them. Even their voices changed. Mannerisms. Like there was too much inside their heads, so the only things they could focus on were the ones that have been constant for a hundred years. Strengthen the Corp at all costs. Keep people high and paranoid. Build complacency from fear so there isn't another war. Citizens are temporary, the Corp is eternal. *I* was temporary."

My fingers hover over the keypad, frozen. What the hell am I supposed to say about this?

"This one's done." The halo of lights blinks and reforms into a person, a man I've never seen. She holds out her hand and I give her another chip, together we walk to a different viewer. One by one, she loads the data held on them, saving her parents for last. They'll live on, sort of, unable to harm anyone, but the passwords encrypted on them—unknown even to their owners—will fool the mainframe into thinking its protection is intact.

"The system will still ping them twice a day," she says, ejecting the last of them. "As long as they stay here, plugged in, the viewers on, the mainframe won't trigger a shutdown. If we make any major changes, it will check on them all at once. Mage is going to reprogram the lock after we leave, so it only answers to my code and his. We'll move out the other chips later and put them somewhere else so people can still visit their families."

"Haven," I whisper. It doesn't matter that she can't hear me. I wrap my arms around her, and she clings to my waist. Her shoulders tremble.

"Let's go get the twins," she says.

I shut my eyes for a second when we pass Pixel's old club, the pod slowing a little, and when I open them again we're on the South Shore, pulling to a stop outside the warehouse. Haven lets me go, and I move with the last of my energy through the gap in the fence and into the building. My usable hand yanks open the trapdoor and this time I do jump, forgoing the ladder altogether.

"Ant!"

Well, the crash of the statue had been my favorite sound. "Alpha," I breathe. "Omega. Come here."

They do, running into my arms and letting me almost crush them. "We slept for a long time," Alpha says. "And I feel funny."

"I know," I say. "It'll go away soon." Not completely, but eventually the itch of addiction will, I hope, fade into the background.

"Can we have some more music?" Omega asks. "That was fun."

"Not yet, okay?" My voice cracks. "But I have something better. Someone who wants to see you." The footsteps overhead don't make me nervous this time.

"Who?"

Haven descends the ladder. Two pairs of eyes widen and huge

smiles spread across safe faces. "Haven!" They let me go so suddenly I should probably be offended, but I can only laugh in hysterical relief. She wraps lace-coated arms around them, and for the first time—probably the only time—I'm glad she can't hear me or my voice break as I tell the twins she can't hear them. I tap Alpha on the shoulder and give her my tablet.

In the gloom, I find Isis and hug her tight, whispering, *Thank you, thank you, thank you.*

"What's going on up there?" she asks.

"It's over." I let her go, sensing Pixel's impatience behind me. Bee, watchful and silent, steps from the shadows and examines our faces. A slow, rapturous smile spreads across her face; her eyes close and her hands fold together over her chest.

"Anthem, you're hurt," Isis says, extricating herself from Pixel. The gash on my arm has reopened, my head's still bleeding, and my hand is clearly wrecked. "Come here." She rummages in a bag and takes out fresh gauze to clean and dress my wounds. "I'll do a better job when I have more light," she says. "If the medical facility is still there, I can give you stitches and set your hand."

"Thanks." We look at each other. No painkillers. I won't take them. She nods.

"We should get back," I say. "Alpha, Omega, you two want to go for a pod ride?" I don't think I'm up to carrying the twins all the way through the tunnels, and we don't have to hide now.

"Is Haven coming?"

I smile at Omega, my chest tight. "She can stay with us forever if she wants to."

Seven of us cram into a pod designed for four and drive north again, by moonlight. The twins sit across from Haven and me, squabbling over control of the tablet. I don't need to know what they're saying, or what her answers are. I only need to see their faces.

Pixel climbs down a tunnel entrance and reaches to help Alpha and then Omega. Bee moves with surprising agility, and I jump again to save my hand the pain.

The alcove is bathed in green and empty. The monitors and wires are flickering, the last of my stored energy dying out. Haven hands me my tablet.

`What do you want me to do?_`

`Turn the Grid back on._`

She pries herself from the twins and sits down, fingers flying across the keys. For a second we're all swathed in complete darkness.

The hum begins. I can feel it, even from here. The low vibration that settles in my teeth. Monitors burst into light again, blinding, as if I've rubbed my eyes too hard, until I blink the spots away.

She keeps typing and lifts a hand only to beckon me over her shoulder, then point at a screen.

Millions and millions of music files. Her finger hovers over the delete key. I close my eyes, shake my head, and reach out to stop her.

Mage was right. It's not our decision. I've made so many now and I'm just so fucking tired.

`Remove the ones we made, and anything they made in the past year._` That should be safe enough for now.

Haven nods, rests her head against my arm for a second, and gets back to work. Somewhere down the tunnel, I hear footsteps.

"Anthem? Pixel?" Mage's voice echoes until he's calling a hundred of each of us.

"Stay here with Bee and Haven," I tell the twins. "I'll be right back." Pixel and I duck out of the alcove, look for the flashlight beams, and go to meet Mage and Phoenix.

I don't know which one of us stops walking or who sees it first. *Him.* The glow of Phoenix's flashlight illuminates dark hair streaked with red, the body over Mage's shoulder. I search their eyes, see everything I need to, and stop breathing.

No. Not him. It can't be.

My knees hit dirt. I cough on the kicked-up dust, gag, turn my head to puke. Pixel falls too, clutching at me, and I try to hold in the deep sobs shuddering through his chest. Phoenix and Mage gently lay Scope down in the ruts of former train tracks.

"We got worried when he wasn't answering his tabs," Phoenix says quietly. "So we went to find him."

I force myself to look at Scope. Every different kind of love I've ever felt for him fights for control in my chest. Crusted blood rings a single bullet hole at his temple, fading into a streak in his hair. It just looks like the dye ran in the rain. A scrap of something yellow peeks out from his clenched fist.

"Is he . . . ? Both . . . ?" Pixel asks.

"Yes, but we only found one—" Phoenix starts. Mage puts a hand on her shoulder.

"You can look at his memory chip later."

Pixel shakes his head. I don't want to know, either. I lean forward and kiss Scope's dry, cool lips. When I pull back, his face gleams wet in a round pool of light.

Agony, sleep, agony again. I soak clean, soft sheets with sweat and they have to be changed several times a day. For weeks, Haven mops my forehead with cool cloths, swallows my screams with her mouth, pins down my hands when I try to claw off my skin, and calls for help when her own strength isn't enough. Bee comes, then Pixel sometime later, and even through the pain, the nausea, the relentless pounding in my head, I know what it means that he's not suffering through this with me.

I don't blame him.

Finally, painfully, the withdrawal passes. I shower, dress, cross my room on atrophied legs, past a gaping hole in the wall, and emerge to see the twins, happy and cared for, gorging on cookies under Bee's watchful eyes. I can't hug them, or her, hard enough. Now that my brain is my own again, I'll have to decide whether staying here is the right thing to do. Yeah, the Corp put me in this ridiculous apartment, but it's big enough for all of us and I kind of think I deserve it. I don't want to go back to my old life down in Two and forget all the things I'm not proud of.

On the TV, a woman who I guess isn't a Corp spokeswoman anymore is trying to explain the idea of elections to anyone watching. She stumbles through concepts she herself doesn't quite understand.

"You okay?" Haven appears from somewhere and slips past the twins to put her arms around my waist. I stare out the window.

"Yeah." I nod. I turn away from the window and point to the front door. Her eyes widen and she releases me.

"Be careful."

The blue has faded from my hair thanks to Haven's repeated washings, and a cast still covers the chrome on my hand. When I hop a passing trans-pod, no one takes any notice of me. The Vortex, alive in neon again, pulls us in and I step out onto the sidewalk in front of what is now just a big, dark glass building, half-shielded by scaffolds and alive with the activity of repair.

"Anthem." Isis greets me when I find her deep in the medical facility. She kisses my cheek. "How are you feeling?"

"Good." I raise my plaster-covered hand. "You?"

"Better now. Yeah, I'll bet you want that back. Come on." She takes me into a treatment room, makes me sit perfectly still for an X-ray, and pulls out a small electric saw. She sees me staring when she plugs it in.

"Mage and some of the others are trying to find alternatives," she says. "Looking up old technologies, things that can take power from the sun and the wind, stuff like that. But they've only been at it for a week or so. The withdrawal hit you worse because you drained so much of your energy beforehand, but it was almost as bad for the rest of us who quit." Her eyes darken. Maybe Pixel will, eventually.

I hope I live to see the day when there are no conduits anymore, but I get that, for now, we need power from somewhere.

My hand freed, Isis examines it closely, flexes my fingers, and feels the bones. "I'll give you some exercises to do for getting the strength back."

"Okay. Thanks, Isis." She checks the healing wound on my wrist and nods in approval. Just another scar, resting over absolutely nothing underneath. After the revolution, after Scope, after everything, I made her pull the extra chip out before stitching me back together.

"You missed a lot. I'm setting up a lab. We're researching medication, chemical stuff. And I think we can alter tracks so that if we *do* use them, it'll be like it was in the beginning. Just for pain relief. Still a little addictive, but no more so than the prewar kinds of drugs could be." She touches my arm, reading my face. "Only if they need it, and only if they choose."

"You think it can be done?"

She smiles. She's in her element here. "I think we can do whatever we want."

I leave her to what she was doing and head for the mainframe hub. I don't have to swipe my ID chip once. Mage is there, bent so closely over a touch screen his dreadlocks keep getting in his way.

"Hey," I say. He looks up and grins, raising his hand for a high five I take with my left.

"It's good to see you up, man. I visited a few times after I recovered, but . . ."

I remember. Vaguely. "What are you doing with all this stuff?"

"Restoring power—some of the outlying areas were damaged pretty heavy. Going through old tracks, making sure there's nothing too dangerous in there and scrubbing duplicates free of encoding so that there's normal music for anyone who wants. Getting the food supply flowing properly again. Haven did a pretty good job while most of us were sick, and the people who kept tracking helped her, but she was pretty busy looking after you. Truth be told, I don't think she was too comfortable controlling anything."

"You should run this place."

Mage laughs. "Nah, man, not me. I'm happy down here. Her, maybe." From somewhere, I hear Phoenix loudly giving instructions. Probably better not to interrupt that.

"Bring her over later?"

"Sounds good."

In the lobby, I stop, paralyzed, staring at elevator doors. Just a short ride to the studio. I turn away and head outside, not ready to face whatever has become of it. Not today. Soon.

I walk down to Two. Not everything is better. There are no guarantees that whoever takes charge next will be any better than President Z or the people who came before her. Without the requirement of tracking or clubbing, life expectancy will extend and the population will grow past the point the island can sustain or hold. Conduits in the Energy Farm are still giving their lives for neon lights and banks of computers.

There's no way to reverse the effects of the music, even in those who choose never to track again, and so people will still come home to find loved ones attached to consoles, chests motionless in blood-ied bathtubs, or on frayed rugs on top of spreading stains.

But around me, there are signs of hope. Pulled from a drugged stupor for the first time in generations, we are awake, seeing what we have and what we can be. The damage sustained in the fighting is slowly being repaired; we care again. I won't help with the rebuilding efforts. I've done enough, both good and bad, and I'm tired. The twins are safe, and I can content myself with the knowledge that they will never have their minds, their wills, their *selves* stolen beyond what they've already suffered.

I have to accept the possibility that, one day, they will choose to track, to satisfy that yearning awakened by the evil, poisonous Ell.

My legs ache. I stop and lean against the window of a water bar, its door locked. I let my eyelids drift closed, stand there for a minute until, undirected by conscious thought, they open again.

Somewhere, someone—a woman—is singing, a rich alto filters down from an open window. Her voice would be beautiful anyway, but strengthened by an utter lack of fear that a guard will drag her away, pin her down and cover her ears with headphones, it sucks all the tiredness from me. I push away from the window and keep going.

Pixel answers his apartment door; his skin sallow against blood-shot eyes. Déjà vu sweeps through me like sickness, and I force myself to remember that Scope is not hiding in his bedroom.

"I loved him, too," I say. My voice cracks.

"I know."

We sit on the old, battered couch, saying nothing more for a long time. Scope is everywhere; a good, trusting, infectious ghost. "Have you gone to see him?"

His breath hitches. "I got as far as the front door of the CRC."

We're all going to need time. The door to his mother's bedroom stands open, the bed empty. "I'm so fucking sorry," I whisper. So much death. So much damage and horror and fear.

"Don't you dare." The tightly restrained anger in Pixel's voice grabs my ears and forcibly turns my head to face him. "Don't you *dare* think what we did wasn't right, or they died for nothing and all the people we killed died for something. Do you get that?"

He's right. I know it, maybe one day I'll feel it, too.

"Thanks for helping Haven," I say just to kill the silence. "Mage and Phoenix are coming over later."

"I'll be there."

The trans-pod back up to One detours around a street too wrecked to traverse. It takes me up through Four, along the edge of the river. A crowd of people are gathered in an empty space, mean-ingless except that it's where one of the bridges used to be. Maybe that's next. There's nothing stopping us anymore. In one of my more lucid moments of the past few weeks, Haven told me she wants to restore all the memory chips the way she did with my mother's. We'll take our entire past into whatever the future holds.

I tab Haven and ask her to bring the twins to the park. Schools will be open again soon, and I want to spend as much time with them as I can. There are other people I should check on, see, speak to—Crave's wife and daughter, Fable and his mother, Tango, J, Imp and all the others at the depot in Two—but I'll do that tomorrow.

The park is warm, soft, and veiled in a haze of mist. It's almost summer, but the clearest sign that winter has ended is on the faces of people who pass by me on the path. The cherry blossoms are gone. I look only for one hint of pink and spot her walking toward me; the twins are on one side of her and a guitar case is in her hand—the one I took from the studio ages ago and wrote songs with in darkness and silence.

"Ant! Haven says you'll play music for us," Omega says. "Will it sound like the music before that the teeth-lady let us listen to? I want more of that." Beside him, Alpha nods emphatically.

"Um. Kind of," I say through a dry throat. "It will if you let it. You have to use your imaginations, though."

"Okay!" they chime. Music—real music—runs down the curve of my mother's violin bow and along my guitar strings and maybe, maybe, into their veins.

"Give me a minute to talk to Haven, then I'll show you," I promise. They run off, chasing each other around trees.

"You know you want to," she says, tilting her head at the case I've put down on the grass. I take out my tablet, and she stops me. "Remember what I said about treating me like I'm too fragile? Don't hide this from me."

She knows me too well. You have to tell me something first._

Her eyes close, shutting out the only green I was looking at in this blooming, living park. I put the tablet into her outstretched hand and, after a moment, she taps at its screen with her nails. Because

307

I thought you wouldn't do it if you knew, and it had to be done. It's not about how I felt about them._

Did you love them?_

She considers this. They were my parents. It was different when I was a little kid, then they took their positions and became people I didn't know. I could blame it all on the memories they inherited, but it wasn't just that. They knew what they were getting into. They wanted it._

Which one were you supposed to inherit?_

Does it matter?_ She shakes her head. They used to argue about that. Probably my mother, but in the end I was just a means of ensuring the future they saw. They didn't know . . . me._

There's more I could ask, more I could say. Instead I lean over and kiss her, because everything else has changed, but we haven't.

My guitar is calling. *Play me.* It's been so long, and this will be worth whatever pain I suffer in my hand later.

I call the twins over from where they're hiding—not very well—behind a bush. The guitar is warm, heavy in my lap, the color of liquid honey in the sunshine. Alpha and Omega kneel, excited, a few feet away. A hand slips between it and my stomach. I look at Haven and realize what she wants. The vibrations will translate to melody in her head, and she'll be able to watch the sound implants on her arms ripple and glow.

We've lost so much. We might lose more. But for now I can sit here, under the trees and sky, and pull music from the strings. My fingers find the frets easily, effortlessly, and each plucked note is light, breezy—a single leaf on one of the nearby trees. With my voice it begins to grow and stretches up to the sun. I run out of songs I want to play and keep going, making up anything that sounds like the sunshine, the warmth of the day, the quiet knowledge of freedom.

No one stops me.

# ACKNOWLEDGMENTS

Thanks to my family, who I hope will understand that my gratitude for their love and support is too personal and extensive to fully describe here without taking up all the space I have. For now, just . . . thank you. You are everything and I love you all.

To the White Blank Page girls, Angela, Anna, Bec, Melissa, and Tonya—you're among the finest writers and women I know. Thanks for always making me feel like I could do it, and for getting that all words are musical. Several others read this book in its early stages and offered their thoughts: Caren, Jennifer, Leiah, Paula, and Shireen. It wouldn't be what it is without any of you, and neither would I.

Help on some aspects was provided by Adam McHeffey of the excellent band Swear & Shake, who was generous in offering his input to a non-musician. Also thanks to my team of acoustics experts.

I couldn't have written this book without feeling the way I do about music. I put on my headphones before I get out of bed in the morning. Way more bands than I can list inspire me every day, but without Animal Collective, The Antlers, Bright Eyes, The Cure, David Bowie, Placebo, The Sisters of Mercy, and Wolfsheim, *Coda* would still be an unfulfilled idea. Their songs kept me going during 3 a.m. writing sessions and were a constant reminder of why I attempted this insane thing in the first place.

For much needed encouragement during the hardest part, my thanks to John, Vicki, Helena, and Suzanne.

I owe more than I can express to Meredith Barnes, an agent who became my friend, and to Brooks Sherman, a friend who became my agent. Meredith's passion and guidance kept me sane during submission and sale, and Brooks took up the agent baton with speed and grace. Thanks for the hugs—both virtual and real—the laughs, the belief in Anthem and in me. You guys are amazing and I'm honored to know you and have you in my corner. Thanks go as well to everyone at Lowenstein Associates and at FinePrint Literary Management.

Finally, thank you to my wonderful editor, Lisa Cheng, for seeing what this story was and could be. Her enthusiasm and understanding have made working with her an amazing experience. (So did the time she force-fed me cheesecake.) She and the team at Running Press Teens turned a manuscript into a real book and have been kind, generous, insightful, and funny along the way.

**Emma Trevayne** is a full-time writer who is an avid music collector, a lover of computer code languages, and a photographer. She has lived in Canada, England, and America. You can find Emma online at emmatrevayne.com, or follow her on Twitter @EMentior.